THE SURGEON'S CASE

ALSO BY E.G. RODFORD AND AVAILABLE FROM TITAN BOOKS

The Bursar's Wife

THE SURGEON'S CASE

A GEORGE KOCHARYAN MYSTERY

E.G. RODFORD

TITAN BOOKS

The Surgeon's Case
Print edition ISBN: 9781785650055
E-book edition ISBN: 9781785650062

Published by Titan Books
A division of Titan Publishing Group Ltd
144 Southwark Street, London SE1 0UP

First edition: March 2017
10 9 8 7 6 5 4 3 2 1

What did you think of this book? We love to hear from our readers.
Please email us at: readerfeedback@titanemail.com,
or write to us at the above address.

To receive advance information, news, competitions, and exclusive offers online,
please sign up for the Titan newsletter on our website:
www.titanbooks.com

Many thanks to Schona and Angus for their professional knowledge

I

JUST FIVE PEOPLE ATTENDED MY FATHER'S CREMATION.
Other than myself and the young woman from the care home
where he'd spent the last eighteen months of his life, two of
them had never met Dad, and one he'd met at a barbecue.
One of those who'd never met him gave the service; a brief
put-the-deceased's-name-here patter that meant nothing
to me and would have meant even less to my father. I saw
the event as a necessary formality, and declined the offer
of watching his coffin (the cheapest I could get away with
without appearing cheap) being conveyed luggage-like into
the furnace for his cremation. Instead I got a lift back with
Linda, who'd driven me to the crematorium in an egg-shaped
VW Beetle. She was the other person there who'd never met
my father.

I hesitate to call Linda my girlfriend, not least because
it's not a word I can use at my age without embarrassment,
but as she seemed willing to get together every now and
then for a takeaway, a film, and sex (not always all three or
always in that order), I liked to think of her as such. Linda
was the crime reporter for the Cambridge *Argus* and she'd

driven me to the funeral because my ageing VW Golf was nearing the end of its natural life and being kept alive under protest, the mechanics saying the humane thing would be to have it put down. But then I'd have to give up a nice boxy car for something that had no angles and was fuel-efficient and aerodynamic, not to mention safer. Everything had to be curved nowadays except women, who'd been brainwashed into thinking that looking undernourished was better than looking like a woman. Maybe it was odd that this sort of crap went through my mind coming back from my own father's funeral but I'll leave any interpretation to the analysts who live for that nonsense. Linda, who happily erred on the side of curves, was in a rush to get back to Cambridge due to the text she'd received (and unashamedly read) in the middle of the eulogy. Perhaps it should have annoyed me more than it had, but I'd said goodbye to my father a while ago; the person now being cremated had, due to Pick's disease, ceased to be the person I'd known. So there was to be no wake, no speeches, no reminiscing from old pals. What friends he'd had were all dead, and living in a care home with a degenerative disease alongside other people in a similar position had limited his ability to make new ones.

Linda was excited; I could tell from our speed and the breathy nature of her voice, which only manifested when the promise of an ugly crime reared its juicy head. My considerable efforts at getting a similar response in bed had yet to yield results.

"A fisherman has found a body near Grantchester. A girl," she was saying. She overtook a lorry on the A14 dangerously close to the Cambridge turn-off, the result being that as she swerved in front of it to get over to the exit I was flung towards her and had to grab the handle above the window with both hands. Some stitching gave way in the left armpit of my suit, which I had last worn at my mother's funeral and had since expanded into. The lorry driver leant on his horn and I started sweating despite the air-conditioning. Linda compensated for her speed with some powerful braking as we came off the A14, demonstrating the advantages of a modern car as it came to a halt at the roundabout. She grinned and patted my knee as she waited for traffic to pass.

Dropping me kerbside outside my office on Lensfield Road, she accelerated off in pursuit of her story. I shared offices in a converted Victorian building with various other sole traders who came and went, and currently included a relationship counsellor, a nutritionist, a life coach and a reflexologist. We shared a waiting room, which made for an interesting mix of people sitting in it at any one time. My clients tended to be the nervous types sitting on their own who didn't really want to be there.

My third-floor office was empty, as Sandra, my part-time assistant, was making her own way back from the funeral, hopefully at a safer speed than I had. Usually I'm quite happy to have the place to myself, so my disappointment took me by surprise. Sandra was quietly efficient, but she was no shrinking violet, and you always knew when she was around.

I sat at my desk and, before I knew it, a lump constricted my throat and salt stung my eyes. The phone rang and I stemmed the tears with the sleeve of my suit before picking up.

"Cambridge Confidential Services," I said, my voice all over the place.

"Can I speak to George Kocharyan?" An older, refined, white male voice.

"One moment," I croaked. I covered the mouthpiece and cleared my throat. "This is he," I said, hoping I sounded like someone other than the person who had answered the phone.

"My name is Bill Galbraith." He paused as if waiting for me to congratulate him. "You were recommended by Pimlico Investigations in London." I sat up. Pimlico sometimes referred jobs my way when they couldn't be bothered to send someone up to Cambridge to deal with them, and I was keen to foster the relationship.

"How can I help you, Mr Galbraith?" I asked, in my best customer service voice.

"We have a problem with an, erm, employee of ours." He stopped, unsure how to continue. It was very quiet at his end, no traffic, no ambient noise, nothing.

"Who is 'we', Mr Galbraith?"

"My wife and I. We have a domestic, a live-in woman, a Filipino. She's disappeared with some, erm, valuables."

"OK. How long has she been gone?"

"A couple of days. We don't want to call the police; she's been with us a long time. You understand?"

"Sure, you don't want to involve them. It's probably best if we meet."

"Yes, yes of course. As soon as possible. Can you meet this evening?"

"That's fine. Are you based in Cambridge?"

"In one of the outlying villages." Cagey. Not a trait I relish in a potential client. "But I rather thought we could meet in town. I'm going to be in the city anyway."

"Will your wife be there?"

"Erm, no. Does she need to be?"

"It would be best if I spoke to both of you together."

"Shall we meet first and take it from there? To be perfectly frank I haven't decided to hire you yet."

"Fair enough. Do you have somewhere in mind?"

"You know the big hotel on Downing Street?"

"Of course."

"Good. Five-thirty, in the lobby?"

I hung up before I realised that we hadn't agreed on how we would recognise each other.

Sandra appeared in the door, still dressed in her funeral outfit, the same outfit she'd worn when I'd interviewed her for the job several years ago. She looked a little sweaty from climbing the stairs and although the suit hung a little looser on her now than it had at her interview she was nevertheless still large. She calls herself fat.

"Bloody hot for June," Sandra said, appraising me. Could she tell I'd been crying? "Your car's not outside. I thought Linda was going to drop you off at the garage?"

"She was in a hurry. Something about a dead kid." Sandra moved to her desk and sat down with a relieved sigh.

"I didn't get a chance to speak to you at the crem." She removed her shoes and rubbed her feet. "Was that her phone that went off?"

I nodded, assessing the rip in the armpit of my suit;

I'd have to go home and change before meeting this Bill Galbraith. Sandra didn't like Linda, nor, it seemed, any other woman I tried to wrestle with, and she did little to hide it. Before she could expound on Linda's failings I told her I had a potential new client.

"Something meaty, I hope."

"Potentially. Someone who can afford a live-in maid, so there's money."

"Anything I can do?" I wrote down Bill Galbraith's name and asked her to check him out and call me before five with whatever she found. She looked at the name and frowned.

"What is it?"

"Nothing. Seems familiar, that's all." She switched on her computer.

"I think I'm going to head out," I said. "I need to change my jacket." I lifted my arm to show her the rip.

She smiled, a smile like a ray of sunshine on an overcast day. "Shall I order you a taxi?"

"It's a nice evening, I could do with the walk." I paused because she looked like she was gearing up to say something.

"Will you be OK, George?" adding, "Tonight, I mean."

"I'll be fine. Besides, I've got the meeting with Galbraith." She looked unconvinced.

"I'll be fine, honestly. Now do some research." I could have told her that Linda would be round later to provide some sort of solace but I had a feeling this wouldn't reassure her. I stopped at the door. "And, Sandra…" She looked up. "Thanks for coming to the funeral."

She shooed me out.

2

AFTER A NAP, A SHOWER AND A PHONE CONVERSATION WITH
Sandra while I dressed in a blue linen suit that Linda had
insisted I buy, I felt ready to meet Bill Galbraith. Since I didn't
have my car I inspected my dad's bike but it turned out to be
a rusty old steel thing in need of maintenance, and besides,
I didn't want to arrive hot and sweaty to meet a potential
client, never mind ruin the suit. I decided to walk, which gave
me enough time to mull over the information Sandra had
rather excitedly imparted over the phone about Galbraith.
A world-famous surgeon at Addenbrooke's Hospital, he was
probably more well known for hosting a medical programme
on TV, following patients through from diagnosis to surgery.
She couldn't believe I didn't know of him but the only TV I
watch is golf and Formula One racing, both of which send me
to sleep, which is precisely why I watch them. At fifty-four,
Galbraith was apparently a bit of a sex symbol for the kind of
women who liked to present themselves as discerning when
it came to crushes on men, at least the ones they could admit
publicly. This included Sandra, judging by the way she went
on about him. Before I left I had a quick look at his picture

online so I could recognise him at the hotel, and I grudgingly accepted that some women might go for that sort of thing. Galbraith had probably expected me to know who he was when he rang.

I arrived at the hotel with fifteen minutes to spare. A large soulless building with a huge fake portico, complete with pillars which I passed through. I found a seat facing the doors. I'd sat in this lobby a few times, waiting for unfaithful spouses to appear from the elevators. Despite the steady income stream, I was weary of that sort of case, coming to believe over the years that monogamy was an unnatural state where people were trying to force a square peg into a round hole, so to speak. Why else was an army of counsellors and lawyers (not to mention people like me) needed to deal with the aftermath? Perhaps my outlook was jaded because it's all I saw, which is why I was keen to drop the marital stuff. More recently, with Sandra's help and insistence, we'd found a new income stream doing background checks on potential employees for Cambridge-based companies. This was for senior positions where personal peccadilloes were seen to be a liability. Sandra had her own reasons for trying to generate more work. Since I could only afford to hire her part-time, and she was a single mother with two kids, she'd been working for a sex chat line from home to supplement the salary I paid her. But that was drying up with the free availability of porn on the Internet and she was left with half a dozen regulars who just wanted to talk about how their week had gone because they had no one else. So she'd left the sex-chat company and moved these guys over to a mobile phone she'd got specially for the purpose.

I wasn't sure how she was monetising her listening skills; it wasn't something I asked her about.

I recognised Galbraith as soon as he entered, as he must have known I would. He was carrying an envelope and wearing a casual shirt, pressed jeans and deck shoes with no socks. He could carry that sort of thing off; I couldn't. He stood in the lobby self-consciously and ran a hand through his greying blond hair, which was swept back and lay in soft waves on his head. I got up and introduced myself. He stuck out his hand, fixed me with his grey-blue eyes and gave me a white-toothed grimace to indicate this was business, not pleasure. His hand was cool and his grip firmer than expected – I thought surgeons might be more circumspect when it came to their hands.

"I've got thirty minutes," he said. We went upstairs into the bar and he ordered coffee. "I'm in surgery this evening," he said, explaining his choice. I joined him in a coffee; it's always best to mirror the client in this regard. I didn't put up any resistance to him paying and we found a table. In order to look professional I took out a notebook and pen and crossed my legs. He looked at an oversized sports watch and got straight down to business.

"So do you think you can find Aurora?"

"Aurora being your domestic?"

He nodded and put the envelope on the table. "Aurora de la Cruz. She's Filipino. Her details are in there." I left the envelope where it was.

"If you want me to take on the case I'm going to need a little more information."

"Like what?"

"Well, for starters, did she go out at all? Did she have friends in Cambridge?"

"Only to the village shop – most of our groceries are delivered. And no, she had no friends here."

"Did she have a computer, or access to one? Sometimes a browsing history can reveal a person's intentions."

"No, she didn't have a computer. She used ours once a month, to Skype her family in Manila."

"If you've come to me you must think she's still in Cambridge."

"Her English isn't brilliant, she doesn't have any money on her, or credit cards. She can't have gone far. When I talked to Pimlico Investigations they thought it was most likely she was still here."

"No bank account?"

"Yes, we paid her salary into it, but it's not a UK account. All her salary went to her family in the Philippines. We gave her cash for anything she might need, and she used a prepaid card for household shopping."

"Did she take her passport?"

He glanced at the envelope. "Erm… no, she didn't, so she's not planning to go far."

"What about the valuables you said she'd taken?"

For the first time I saw a flicker in his expression.

"It's nothing of any monetary value."

I waited expectantly.

He gathered himself and sat forward. He was used to having control of any situation and this was no exception.

"May I call you George?" I nodded. He clasped his hands and studied the bland carpet as if gathering his thoughts. I wondered if it was a move he'd affected for TV. I looked around the room at the businesspeople, mainly men, filling the bar after a day at workshops or conferences or whatever else they did to make working life seem bearable and give it the meaning it lacked by calling it a career.

He looked up at me, ready for his scene. "The thing is, George, Aurora's taken my briefcase."

"I see. And what was in it?"

"It's a little embarrassing."

"Rest assured, I've heard it all before."

He grimaced, not seeming to take comfort in this. "The briefcase contains patients' notes – their medical records. It's a bit of a problem surgeons have. We're notorious for taking notes home with us to look at, because there isn't enough time in the day at work. It causes problems at the hospital when staff need to see them."

"I thought it was all electronic now," I said.

He snorted. "Far from it."

"So she took the briefcase with what aim, do you think?"

He folded his arms and sat back. A couple of young women in suits were staring at our table but I was acutely aware that I was invisible to them.

"Maybe she thought it had money in it. I don't know. I do need them back, though." It didn't seem to me that missing medical records was that embarrassing, but perhaps to someone with his public profile it was a potential tabloid headline that he could do without. Maybe he just needed to check the cut of my jib before divulging himself; private investigators had been known to work for tabloid newspapers. I decided I'd give him the benefit of the doubt on the matter. He checked his watch and asked, "So, do you think you can find her?"

"Maybe, although there isn't a lot to go on. Why did she leave, do you think? Did you or your wife have a disagreement with her?"

He looked surprised – or feigned it – and shook his head.

"If I do take this on I'll need to talk to your wife. I'm assuming, given your schedule, that she deals with Aurora on a day-to-day basis?"

"Yes."

"When can I speak to her?"

He hesitated before saying, "She's away. Why not see what you can find out and come to the house on Monday, say five o'clock?" He wrote something on a card with a fountain pen and handed it to me. "Our address." I glanced at it. An address in the village of Fulbourn. I pocketed it as he stood up. I stood up too. I supposed I'd just been hired.

I gestured at the envelope. "Is there a photo in there?"

He nodded.

"We should discuss my fees and expenses. I'll draw up a contract and—"

He pulled a face and waved his hand dismissively. "Let's keep it casual for the moment. There's three hundred in the envelope to get you started – call it a retainer. The rest we can sort out. With any luck I'll only have to pay you for the next couple of days anyway." He paused. "If you do find her, don't approach her yourself – she might be a little skittish. Just let me know. My medical secretary's number is on the card." We shook hands. He smoothed his hair as he walked off, nodding at the women who'd been staring at us, or rather him.

"I'm sure that was him. Did you see?" one of them said.

Feeling cheapened by the cash in the envelope, which was perhaps the intention, I picked it up and went to the bar to order a beer but remembered how much Galbraith had paid for the coffees. It wasn't my type of place anyway.

3

AT HOME I CHANGED OUT OF MY SUIT AND SUPPLEMENTED THE beer I'd had in the pub on the way back with a bottle from the fridge. In the back garden I enjoyed the tangle of brambles and weeds that used to be a garden when my parents had owned the house. My mother would be horrified at its state, but after her death and my father's incarceration in a care home my wife Olivia did all the gardening. But since she'd left with a woman from her book group for a Greek island (not Lesbos, but it might as well have been), nature had taken over.

Overwhelmed with sudden tiredness I sat on a rotting bench and opened the envelope Bill Galbraith had given me. Aside from the three hundred pounds, it contained a folded sheet with a picture – a photocopy of a passport page to be exact. The passport was for one Aurora de la Cruz, a Filipino national who looked rather studious as she stared unsmiling at the camera. Born in Manila in August 1982, her photo was four years old, judging by the issue date of her passport, which would expire next year.

The doorbell rang. I let Linda in. Still in her dark suit

from the funeral, she was hot and sweaty and had stale breath, but I was pleased to see her. She pushed past me with a plastic bag of groceries into the kitchen. I closed the door and followed. She was unloading a glistening bottle of white wine, a bag of salad and a couple of supermarket pizzas.

"Put the oven on, will you, I'm going to jump in the shower." Following her instruction I took the pizzas out of their cardboard boxes and plastic wrapping and unbagged the salad into a bowl. I could hear Linda make oohing and aahing noises as she enjoyed her shower.

I'd met Linda via her husband, who hired me to follow her. At the time he was a Labour member of the city council and had come to see me, convinced she was having an affair. I'd dutifully followed her around town and into London but all I discovered was that she was vivacious and friendly, the very things, in my experience, that men found attractive in a woman until that woman became their main squeeze and they realised other men found them attractive as well. He became psychopathically jealous, unable to deal with the fact that she spoke to other men and sometimes even smiled at them.

Somehow she found out that he'd had her followed and dumped him pronto, but he wouldn't let her go that easy. She'd acquired my details from him and came to see me about his continued harassment, arguing that, because I was partly responsible for her predicament, I should speak to him. I refused; in my experience of these matters, the only thing that would work was a complete break. He was calling her several times a day and she would ignore him for a few days but then take a call in order to plead with him to stop. Or he would turn up at her work and she would agree to talk to avoid a scene. I told her to move, preferably to another city, but she didn't see why she should. Instead she moved within Cambridge, and changed jobs, telling nobody from work where she'd gone. I advised her to get another mobile phone, give the new number to everyone she trusted, but to keep the existing one switched off just to record voicemail messages from him, which she should never respond to under any circumstances. I hoped that her refusal to respond to his calls would send a clear message to him, which would, in the majority of cases, be the end of it. Just one returned call, even if it was a plea to be left alone, would give him the contact he craved. A visit by me would be a visit by proxy, and would just feed his febrile imagination with ideas about our relationship. Once a week Linda and I got together and monitored any messages on her old phone, mainly to see if he was one of the minority that didn't give up, who became threatening and potentially violent. But his calls diminished over time then stopped, and when I looked into it I discovered that he had moved to London, no doubt to disturb another hapless woman suckered by the initial and pleasing over-attentiveness that harassers initially exhibit.

When Linda stopped being a client I realised I missed our weekly get-togethers and we formed a liaison of sorts which settled into her coming round to mine or us going to the cinema. I have never been to her place, nor have I met any of her friends – with whom she spends a lot of time – but it doesn't really bother me, I don't think. It is, as they say, what it is.

She came down wearing one of my T-shirts and not much else as far as I could tell, clutching her phone, which rarely left her person. The smell of the pizzas filled the kitchen. I poured her some cold white wine and doused the salad with dressing from a bottle in the fridge. She looked up from her phone, putting it aside.

"How are you doing, Georgie?"

"I'm OK." Like Sandra, she didn't look convinced.

"Sorry I rushed off this morning after the funeral."

"You're here now, for which I'm grateful."

She smiled and sipped her wine while I took the pizzas from the oven.

"What's the story with your dead girl?" I asked, slicing the pizza.

"Could be juicy. She was found at Byron's Pool?"

"I know, on the Grantchester Road."

"Yes. Dumped by the side of the car park, in some long grass."

"How old?"

"They're not sure yet. They've not even ID'd the poor kid and until any family are told we can't publish anything." She looked at me. "Detective Inspector Vicky Stubbing is leading the case."

I concentrated on trying to keep my slice of pizza from shedding its topping before it reached my mouth while she peered at me.

"Don't you know Vicky Stubbing?" she asked. I did indeed know Stubbing – we'd become acquainted on that unpleasant business with the bursar's wife at Morley

College. I'd sworn off taking cases related to the university after that, and thus far had been successful. I didn't tell Linda that I'd once shared a condom with Stubbing but the sordid circumstances of that desperate liaison were such that relating it would take longer than the encounter itself.

"Our paths have crossed, as you might expect."

"She can be a cold fish."

"She's OK once you break the ice," I said, not sure why I was defending her.

"Must have taken a sledgehammer to get through that," she said, studying me. I remained impassive. Linda smiled. "I like that you're not a kiss-and-tell kind of guy, Georgie."

"So do you think this is the big one?" I asked, steering the topic onto safer ground. Linda was convinced that because she was forty-something and still worked on a provincial newspaper, her only chance at moving up in the world (in other words, joining a national paper based in London) meant getting hold of a big fat juicy story. Not an everyday catch in Cambridge.

"Time will tell. It might be an accident, of course. She may just have drowned." She drained her glass. "Jesus, if people could hear us they'd think we were ghouls."

"We both make our living off other people's misery, so I suppose we are ghouls."

"That's a bit dark. If that is the case, then so are doctors."

"Doctors try to alleviate misery; we often make it worse."

"Jesus, if you're going to be a miserable bastard, Georgie, I'll take my *joie de vivre* elsewhere." She cleared the plates and I finished my beer. She stood at the sink and ran some hot water. My dad used to wash up, every night. This house was pretty much as my parents had kept it, untouched from the fifties, and a constant reminder of them. I thought about selling it, making a fresh start. In today's market and in this gentrified area I would make a small fortune. I could buy a nice apartment overlooking Parker's Piece, maybe even a small sports car like Galbraith's. No, I would never buy a sports car.

I watched Linda at the sink before getting up to stand behind her, putting my hands on her waist.

"Are you wearing my underwear as well as my shirt?" I asked.

"Check for yourself," she said, squeezing washing-up liquid into the water. I moved my hands over her behind, and could find no evidence of underwear.

"Hello, I think I've just found your *joie de vivre*," I whispered into her ear.

4

"SO WHAT WE GOT?" SANDRA ASKED ME IN THE OFFICE THURSDAY morning. It was a beautiful day, and going to be another hot one for June, but I was feeling out of sorts after a restless night. I'd dreamt about the funeral, except in the dream the crematorium was full of people, and when the time came for the casket to disappear it rolled the other way instead and crashed onto the floor where it continued to move towards the mourners who screamed and panicked and were climbing over each other to escape. I tried to stop the coffin but was carried along, crashing through people towards the exit. I made no efforts to analyse the dream, because trying to do so would lead nowhere fast.

"Hello, anyone there?" Sandra waved at me.

"Sorry." I sat up. "We have a missing person. Or more accurately, a person who wants to be missing. Her employers say she stole from them." I showed her the sheet Galbraith had given me, with the photo of the passport page.

"Aurora de la Cruz," Sandra mouthed, looking at it. "What did she do? I mean, as a job."

"He called her a domestic, so cooking and cleaning, I'm guessing."

"A nanny?"

"There was no mention of kids."

"What did she take?"

"A briefcase containing patients' notes apparently."

"Not much of a haul. Did you meet the wife?" Sandra asked, handing me the sheet and going to her computer. "Was she gorgeous?"

"What are you on about?"

"I did a bit more digging after I rang you yesterday. The wife was a beauty queen, once upon a time," she said, pointing at her screen. "Miss Russia 1995." I stepped behind Sandra's desk to have a look at a picture of her. She was stunning despite over-the-top makeup and elaborately coiffed hair.

"I'm seeing her Monday, I think."

"Bet you're looking forward to it now."

"So what has she been up to since?" I asked, moving to my own desk.

"Advertising deals, perfume, jewellery, that sort of thing. Did a business degree after winning the beauty contest, then moved to the Persian Gulf where she set up a business and met the dashing Dr Galbraith. What's he like, in the flesh?"

"He's aged well. I'll give him that. A little too good-looking for my tastes."

"He looks yummy on TV. So, any ideas on where to start?"

I picked up Aurora's picture and looked at it, in case it should provide some insight. None was forthcoming. I put my feet up on the desk to improve blood flow to the brain.

"So, this is what I'm thinking," Sandra was saying. "This Aurora, does she have money?"

"Not a penny. No credit card, nothing."

"So if she's still in Cambridge then she will have to be working. Either that or she's shacked up with someone."

"But why did she take the briefcase?"

She ignored me and ploughed on. "So, going with the fact that she is some sort of domestic then she'll be looking for a cleaning job," she said.

"Anyone hiring a cleaner would probably want a reference, which in her present circumstances would be difficult," I said.

"Exactly, so she'd have to do something off the books, or cash-in-hand…"

"But where would she go? Who would she go to? Where would you go if in a foreign country and in trouble?" I asked.

"The embassy I suppose."

"Not if you've stolen something from your employer."

"OK, then to someone I knew, someone I'd built a relationship with," she said.

"She didn't know anyone, according to Galbraith. She hardly went out."

"Then you go to your own, to someone who at the very least speaks your language."

"Exactly. We need to find the Filipino community in Cambridge."

"Is there a Filipino community in Cambridge?"

I took my feet off the desk as the blood had suddenly rushed to my head.

"Which organisation, in Cambridge, is the biggest employer of workers actively recruited from abroad?" I asked.

I let her think for a moment until she clicked her fingers. "Addenbrooke's Hospital, of course. Nurses, technicians; I remember seeing something about them recruiting from the Philippines in the paper. Haven't you got a friend who works there, a porter or something?"

"I'm way ahead of you," I said, picking up the phone and dialling Kamal's mobile number. Sandra got up, picked up her mug and then mine which she waved at me questioningly. I didn't have time to decline her coffee as Kamal's phone went to his annoying voicemail message: "You're better off texting if you want a quick response." Idiot. He worked funny shifts at Addenbrooke's, fitting them in around his writing, so he could be either at work or asleep.

I switched on the new office mobile which had two SIM cards in it, one with a number we gave to clients, the other my personal number, something I was still getting used to having. Using my number I proceeded to tap out a message to Kamal, saying that I wanted to meet up and pick his brains. Sandra came back with coffee. Her coffee-making followed a path of least resistance that led nowhere particularly good. I suffered a few sips to avoid giving offence then stood up.

"I'm going to see what's up with my car. The garage aren't answering my calls."

Instead, I walked up Lensfield Road and turned right at the Catholic church on the corner and as soon as I was outside Antonio's I stepped in for a proper coffee. Unfortunately young people – bearded males and women with androgynous haircuts – had cottoned on to the fact that Antonio's was an indie coffee shop and had occupied it, tapping at expensive laptops or pretending to read battered Penguin classics. I had advised Antonio to turn off the free Wi-Fi to get rid of these posers.

"Adapt or die, George," he'd said. "Like you, I have to make a living." Which explained the unreasonable hike in prices and the new decor and, to my mind worst of all, an actual menu which proclaimed Antonio's Italian credentials and therefore his innate mastery of all things coffee related. I was disappointed in him, but still I came.

I nodded at Antonio as I entered and he handed me the Cambridge *Argus* from behind the counter. I managed to find a seat among the hipsters as they hunched over their laptops and iPads. Waiting for my usual, I calculated that a simultaneous raid of coffee shops in central Cambridge would yield a lucrative haul of high-end computer equipment. You could clear ten grand in this place alone.

The *Argus* had an article about the ongoing Cambridge punt wars. Rival companies were flooding the town with young, good-looking touts, male and female, all trying to convince the same tourists that they should spend a small fortune on a punt tour of the colleges with a historically dubious commentary from a clueless guide. Sandra's son Jason was earning extra cash doing it. Scudamore's were the top player in town but smaller enterprises sprung up every summer. If you had the capital outlay for a couple of punts, and recruited students to do the touting and punting, it was potentially a good little earner. Competition was fierce; one punt was found sawn in half at the start of the season.

The mobile chirped and I picked it up to read a message

from Kamal – he happened to be free now and could meet me at Antonio's. I replied to tell him I was already here and asked what he wanted to drink. After placing his order I read some more newspaper and watched the other customers. They seemed oblivious to anyone else, each wrapped in their own world. Two men sat opposite each other, looking at their phones, occasionally talking without looking up.

Kamal arrived to find his coffee on the table. He looked tired.

"I did a long shift yesterday," he explained when I pointed it out. "Sorry I couldn't make the funeral, my brother. How was it?"

"You didn't miss anything." I felt a constriction in my throat. "So, book sales aren't enough to live on? You still need to work?"

"Ho ho ho. Very funny." Last year he'd had a collection of his short stories published. It was well received, as they say, but apparently good reviews mean nothing in terms of sales. I'd read them out of duty: slices of life in which not a lot happens but much is implied. I enjoyed them but he wasn't exactly giving Dan Brown a run for his money.

"The cleaners at a publishing firm earn more than most of the writers they publish," he said. "Besides, I'd still work even if I didn't need to. What would I write about otherwise? I see and hear all of life at the hospital, people are at their most vulnerable. You should hear the things patients tell you when you're wheeling them about. And with the medical staff I'm like a fly on the wall. People tend to ignore porters and cleaners; it's the perfect job for a writer."

"That's exactly why I want to pick your brains. I'm wondering whether you know any Filipino staff at the hospital?" He stroked his moustache, a recent accessory which in my view was an unfortunate appendage to his face – a view I'd shared with him freely and often, to no avail.

"I know a couple, yes. What do you want to know?"

"I'm guessing they have some sort of community outside work? Where do they hang out, what do they do for fun, that sort of thing."

He nodded. "I have a bit of banter going with one of the nurses who works in the outpatient clinics. I could ask her. Is it for a case?"

"Not much of a case at the moment, but it's the only place I can think to start." We savoured our coffees. "Have you ever crossed paths with that TV surgeon, Bill Galbraith?" I asked him.

"No, he's above my pay grade. They call him the Hugh Grant of surgery."

"That makes sense. Do you hear any gossip?"

He shook his head. "Would you like me to ask around?"

"Discreetly."

"Is there any other way?"

5

AFTER AGREEING TO MEET AT KAMAL'S THE FOLLOWING NIGHT before our regular poker game, I walked over to Densley's garage to see what he was doing with my car. Densley's was incongruously situated in a residential area off Mill Road with just enough room for two cars out front and one in the workshop. If I have to pay money to businesses I prefer to give it to those with the owner's name on the front; they have more at stake and will usually do a good job. Densley was fighting a constant battle against the newer residents who believed having a car mechanic in their midst brought the value of their properties down – something that hadn't concerned them when they'd bought their properties. On the other hand, he had developers offering him huge amounts of money to sell up so they could build a couple of homes on the plot and call them town houses.

But Densley had been there thirty years and wasn't moving. When I got there my car was up on the ramp and someone was underneath, tinkering with it. I went into the small cubicle that was Densley's office. He was fixing a form onto a clipboard which he placed on the wall with the corresponding car keys alongside some others. I spotted my familiar key fob: a small blue Swiss army knife which Olivia had given me. He looked surprised to see me, which was my intention.

"Alright, George? Did we call you?"

"No, that's the problem." He laughed.

"So you thought you'd come and make sure work was being carried out on your car."

"Something like that." He stood up, his ancient office chair gasping after too many years of service. He was a gangly fellow who I'd only ever seen in filthy dungarees. "I heard about your dad passing." I nodded. "Condolences."

"Thanks."

"He brought his first car in here to be serviced, a Hillman Avenger."

"Yes, I remember it." We stood for a few seconds, thinking our own thoughts until he gestured through the dirty Perspex window that looked out onto the workshop.

"Well, as you can see, work is ongoing on your piece of crap. Do you want me to explain all the different ways it's fucked?"

"No, I just want to know when it'll be ready and how much all this is going to cost me."

"My dear George, I believe I advised you to sell the thing and get something relatively new. But no, you wanted to resurrect the beast. Unfortunately it isn't old enough to be a classic, but is old enough to be a pain and a drain."

We went back and forth like this until I got out of him a commitment to have it ready by lunchtime Monday.

* * *

I left Densley's and walked towards Parker's Piece. A group of young men (language students judging by their appearance and shouts) were playing football. Some teenage girls sat in a circle on the grass, heads bowed, thumbs twitching, engrossed in their little screens. When I got to the other side of the green and crossed the road opposite the police station, a bicycle bell rang urgently and I stepped lively onto the kerb. The ringing resumed and I turned, preparing to engage with one of those aggressive cyclists who go around in a constant state of anger, looking for people to gesticulate at. It was Detective Inspector Stubbing, who stopped by the kerb. She looked different. Maybe her hair wasn't pulled back so severely and maybe she'd put on some much-needed weight.

"Stubbing?"

"I thought that was you, Kocky."

We had last parted as George and Vicky but that had been in a rare and misguided show of sentimentality at the end of that nasty case regarding Morley College, which had involved both my father and her then boss, now promoted to pastures new.

"They haven't got rid of you then?" I said, gesturing at the squat brutal building behind her, ever more anachronistic among the shiny new apartments taking over Cambridge.

"I know where all the bodies are buried."

"I don't doubt it." I gestured at her bicycle. "I know public services are being hit by austerity measures but do detectives now have to cycle to crime scenes?"

"I see your levels of wit haven't improved. I'm on my way home as it happens. Trying to keep fit." I still struggled with the idea that Stubbing actually had a home; I imagined her to be permanently moving between office, crime scene and suspects in a state of continuous sordidness. Much like myself. I was about to tell her she looked fit before I realised she might misconstrue it as an invitation to engage in verbal foreplay leading to God knows what. We stood awkwardly for a few seconds before I came up with some suitable small talk.

"You have a juicy case on, I hear. A dead kid."

"Heard from your girlfriend, I suppose. I'm surprised – I didn't think educated professional women were your type."

How the hell did she know about Linda? "I don't really have a type," I said, despite my better judgement.

"It's anyone who puts out, I'm guessing." She smirked, then prepared to move off.

"Shouldn't you be wearing a helmet, as an example to the rest of us?" Hardly the devastating parting shot I was looking for. She showed me her middle finger as she sped away. I walked on, feeling annoyed with myself that I let her get under my skin like that.

To get Stubbing out of my system I went for a pint at the Green Dragon on the river then stopped for groceries on the way home. Linda's car was parked on my drive. She was busy scrolling through her Facebook newsfeed on her phone when I tapped on the window.

"Can't you leave a key under a plant pot or something?" she asked when we were inside.

"I don't have any plant pots," I said, ignoring her real question. Childish, I know, but if she wanted to keep me out of the rest of her life, then I wasn't going to hand over all of mine in a big hurry. Part of me was happy with this ad hoc arrangement, but part of me yearned for something more.

"Hungry?" I said, lifting the carrier bags. "I've got fresh pasta."

After dinner Linda filled me in on some more details regarding the dead girl, although they were scant. She was a teenager, although the cause of death hadn't been established, or at least hadn't been released. "This is according to Vicky," Linda said.

"You're on first-name terms with Stubbing?" When she just shrugged I said, "I ran into her today, or rather she nearly ran into me."

"That's nice for you."

"She seemed to know about us. Any ideas how?"

"She's the police," she said, smiling.

"Hmm. That makes it sound like we're committing a crime."

"When it's good, yes." She laughed when she saw my face. "You're such a prude, Georgie."

"Is that right?"

6

KAMAL SUBLET ONE OF HIS ROOMS TO PAY THE RENT AND HIS
latest lodger was a pale young chap with wispy brown hair
who nodded shyly in greeting as he squeezed past me to
leave Kamal's small flat. Kamal found most of his lodgers at
Addenbrooke's, advertising on the staff noticeboard. Nobody
could afford their own place any more, even if they had
proper jobs. This guy was a statistician or something, a recent
graduate in his first job, or so Kamal told me as we went into
his room. I sat at the two-person table under the window that
looked out over Mill Road.

"Beer?"

I nodded and watched the street while he fetched them.
Muslim men were heading towards the mosque off Mill
Road for Friday evening prayers. The traffic was crawling
at this hour and cycling commuters weaved amongst the
stationary cars along the narrow road. I liked this road, the
mix of people and the cafés and restaurants to go with it.
Kamal loomed into view and handed me a sweating bottle of
something from the Czech Republic.

"Cheers." Behind him were floor-to-ceiling paperbacks on

cheap bookcases sagging under the weight. He kept trying to lend me books to read, like Olivia had, presumably because he also thought I was culturally stunted. His choices were usually a better read than hers had been, which mostly seemed to have been written with the purpose of telling the reader how clever the writer was. He sat opposite and swigged his beer.

"So, I've got some good news for you."

"Yes I know, I could tell from your voice on the phone. It's why you're not very good at the poker table." He pulled a face and fondled his misconceived moustache. It was another poker tell that he had acquired with the lip hair and one I would keep to myself for a while.

"So," he said. "I spoke to one of the Filipino nurses in Outpatients, and guess what's happening this weekend?" He put the beer bottle to his mouth and guzzled.

I shrugged. "I don't know. A beauty contest?" He coughed and spluttered, spraying beer all over the table. His eyes watered as he struggled for breath. "Easy, fella, it wasn't that funny," I said. He started to breathe.

"How did you know?" he rasped.

"Know what?"

"About the beauty contest?"

"What are you on about?"

"This weekend is Philippine Independence Day. It's a big thing apparently, for the ex-pats, anyway. They're celebrating in Cherry Hinton."

"With a beauty contest?"

"A Little Miss Philippines pageant, to be exact, for girls. That's just a part of it. They'll be singing hymns at the church, and there's bingo, a basketball tournament, a bring-and-buy sale, that sort of thing. I've been invited to the bring-and-buy on Sunday. You want to come?"

"Of course, although I'm not watching a parade of little girls."

"Don't worry, that's on Saturday."

I nodded, relieved. "My car's out of action at the moment."

"We'll cycle; it's not far. It'll be a nightmare to park anyway." He paused. "I've never seen you cycle. Have you even got a bicycle?"

"I've got my dad's old sit-up-and-beg bike. Weighs a ton and needs some tidying up."

"I'll have a look at it. I've become a bit of a bike mechanic out of necessity."

"That would be great." I drained my bottle. "The others will be here soon. Shall we set up the table?"

A few hours later and we were collecting chips into their respective colours. It had been an unusually good game from my point of view; I came out on top by ten pounds. Nobody could lose more than twenty pounds and the winning wasn't that important. It was an eclectic mix of people from different backgrounds that you wouldn't normally find sitting together around a Cambridge dinner table – everyone was here just to play poker and engage in a bit of banter.

The next afternoon I was lying on the bed, naked, the sweat drying on my chest. Linda had already been in the shower and had gone to make some tea, or more likely open some wine since it was after five o'clock. It was good to hear kids playing outside for a change, in the same street I had. At the weekends our mothers used to kick us out of the house and we were only allowed back in for lunch. Nowadays they were in their bedrooms all day, talking to each other online. A breeze came through the window. I had that pleasant dreamy feeling you get just before you drop off. The doorbell ruined it. I sighed. I was damned if I was going to get dressed and then undressed again before showering – then I remembered that Linda was downstairs. Maybe it was just the kids. Who else are you going to play "ring and run" on if not the sad old guy who lives on his own with the overgrown garden and battered car? I heard the front door open and there were loud exclamations that only women can make when opening a door to someone they know. Who would call here who knew Linda? I resigned myself to not getting a glass of wine and dragged myself into the shower where I had to hang up the towel Linda had used. Domesticated she was not and in some respects I was glad she never stayed for more than a night at a time.

As I went downstairs, scrubbed and in my finest tracksuit bottoms and T-shirt with holes in it, I heard voices from the kitchen, one of them Linda's, the other disturbingly familiar. I stepped in to see Linda and Stubbing sitting at the kitchen table, a bottle of wine already half-demolished. Stubbing, her hair loose, looked me up and down in a manner that made me feel I was standing in my underwear. She was in her civvies, skinny jeans and a button-down shirt.

"Hello," I managed, glancing at Linda for clues.

"Kocky," said Stubbing, smirking. She never just smiled, always smirked.

"Kocky? Is that what you call him?" Linda asked her, smiling in a knowing manner I found unsettling.

"You've got a dirty mind, Linda. It's not what you think. I misread his name once and it's stuck."

"What's going on?" I asked, trying to regain ownership of my kitchen by finding a glass and pouring some wine.

"Vicky just came round to talk about work."

As I turned I saw Stubbing give Linda a warning look. She stood up and smoothed down her jeans; she'd definitely put on some weight and it suited her. My eyes met hers and I knew she'd caught me looking.

"I was just going," she said. "I'll leave you two lovebirds alone."

I forced a smile as Linda showed her out. There were lowered tones in the hall and some laughter before the door opened and closed. Linda reappeared.

"Sorry about that. She rang me and I asked her round."

"I didn't know you two were mates," I said, refilling my glass.

"I didn't know you two were either."

"We're not."

"Well I didn't tell her where you lived," she said.

"I told you, we worked on a case together."

She laughed. "Alright, whatever you say... Kocky."

I shook my head. "Please don't."

She put her hand on my face. "Still hurts, eh, Georgie?"

"What can I say, she broke my heart. What did she want, anyway?"

She moved to pick up her glass, her face serious. "I was just discussing my piece on the case, you know, the kid at Byron's Pool?" I sat at the table, as did she.

"You were running it by her?"

"No. She wants me to write about it, but she's acutely aware that it's going to be read by the killer."

"Killer?"

Linda grimaced and refilled her glass. "Look, I'm not supposed to talk about it. Anyway, there's something else."

"What?"

"I can't really talk about it. Anyway, you'll read it soon enough."

"I must get some perks sleeping with the reporter. I won't break the story, promise."

She smiled. "There's a London girl missing. Young, fourteen or fifteen. She was in Cambridge Tuesday and apparently never got home."

"What was she doing up here?" I asked.

"She was at a medical students' open day or something."

"Sounds a bit young for medical school, doesn't she?"

"Maybe they got the age wrong."

"And Stubbing thinks the body at Byron's Pool could be—"

"Vicky's not making any connection."

"Fair enough. I would advise caution, though, colluding with Stubbing."

"She's OK. She's a good detective."

"I didn't say she wasn't. But you're the one who'll be compromised as a journalist if you start running stuff by her."

"I'm not running anything by her. I think I know what I'm doing, George," she said. "I don't tell you how to do your job, do I?"

I raised my hands in acceptance. "You're right." I got up to open the fridge, took in all the wasted space and closed it. "Takeaway for dinner?" I asked, but she was standing up.

"I've got plans, I'm afraid. Girls' night out."

7

KAMAL, AS PROMISED, DID A MAINTENANCE JOB ON MY BIKE which meant that Sunday mid-morning he and I cycled down to Cherry Hinton, previously a village in its own right, now a suburb of Cambridge. It was here that the Filipinos were celebrating Independence Day. We tied our bikes up near the Catholic church at the top of the high street. I was sweaty from riding the heavy bike, and had to pull my trousers from between my buttocks.

We walked up to the church where there was a lot of activity. Filipinos, I assumed, were emerging from the church, dressed in their finest. Shrieking kids were running around, but there were no elderly people, reflecting the fact that these were contract workers and their families. Kamal went to look for the nurse who'd invited him while I watched people putting the final touches to the stalls of bring-and-buy foodstuffs set up in the churchyard. A hog roast was already being sliced, the aroma of which made my mouth water. I removed Aurora's photo from my pocket and had a surreptitious look at it. I studied the people sitting behind the stalls. There was some English being spoken but also a language I didn't recognise, with a sprinkling of English words thrown in. I realised that I was attracting a little attention since I was one of the few non-Filipinos on my own. It wasn't unpleasant scrutiny, simply a sort of "I wonder who he is here with?" type of curiosity. Trying to find Aurora (assuming she was here) from a photocopy of an old passport was going to be difficult.

Kamal appeared at my elbow.

"Any luck?" he asked.

"It's going to be impossible, based on the photocopy."

"Maybe we should try a more direct approach."

"What do you mean?" Before he could answer, a short, plump woman with black hair and large glasses appeared at his side. She smiled, friendly, as he introduced me. Her name was Dolores.

"George is looking for someone, a woman," Kamal told her.

Dolores laughed. "A bride, perhaps? There are many women here looking for a husband."

"No," I said, thinking it best to intervene. I took out the photocopy and handed it to her, shooting Kamal a withering look for blindsiding me. Still smiling, she lifted her glasses to look at it, promptly losing the smile.

"What do you want with her?" she asked, suddenly wary.

Kamal made to speak but I put a hand on his arm.

"Her employer wants to speak to her. That's all."

"Are you the police?"

"No, he's not the police, he's a friend," Kamal said.

"I'm a private investigator," I said, taking out a business

card and swapping it for the photocopy. "I just want to speak to Aurora."

"You work for those horrible people?" Dolores asked. Her voice had risen an octave and a few people stopped to listen.

"Is she here?" I asked.

"What do you want with her?" Dolores said. "You know, she should go to the police and report them." A small crowd had now gathered. I tugged at Kamal's sleeve and nodded towards the churchyard gate.

"Please just give her my card. She can call me, just to talk." We turned towards the exit but found ourselves blocked by a group of Filipino basketball players. They were hot and sweaty and must have walked up from the leisure centre down the road where they'd been playing. One of them, holding the basketball, pushed it against my chest. I put my hands on it so we were both holding it and took a step back to remove it from my chest. I didn't push back, just held the ball there and held his gaze, smiling, simpleton-like. I could feel Kamal clenching beside me. Realising that we looked silly, both holding the ball mid-air, he snatched it away and tucked it under his arm. I stood with my hands beside my sides, trying to appear non-threatening.

"What do you guys want?" he asked, looking at me.

"Nothing. We're just leaving."

He spoke to Dolores in the same language I'd heard being spoken and she replied at length, the word "passport" thrown in.

"Tagalog," Kamal said in my ear.

"What?"

"It's what they're speaking." Basketball guy glared at Kamal then turned back to me.

"What's your business with Aurora?" he asked.

"I just want to talk to her, that's all."

He gestured at Dolores. "She says you have Aurora's passport."

"I don't. It's just a photocopy." I took it out and showed him.

"So you have the original?"

"No, her employer gave this to me." The woman spoke to him and there was some back and forth. She was trying to convince him of something. He nodded to her and she disappeared.

"Let's move, we're making a scene here," he said to me, his tone a little more conciliatory. He dismissed his mates and we walked over to the wall of the churchyard.

"Go mingle and let me do my job," I told Kamal. "Before you start any more fires."

He raised his hands, muttering, "OK. OK."

As he wandered off I could see Dolores approaching with someone small enough to be a teenage girl in tow. I recognised the face – it was Aurora. Up close she looked older than her photo, and her dark hair was longer, but it was her, in a floral dress and nice shoes, dressed for church. A head shorter than me, she looked up at me guardedly as I offered my hand. She ignored it.

"They are here?" she asked in a high-pitched voice, looking warily to the road. She was worried, I could tell that much.

"Who?"

"Mr Bill and Mrs Kristina."

"No, they don't know I'm here." She relaxed a little and spoke to Dolores and basketball guy in Tagalog. They nodded.

"I'll be over there," basketball guy said to me, in an I'll-be-watching-you tone and made his way with Dolores towards the hog roast, bouncing his ball. Aurora gestured to a bench and we sat, watching the kids running around in circles together, temporarily free from adult control. She sat with her hands tucked between her thighs.

"They're protective of you, I see," I said to her.

She shook her head, not understanding.

"They look out for you."

"Yes."

"That's good."

She looked at me, surprised, and nodded. "They pay you to find me?"

"Yes. They're worried," I said, although I wasn't sure to what extent.

"And if I don't want them to find me?"

She wouldn't be the first person to say that. Often people don't want to be found, and I deal with the situation as circumstances present. Sometimes all that is needed by those hiring me is reassurance that the person they are seeking is OK. Sometimes they want something more. Certainly I wouldn't put anyone in a situation they didn't want to be in, especially when women were running from men.

"Well, I have found you, so it's a matter of what happens now."

"What happens now?"

I contemplated the busy scene, especially the hog roast, which I could smell from where we were sitting.

"That's up to us, you and me, to decide." She took a long breath and let it out slowly. She still wasn't sure she could trust me.

"What's your name?" she asked.

"George. George Kocharyan." I produced another card and gave it to her.

"What she want, Mrs Kristina?"

"He wants his briefcase. I haven't spoken to her yet."

She didn't look at me but studied the card, flipping it over in case it provided information regarding my intentions.

"What about the briefcase?" I asked. "He says it has medical notes in it."

She shrugged.

"Why did you take it, Aurora?" She wrinkled her small nose. Basketball guy, clutching a hog-roast roll, nodded a question at her and she nodded at him. She turned to me for the first time.

"I can give it, but I want something."

"This isn't a negotiation, Aurora. You stole the briefcase."

She flinched. "My passport," she said.

"What about it? You mean you left it there?"

She sighed, perhaps with exasperation.

"Why not just go back and get it?"

"They have it. They keep it since I come here."

"You mean they've kept it from you?"

She rolled her eyes as if I was stupid. A faint bell rang in my head regarding domestics who'd been brought into the country. I would have to get Sandra to look into it.

"I thought passport was in briefcase," she said.

"But it wasn't?"

She shrugged. "Need numbers to open." I assumed she meant a code. Did people still go around with locked briefcases? Maybe if they contained confidential patient information they did.

"You haven't forced it open?" I made a motion of pulling something apart with my hands.

She looked shocked. "No. I don't break it." She wrung her hands together, her knuckles white. "So, you ask them for my passport?"

"I can ask them about it. I'm seeing them tomorrow afternoon. Mrs Galbraith is away until then."

"She often away."

"On business?"

She snorted. She stood up, straightening her dress. I stood up too but wish I hadn't because I towered over her.

"If I take the briefcase back to Mr Galbraith, Aurora, I can ask for your passport."

She shook her head vigorously, saying, "They give passport, I give case." She held up my card. "I call you. After you talk with them." I didn't push it. I stuck out my hand and this time she took it, but without much enthusiasm. It was like shaking hands with a child. She disappeared into the crowd and Kamal appeared from the same direction clutching a half-eaten hog-roast roll. We went to find our bicycles as he stuffed his face.

"Sorry about messing that up," he said, mouth full of

pig. "But I got carried away with the excitement."

"It's not a game, Kamal, it's my job." He looked genuinely remorseful. "But, as it happens," I conceded, grudgingly, "it turned out OK." We unlocked our bikes.

"Dolores told me that Aurora came to Outpatients a few weeks ago," Kamal said, as I struggled with the lock.

"What for?"

"I didn't ask that, of course, but she did say that they'd had a brief chat. Then Aurora turned up at the clinic out of the blue this Monday saying Dolores was the only person in Cambridge who she could turn to. She said Aurora had walked all the way from Fulbourn." As I cycled home I wondered how much truth Aurora was telling, and indeed how much Bill Galbraith was. People lie to me all the time. All the fucking time.

8

AFTER A DULL BUT NECESSARY MORNING OF PAPERWORK I
picked up my car from Densley's that afternoon. His bill, even
after fifteen minutes of back and forth, was eye-watering, and
ate into my small reserves. So as I headed out to Fulbourn
I hoped that I could draw out the case a bit longer and not
have this meeting be the end of it. That's how you think when
you're self-employed.

Fulbourn is just a few minutes' drive east of the city. I
drove past Fulbourn Hospital, once a Victorian lunatic asylum,
later a mental health facility. After a lot of its inhabitants had
been released into the community, most of the grounds were
turned into a business park and admin offices for the health
authority. It's true that places like that had their problems
but one of their functions was to be somewhere people could
seek refuge from a society that couldn't cope with them –
somewhere they could be themselves without judgement.

Once on the right road in Fulbourn I drove slowly and
passed a pub, the Weasel and Stoat, with a garden busy with
drinkers. A hundred yards beyond it I pulled up outside a
black metal gate in a modern design on which was fixed a

slate sign proclaiming it to be the entrance to The Willows. I turned around and drove to the pub where I parked in the car park. I walked back to the gate and a small camera eyed me from its perch above a metal keypad, buzzer and speaker grill. I pressed the buzzer. Beyond the gate I saw a short drive leading up towards a contemporary-looking house obscured by some large trees. Willows, I presumed. A crackly voice I recognised emerged from the metal grill.

"Come in, Mr Kocharyan." The gate started to slide open. I stepped through the widening gap and it immediately started to close behind me. I walked up the drive to see a flat, architect-designed house on two levels, the upper level jutting out over the first. There was more glass than wall. On the second floor I could see Bill Galbraith standing at a large window. He nodded and pointed beneath him to the front door. He then turned and disappeared. Two cars were parked under a carport, a silver Range Rover with personalised number plate, KR15 TIN, (Bill's wife's car presumably) and an orange Porsche 911 with the top down. It was an old model rather than new, and the leather inside was pleasingly cracked and worn, like the armchair I snoozed in when watching rich men play golf. I wasn't much of a car guy but of the two cars on offer I could see myself sitting in the Porsche; I like to think I have the hair for a convertible.

Instead of swinging open, the wooden front door slid into the wall to reveal Galbraith standing in a very white entrance hall. He greeted me and I stepped onto a white marble floor. Everything was white. Teeth, walls, fittings. Like an operating theatre. He was even dressed in white linen trousers and matching shirt, the only colour a thin blue jumper hanging over his shoulders, the sleeves tied at his chest in a manner only seen in aspirational lifestyle magazines.

"Let's go up," he said. "The house is designed upside down to take advantage of the view."

He wasn't wrong. Upstairs, from the minimalist open-plan living area the size of a tennis court, the back of the house looked out over a large garden bordering a field which in turn gave onto a woodland area. The floor-to-ceiling glass gave the room a feeling of being exposed to the outside but without the messy inconvenience of nature spoiling things. It was cool, despite the afternoon warmth and windows that looked like they didn't open. The kitchen and dining area was in one far corner separated by a granite worktop long enough to park the Range Rover behind. A glass table, complete with acrylic chairs, was set against this. In the seating area where we headed a whole wall was given over to a collection of vinyl records. A pair of large white curvaceous floor-standing speakers, sculptures in their own right, stood guard either side of an expensive-looking turntable and amplifiers. I made some noises about the view since he was expecting me to and we sat in squishy white leather armchairs where I could look out at it. He glanced outside and checked his watch.

"Is your wife going to join us?" I asked.

He shifted in his chair. "She's out running at the moment. I was hoping to catch you first in case we could resolve things before bothering her with it." He couldn't help looking outside. I looked too and could see a runner on the horizon, a woman, judging by the bright purple gear.

"Well, I have made some progress," I said. He turned back to me, looking hopeful.

"And?"

"I've found Aurora." His attention on me was now a hundred per cent.

"So where is she?"

"She's in Cambridge, you were right about that."

"Where? Where in Cambridge?"

"I don't know. But before we get into that there's something we need to discuss."

He looked at me distastefully. "Are you after more money?"

I counted backwards from ten. "I'd like to ask about her passport." His pale face turned the colour of pickled beetroot.

"What? Did you talk to her?"

"Yes."

"I thought I asked you not to."

"I hadn't planned to, but that's how it happened. She approached me, actually."

He looked outside again and I followed his gaze. The runner was now along the border of the woodland and field and heading towards us. Definitely a woman, with long dark hair. Galbraith looked anxious.

"Has she got the briefcase?"

"Yes. She says she thought her passport was in it."

"Has she opened it?"

"She says not. It's locked, according to her."

"Did she say anything else?"

"No."

He held out his arm as a gesture for me to rise and simultaneously looked outside, prompting me to do the same. The runner picked up speed as she approached the waist-high wooden fence at the boundary of the garden and hurdled it. She slowed up once in the garden. Her dark hair was tied back but was long enough that it swung from side to side as she ran. She was dressed in running shorts and top, bare-limbed, pale-skinned. As she approached she looked up, saw him and faltered. Galbraith raised his hand but she didn't respond. I wasn't sure if she'd seen me as I was seated. He turned to me and I stood up.

"Is that your wife? It would be useful to talk to her." But he had me by the arm and was leading me quickly to the stairs. A door slammed somewhere as we descended.

"Bill?" She was at the bottom of the stairs, doing stretches. She saw me and stopped.

"I didn't know we had company."

"This is Mr Kocharyan," he told her. Her expression told him this wasn't quite enough information. "He's an investigator," he added, somewhat reluctantly, as we drew level with her. She shot him a look which I couldn't interpret.

"I didn't realise you were going ahead with that." She still had a Russian accent. She appraised me without smiling and I reciprocated. After running most people look like they've been sitting for ten years in a sauna – but she didn't: she looked like she'd been for a stroll. I could see the likeness from the picture Sandra had shown me, but she looked better now, more natural and settled into her face, less brashly pretty. Late forties, I guessed. Dark, long eyelashes leading to black wells for eyes in which the moon seemed to be reflected. Her face broke into a practised smile and she stuck out a hand to let it rest stickily in mine for a second. "I'm Kristina, Bill's wife. Sorry, I'm a bit sweaty."

Her teeth were perfect, too perfect, like his. I was made aware of my own dental shortcomings.

She placed a hand against the wall and pulled a foot up behind her to meet a well-formed buttock, studying me all the while.

"And Kocharyan, that's Armenian?" I nodded. She turned to her husband. "So, you still insist on finding her. I say good riddance to the ungrateful bitch. I told you I don't care about the pearls."

Bill flushed and covered by laughing like a startled pony. It seemed I was missing some vital information.

"What pearls?" I asked.

Her face went dark. "The ones she stole. The ones he," pointing at Galbraith, "gave me. I never wore them anyway. Do I look like the sort of woman who wears pearls?" She gestured dramatically at her slender neck, as if inviting me to assess it for suitability.

Bill, a pained look on his face, raised a hand in a placatory manner and said, "Kristina is still angry, she feels betrayed by Aurora."

"Bill is wasting his money," Kristina said, ignoring him. "She'll come crawling back. She can hardly speak English and has no one else to go to."

"She seems to have found someone."

Kristina looked genuinely surprised. "Who?" When I

didn't elaborate she carried on. "I brought her with me from Dubai," Kristina said. "We're her family, we look after her."

"So why did she leave?"

"Because she is like a little girl. She doesn't know what is good for her."

"She says she would like her passport," I said.

There was a silence as they both pretended I hadn't spoken. I might as well have broken wind. Rather perceptively I was getting the impression that nobody wanted to talk about the passport.

"Is it true that you have it?" I persisted.

"I have it for safekeeping," she said, shrugging.

Before I could probe further a rapid clicking of claws on the tiles caused Kristina to exhibit genuine delight. "Misha," she cried. A tiny hairless dog the size of a large rat with disproportionately large ears and bulging eyes came scampering up to her on legs made of Twiglets. It caught sight of me and bared its fangs. She scooped it up, cradling it in her arms and making cooing noises. She started kissing it on its mouth as it licked her lips and waved its little legs. It was as if Galbraith and I weren't there. He looked uncomfortable at this display. I empathised; I wouldn't want to be next in line on those lips, however inviting. She stopped long enough to say to me, "If she doesn't come back I will call the police." Mixed messages, to say the least. She moved into another room, muttering baby talk to the bald rodent. I turned to Galbraith.

"You didn't mention any pearls to me."

He glanced to check that Kristina had gone and leant into my personal space, speaking softly. "The pearls don't matter, they're replaceable." His breath smelled sweet, like liquorice. His eyes had narrowed. There was a dark fleck in the left eye, an island in a sea of blue. "Now, just tell me where she is and we can conclude our business."

"I honestly don't know where she is, nor can I contact her."

"I thought you'd spoken to her."

"In a public place. She's going to ring me later."

"Just get her to bring me the briefcase. I need to speak to her."

I took a step back. "If the purpose of finding Aurora is to retrieve the briefcase, why don't I just arrange a trade?"

"What?"

"Her passport for the briefcase. Maybe even the pearls. Everyone's happy." Except his wife, possibly, but he was the one paying me.

He crossed his arms and pondered this as he studied me, calculating something. Then he nodded. "I think that's doable, George. Arrange it as soon as possible."

9

AGREEING THAT I WOULD RING HIM LATER, ONCE I HAD SPOKEN
to Aurora, I left Galbraith and walked back to the pub where
I'd parked my car. It was a nice evening so I ordered a drink
and found a table in the garden which overlooked a rugby
pitch where some enthusiastic amateurs were playing. As I
watched them, nursing a pint and mulling over the strange
conversation I'd just had, I looked round at the throaty
sound of Bill Galbraith's Porsche as it zipped past. He had
sunglasses on, his hair in the wind. Several minutes later
Kristina's Range Rover followed, her sunglasses even bigger
than her husband's. Obviously not a stay-at-home-and-
watch-TV kind of couple.

The mobile phone rang on the office number as I got
in the car. I hoped that it was Aurora, but Dolores's voice
emerged from the earpiece.

"Mr Kockaryan?"

"Kocharyan," I corrected, not for the first time. Was it
really that difficult to get right?

"This is Dolores speaking."

"Hello, Dolores, is Aurora with you?"

"She wants me to check that this is your number." Whose number did she think I'd given her? Perhaps she thought I would trick her into calling her employers.

"This is me," I assured her. There was a short whispered conversation in Tagalog off-mike between her and someone I presumed to be Aurora. After some rustling I heard the definite high-pitched voice of Aurora.

"Mr George?"

"Please, call me George."

"Did you see them?"

"Yes I did, and I need to ask you a question, Aurora."

"OK?"

"Did you take some pearls from Mrs Galbraith?"

"Pearls?"

"Yes, a necklace, jewellery."

There was a pause. "I gave him pearl," she said.

"What do you mean you gave him the pearl? You mean the necklace?"

"I found it in office, when I clean. Under sofa."

I rubbed my temples with my free hand. Was I getting through the language barrier here?

"When you say pearl, Aurora, do you mean pearls, like a necklace?"

"No, just one pearl."

"Just one pearl?" I echoed pointlessly.

I watched a thirty-something couple in work suits kiss passionately in the car park before getting into their separate cars. They each checked themselves in the rear-view mirror before driving off in opposite directions. My immediate thought was that they were lovers sharing a snatched moment before heading home to their spouses. Such is my world view.

"Mr George, I only took briefcase. I am not stealing."

I refrained from pointing out the lack of difference between stealing briefcases and stealing jewellery. She must have heard me thinking.

"I took briefcase because maybe my passport in it. Did they say I stole necklace?"

"You can see how it looks to them, Aurora. The pearls go missing, then you disappear with the briefcase."

"Yes," she conceded. "It look bad. But I not take necklace. She broken it maybe. He knows it broken because I gave him pearl. Honestly. I swear to God. I just want passport. I need to go home."

"To the Philippines?"

"Yes. My girl…' Her voice broke and faded and Dolores came back on.

"Mr Kockaryan. This is not acceptable." Nor is constantly mangling my name, I wanted to say.

"Is her daughter ill?"

"Yes," her voice dropping to a whisper, "she has cancer. She hasn't seen her for many years." There was more whispered Tagalog and Aurora came back on the phone.

"Can you please get passport?" she asked in a broken voice.

"Yes. If you give me the briefcase then I can get the passport in return. He said he was happy to trade."

"Maybe you tricking me?"

"To do what?"

"To give him case and no passport for me."

"Aurora, why can't you just ask for the passport yourself? If you just explained the situation to them—"

"No, you not understand."

"What is it?"

"I will not go there," she said emphatically.

"To the house?"

"I will not."

"OK then. Do you want me to exchange the briefcase for your passport? Can I pick it up this evening?"

"No no no. You trick me. We meet somewhere, tomorrow. I will call you." With that she hung up. Blimey, hard work.

I started the engine then turned it off as the phone rang again. Different number.

"I've been trying to call you." It was Galbraith, in an assertive mood.

"I was about to ring you. I've just come off the phone with Aurora."

"You've already spoken to her?"

"Yes I have. Isn't that why you're ringing?"

"I wanted to make something clear before you spoke to her. What did she say?"

"I can get the briefcase back to you. I'm just arranging for her to hand it over to me, hopefully tomorrow."

"I thought so, that's why I rang. No, that won't do at all."

"What do you mean?"

"I need to speak to her in person. Just tell her to come home and we'll sort it out."

I massaged my temples again, willing the woman who worked behind the bar in the pub to come out on roller skates with a cold beer held aloft and pass it to me through the window. It didn't work.

"I have to tell you," I said. "She doesn't seem overly keen on that idea."

"I don't care whether she's keen or not. I'm paying you, not her."

"True, but that doesn't include me compelling her to do things she doesn't want to."

"Why don't you just tell me where she is, like I paid you to."

"Because I don't know where she is. Like I said earlier, I met her in a public place."

"But being a private investigator, you could find out, presumably?"

No hint of sarcasm in his tone, just a slight pause before "presumably". He was right, of course; if she was staying with Dolores then I could, since Dolores worked at Addenbrooke's. But before I could come up with a half-decent deflection he was speaking again, this time in a more conciliatory tone.

"You'll be seeing her tomorrow, then?"

"Yes."

"Tell her we would like to speak to her. She is family to us and we wouldn't want things to end on a sour note. Tell her we'd also like to give her compensation. Call it redundancy pay. And she probably wants to pick up her things – she left everything behind. Could you pass that on?"

I told him my passing that on was entirely possible before I moved on to something more meaty.

"She is adamant that she didn't take the pearls. She says

she found a single pearl which she handed over to you."

There was a lengthy silence at the other end and I could hear the muted sound of some dreadful symphony coming to a crashing end, followed by the monotonous tone of an announcer, whose words I couldn't make out. I envisaged Galbraith sitting in a car, in a car park, just like I was.

"Tell Aurora it's not too late for us to call the police," he said before hanging up. Blimey, they were both hard work.

I drove home and called Sandra. I could hear the TV, and her boys laughing in the background.

"Do me a favour, will you, tomorrow morning?" I asked.

"Hang on, George. Turn that bloody thing down!" she shouted. The TV sound was lowered and she came back on. "What is it?"

"Foreign domestics. I need to know what the situation is with visas and passports for people brought here as domestics by their employers."

"OK. I hope you're not being sucked into something you don't need to, George, 'cause I've just taken on another background-check job this afternoon."

"Just doing some due diligence, Sandra."

"I know you, you're a soft touch for women in trouble."

"Get Jason started on the online aspect and I'll take it from there." Jason's role with the agency was now limited to doing online research and computer support. In the past I had used him on some cases but the last one he was involved in resulted in his fingers being broken by a sadistic hoodlum which put the kibosh on his burgeoning music career as a keyboard artist, such as it was. Sandra had forgiven me, eventually, but he was no longer allowed to wear out any shoe leather for me, that was made clear.

"I'll look into it. I'm in the middle of making supper if you want to stop by? Nothing fancy."

"Thanks, Sandra, but I've already eaten."

She let out a sigh as if she were being slightly deflated and I ended the call. I'm no gourmand but Sandra's cooking was just an extension of her coffee-making. One of the things I missed about Olivia was her cooking. Her cookbooks were one of the few things she'd taken with her to her new life in Greece. She was probably cooking the same meals for that woman as I stood in my empty house, my empty stomach rumbling. Adept at recognising the onset of self-pity, I went to the kitchen, put on the radio to a station that was playing some Bach and rustled up a cheese omelette which was gooey in the middle and perfectly folded. I washed it down with the dregs of a bottle of white wine left by Linda and decided that my life was, at that very moment, OK.

10

I WOKE ALONE — SOMETHING I'VE BECOME USED TO, AND NOT an altogether unpleasant feeling. I liked having Linda over, but I'd lost the knack of domesticity that I had acquired with Olivia. Linda kept none of her stuff here, preferring to bring an overnight bag. This suited me on the one hand, but on the other hand something was lacking, and I was left feeling dissatisfied. These contradictory thoughts bounced around as I showered, shaved and made coffee before driving to work.

As I turned onto the drive of my office building I noticed two guys standing against a black Ford Focus parked on the other side of the road. One was white, blond, bearded, longish hair tied at the back. The other was darker and smaller, squat but with a weightlifter's torso and shaved head. He wore a T-shirt tight enough to show off his gym membership. His blond companion was dressed like a preppy. Any health consciousness was offset by the fact that they were both smoking while ostentatiously checking their phones. In my mirrors I could see them looking at my car as I parked. Over the years, in my game, you get a feel for people who are up to no good, and to be frank a lot of career-criminal types are not of the highest intelligence, lacking any subtlety or finesse. These two seemed a little out of place; there was nothing on this road one would hang around for. There was a doctor's surgery next door but that had a car park. On the side they were parked was a department of the university but that also had its own car park.

I wrote down the number plate as Maggie, one of the women co-occupiers of the building, arrived on her bicycle which she locked onto the covered bike rack. She smiled as I got out of the car. In her fifties, she had a full head of striking grey hair, plaited down to her waist. I liked the fact that Maggie didn't colour her hair, and wasn't trying to recreate a younger version of who she was. She was a relationship counsellor, and sometimes I referred people to her when the shit hit the fan and I thought they could still make a go of it, which to be honest wasn't often after they'd been through my office. She was the only occupant of the building who gave me the time of day. The others thought I disturbed the flow of the building's chi; a walking black hole of negativity that sucked at the positive energy of their holistic endeavours.

"Morning, George! You ruin any marriages yet today?"

"No, but it's still early. What about you? How's the relationship business?"

She checked around her before saying, "Cambridge has a never-ending supply of troubled couples with disposable income so I'm not complaining."

I laughed as I opened the building door for her. "Let's go get 'em." I left her in the communal kitchen and headed up to the top floor. Jason, Sandra's son, was in the office hunched over her computer, tapping away.

"Boss," he said, by way of greeting, without looking up. He'd taken to wearing his hair shaved at the sides but long and slicked back with gel at the top. Coupled with his stubble he looked like an arse. I didn't say anything but his mother characteristically didn't hold back and to his credit he weathered her scorn with stoic self-assuredness. He loved the investigation business; and if it wasn't for his mother he'd be doing a lot more, were it not for that finger-breaking incident. Since he was over eighteen, and I was an adult, we could have overruled his mother, but you did that at your peril.

"What's the rumpus?" I asked him, going behind him to the window, where an obsolete fax machine waiting on the floor to be taken to recycling got in my way.

"I'm just doing some online research on this guy you've been asked to background check."

"Who's the client again?"

The two men, whom I nicknamed Bill and Ben, had now got into the Ford Focus and were blowing cigarette smoke out of the open windows.

"It's the software company," he said. "In the Science Park. They think the guy they're hiring, some computer whizz, might be working for a rival."

I moved to my desk as the phone started to ring. "It's good to know that industrial espionage still needs bodies on the ground in this digital age." I silenced the phone.

"Cambridge Confidential."

"Mr George?" The high voice was becoming familiar.

"Aurora. How are you?"

"We meet today?" There was some general hubbub at her end.

"Of course. Where and when?"

"At hospital. In the main area. Twelve o'clock."

"At Addenbrooke's? Are you sure you want to meet there?"

"Yes, why not?" she asked, sounding unsure.

"Mr Galbraith works there, remember?"

"Oh! No, he not here today, he making TV show."

"Fine, I'll see you at midday." Sounded like she was already there – probably went in with Dolores.

I hung up and looked through the post that Jason had put on my desk. Nothing that Sandra couldn't deal with, although where was she? I could never remember when Sandra was supposed to be working. Jason took out a metal comb and ran it through his hair. I stared at him in distaste.

"Where's your mother?"

"She's on her way. Said she had some phone calls to make." I didn't ask what calls in case it was her other job, although I thought those would be nocturnal events rather than straight after breakfast, but what did I know about it?

"I'm off to Addenbrooke's," I said.

"But you're not meeting until midday, boss. It's only ten."

"Should you be listening to other people's conversations?"

"I thought that's exactly what you did in this line of work." I showed him my middle finger and headed out.

The Ford Focus was still there and I watched the occupants in my mirror as I reversed onto the road. I pulled out parallel to their car but pretended not to notice them. Heading in the direction they were parked, just to make it easy for them, I drove down to the roundabout then turned round and headed back the way we'd come. They were right behind me, not even leaving a car or two between us. Amateur hour, unless they wanted me to know they were there, but judging by their feigned disinterest when parked on my road I'd say they just didn't have a clue; they certainly weren't trained in surveillance. I had no idea who these guys were or what they wanted but right now wasn't the time to find out. My priority was to meet Aurora without taking them with me.

I headed slowly to Densley's garage, making sure I didn't lose them, and backed into his forecourt. The Ford Focus parked in a residential parking space on the street.

Densley obviously wasn't pleased to see me.

"What's wrong?" he asked.

"With the car? Nothing. I need a favour."

He looked relieved. "What is it?"

"I've got unwanted company and need to borrow one of your guys." I explained what I had in mind and Densley called one of his men in. I handed him my car keys and stepped onto the street where I stood for a second before walking off. I could hear the Focus start up and crawl along behind me as I turned left at the next junction. It was a dead end. For cars that is. There was a gap at the end with bollards, a gap wide enough for bicycles and pedestrians. I walked through it and stopped the other side long enough to hear the car door open and close. I risked a glance to see the smaller, top-heavy Mediterranean-looking guy coming through the bollards, looking at the ground. I decided he would be Ben. The blond driver of the Focus, now called Bill, would be desperately trying to do a three-point turn, but if things went to plan Densley's recovery truck would be blocking his way for a few minutes. I walked on and turned a corner to see Densley's man walking towards me, my car parked further along. He grinned as he passed and I nodded discreetly. Getting into my unlocked car I found the keys in the ignition as agreed. In the wing mirror I could see the guy following me react in panic. He got out his phone and stabbed some buttons, putting it to his ear. Starting the engine I slowly pulled out. I couldn't resist sticking my hand out of the window and waving jauntily as I set off for Addenbrooke's. Sometimes my job can be fun.

II

CAMBRIDGE COULD BE SAID TO CONSIST OF TWO WORLDS: THE university, and the rest of the town. The two really don't interact much, except where some of the latter service the former. Plumbers, cleaners, cooks, gardeners, child-minders, electricians and the like, who keep the university grounds looking tiptop, the hot water running, the meals served on time, the drains unblocked, the beds made. They also take care of the domestic arrangements of academics to allow them to inhabit their ivory towers unencumbered by the mundanities of running a home. It is a co-dependent relationship in which both parties couldn't really exist without the other but do so with an underlying resentment hidden by smiles and money. My father had served these people as a butler at Morley College and I was one of those who occasionally (and reluctantly) made their living from the tribulations of those who worked among the hallowed spires – spires that were being increasingly undermined by the continued erection of architecturally challenged blocks of tall apartments that mysteriously made it through the council's planning committee.

There is, however, a third Cambridge world that

straddles both town and gown, serving and employing both: the large complex on the south of the city that I now drove into – Addenbrooke's Hospital, or, to give it its proper title, Cambridge University Hospitals. It was now big enough that its chief executive was more a mayor than CEO of this sprawling mini-city, complete with its own power source and network of roads and buildings. Given it was a teaching hospital and linked to the university, many of its consultants were also university professors and, according to Kamal, begrudged the fact that Addenbrooke's was a general hospital that provided the local population with mundane medical care that got in the way of being a cutting-edge medical research facility.

I parked in one of the staff car parks using a cloned parking pass acquired through one of Kamal's flatmates who used to work here. Parking in the visitors' car park was exorbitant, and although I could reclaim it as an expense, it was paperwork that I could do without.

The concourse in Addenbrooke's main building reinforced the feeling of a small city. There was a food court complete with all the fast food chains you could find on any high street (surely a reason for many of the admissions?), as well as a bank, travel agent, dry cleaner, newsagent, hairdresser and solicitor. If you worked here and lived on site you need never leave.

After a long wait I saw Aurora, wearing jeans and an oversized T-shirt, standing next to my basketball-playing friend, now dressed in scrubs. Was he a surgeon? Up close his staff badge told me he was a theatre orderly, and that his name was Joshua. This time he shook hands with me and we looked for a table in a quieter part of the food court, Aurora like a small child walking between us. I was disappointed that she didn't have the briefcase with her, but perhaps it was with Dolores somewhere in the hospital.

"I'll be over there," Joshua said to Aurora, pointing to a sandwich bar. Of course you will, I thought. Aurora and I sat down. The place was starting to get busy with both hospital workers and visitors, as well as the odd patient in pyjamas wheeling a drip around, putting people off their lunch.

"You speak with Mr Bill?" she asked, straight to business.

"Yes I did. He's happy to give you the passport but he wants to see you." She started to knead her hands together.

"Why?"

"He wants you to do the exchange in person. He, they, want to talk to you."

Judging by her reaction I might as well have suggested that she had to sleep with him in return for her passport. It occurred to me that maybe she already had, willingly or not. She could have been cajoled into it or worse, forced. It might explain why she'd left and her aversion to going back there.

"Is there any reason meeting them would be a problem?"

She shook her head but her hands said otherwise. I had an urge to put my hands on hers, to reassure her and keep them still, but Joshua was looking at us as he took ownership of a newly created foot-long sub and I doubted he would take kindly to physical contact on my part.

"He talked about giving you redundancy pay." Actually he'd called it compensation at first, which on reflection was an odd word to use in this context. Compensation for what?

But Aurora just looked perplexed.

"He wants to give you money," I explained. She visibly perked up at the mention of money.

"How much?"

"He didn't say."

"Three hundred and sixty-nine pounds."

I couldn't help smiling. "That's a very specific amount."

"That is cheapest ticket for Manila." She wiped her palms together. "I have no money."

"Right. What if I organise a meeting with Bill Galbraith and negotiate a package?"

She reverted to her confused look.

"I mean you would get your passport and at the very least the cost of the ticket to Manila, maybe even some more?"

"I have no money to pay you."

"You don't have to pay me. I'm being paid to return the briefcase, so as long as that happens then everyone is happy." Joshua wandered over and sat at the next table. He was already halfway through his sub and his chin glistened with some green relish. I could have pointed to my own chin so he would get the hint but he might not understand and it could get awkward. Instead I turned back to Aurora.

"Look, I don't know what happened between you and the Galbraiths, but if you want to leave, and frankly I don't blame you, then maybe I can help you. But you need to give me something, Aurora."

She frowned. "The briefcase?"

"No, no. It was an expression. You have to help me to help you."

"How?"

"Do you want to tell me what happened, at the Galbraiths'? Why did you leave?"

She looked at me like a rabbit in headlights, unable to speak.

"Was it Mr Galbraith?" I persisted. "Mrs Galbraith?"

She looked round wildly, and had forgotten to breathe. Joshua suddenly appeared beside her. He spoke to her gently in Tagalog, his hand on her shoulder.

"Is she OK?" I asked him.

"She'll be fine, she gets panic attacks. Are you done here?"

"I guess so."

They stood up and she looked at me.

"I go to the house," she said, then pointed at me. "If you go to house."

"Of course I'll go with you. I'll speak to Mr Galbraith and arrange it. How can I contact you?"

She had a whispered conversation with Joshua and he came over.

"I'll give you my mobile number," he said.

I bought a sandwich to go and headed to the main entrance where I came across Kamal in his dark blue porter's uniform pushing an elderly lady in a wheelchair. He was bent over, talking to her as they trundled along. She seemed amused at something he was saying. He spotted me and stopped.

"Aha, here's a friend of mine. Dorothy, this is George."

She smiled at me, her eyes clear and bright. She stuck out her hand and I took it, her grip unexpectedly firm.

"Nice to meet you, George."

"Dorothy." I pointed to Kamal. "Is he looking after you?"

"He's taking me to lunch," she said.

"Just you watch out, Dorothy, he's got a reputation."

"Maybe I'm the one with the reputation," she said, winking. We all laughed. Kamal leant towards her.

"I just need to have a quick chat with George here, Dorothy. He's a private detective and working on a big case which I'm helping him with."

"Right you are," she said, rolling her lovely eyes at me to let me know that she was humouring him. We stepped aside although Kamal kept one hand on the wheelchair, as if worried Dorothy might decide to make a break for it.

"I've been asking around about our good-looking friend," Kamal said to me.

"And?"

"In a nutshell, his senior registrar does most of his surgery 'cause he's away filming and the consensus is that his TV career is more important to him than his work here."

"Any gossip about his personal life?"

"Curiously nothing. I mean he's a looker and there are no shortage of women in this place who wouldn't have a go, married or not, but there's not a hint of it. You'd expect at least some speculation."

"Perhaps he's gay," Dorothy said, looking at us like butter wouldn't melt in her mouth. Kamal and I stared at her. Clear eyes, a firm handshake and perfect hearing; what exactly was wrong with the old bird? Kamal turned to me and shrugged.

"Maybe she's right."

"Maybe he's just happily married," I said.

For some reason the three of us found that funny.

12

TO MY RELIEF THERE WAS NO FORD FOCUS PARKED ON THE street when I got back to the office. The first thing that sprung to mind as to why I would merit such attention was some grudge from a previous case, an errant husband perhaps. Of course it could also be related to my finding Aurora – maybe Bill Galbraith was keeping tabs on me. Although to be honest the idea that someone of his social standing would know people like those two seemed unlikely.

Upstairs, Sandra was eating some leftovers from a Tupperware pot. Something fish-based, judging by the smell. I ought to have rules about smelly food in the office, just in case a client comes in. Her mouth full, she raised her eyebrows at me in greeting as I put my hospital-bought lunch down on my desk. Jason's report was sitting there, neatly presented in a plastic folder, the name of the target printed on the front. He'd compiled all the information he'd gleaned going through their social media and other online activity, what Jason called their "digital footprint". It's surprising what information people give away online. You can build up quite a picture from a variety of sources. Of course some people are canny, and only reveal what they want to reveal. I remember some philosopher saying that we erect a statue of ourselves in our head, and spend all our time trying to live up to that image – an accurate definition of the sort of narcissism that appears to make up a lot of Facebook, it seems to me. Jason had set up fake Facebook and LinkedIn accounts so we could connect with them and check their professional profiles. Sometimes, if we were given a password (by a suspicious/ disgruntled partner) and had an email address, we could log on to a variety of websites (people use the same email and password for everything), like Amazon and eBay, just to see what sort of items they were buying or browsing. Even looking at someone's Netflix account gives you a window into their personality. It's scary stuff and I'm glad that I avoid taking part in all that shit.

I read through the report while eating my sandwich. The interesting thing about this particular target was that he'd gone quiet online after applying for a job at the software company that had hired us to look into him. He'd been prolific before, posting something several times a day, but then he'd gone off the radar. This led Jason to dig a little deeper and he discovered an old post on a Reddit subreddit (whatever that was) – one used by coders to exchange code and tips – by someone using the same username and avatar that the target had used on another social media platform. In the post he'd been unable to resist boasting about who he was working for on contract, which happened to be the main rival company to the one who'd hired us. This wasn't an issue in itself; except when I double-checked his CV he'd omitted it for some reason.

I made a call to the company and agreed to come up to the Science Park later that afternoon, as they needed to make a quick decision as to whether to hire or not. I then tried to call Galbraith but the mobile he'd called me from was switched off and his medical secretary confirmed that he was away. I told her to ask him to call me if he checked in.

"You asked me to find out about foreign domestics?" Sandra said.

"Ah yes, I'd nearly forgotten about that."

"You are still interested?" she asked, a little edge to her voice.

"Yes, of course." I sat up and gave her my full attention.

She consulted a piece of paper on her desk. "Well, I spoke to a charity based in London that deals with foreign domestic workers. It's a thing, apparently, bringing in domestics from abroad. They come in under something called…" – she glanced at the sheet – "… the Overseas Domestic Worker visa, which basically ties them to their employer; they can't work for anyone else. There are high rates of physical abuse and a lot of them say they're not allowed to leave the house and don't get any time off. Often they have to sleep in the kitchen or share with the kids. Most of them are on less than fifty pounds a week."

"Modern-day slavery, then."

"Pretty much. Do you think this Filipino woman is one of those?"

"It's possible. They have her passport."

"Really? Yes, that's common with this type of worker. The employer holds onto the passport so they can't leave.

She might not even know she was on such a visa and it might have expired. How long has she been in the country?"

"I don't know."

"Are you going to help her?"

"First you tell me I'm an easy touch for women in distress, now you want me to help her?"

"I don't see the contradiction."

"Never mind. I'm trying to get her passport back, and some money so she can go home. Beyond that…" I shrugged, not having really thought any of it through – I didn't know whether she'd be able to travel if she was here illegally, *if* she was. I stood up and stretched.

"I'm going to grab a coffee from Antonio's then head over to the Science Park with this," I said, picking up Jason's report. "Jason's done a fine job. Ask him to do a digital footprint report on the Galbraiths, will you?"

She raised her eyebrows. "But they're the clients."

I smiled. "I thought you wanted me to help the maid?"

"OK, I'll tell him. Why don't I prepare an invoice for the Science Park job for you to take? That way it's done and delivered." That right there is how Sandra kept this business afloat. Or maybe she just needed to make sure she got paid each month.

After two rejuvenating coffees and a perusal of the Cambridge *Argus* (still nothing on Linda's dead kid), I drove to the Science Park, delivered a verbal report to the director of human resources and gave them the invoice that Sandra had prepared. The company decided they wouldn't give him the job, "just in case".

As I waited in the right-hand lane at the traffic lights to exit the Science Park I spotted the distinctive KR15 TIN number plate on the silver Range Rover as it headed out of town towards the A14. Being in the wrong lane to follow her I pulled into the left lane, just as a shiny Merc approached the lights, and ignored the horn-blowing and hand-waving that this generated behind me. My car was old and battered and hopefully gave the impression that I didn't give a toss, so the sort of respectable person driving a nice Merc was likely to stay within the safe comfort of their car. I was wrong. A bald, pugilistic-looking fellow in an expensive suit emerged from the driver's door and headed my way. He didn't look like he wanted to talk about the weather. Luckily the lights changed so I didn't have to hang about to find out.

I could see Kristina's car waiting at the lights on the roundabout that leads onto the A14. I was three cars behind her as the lights changed. The Merc was two behind me. Apparently he was the sort of driver whose road rage got the better of him; he wasn't going to let it go. I followed the Range Rover onto the roundabout and we went all the way round and back onto the road we'd just come off. Had she spotted me? No, she was turning off into the grounds of a new hotel, part of a cheap chain that springs up on major routes to provide rest to the weary traveller, a Premier Lodge or Travel Inn or some such thing. She drove into the car park and I followed, as did the bloody Merc driver. Rather than park and risk a confrontation I did a slow circle round the car park, watching Kristina, dressed in a trouser suit and large sunglasses, enter the hotel carrying nothing but a large shoulder bag, the sort that had a silk scarf tied to it as a style statement. I had to do three loops of the car park before the Merc driver, hooting furiously, finally decided to call it a day in his pursuit of justice. I hoped he didn't give himself a heart attack while driving, if only because he might cause an accident and kill some poor innocent.

I parked up where I could see the entrance and Kristina's Range Rover, put the seat back and waited, wishing that I hadn't had that second cup of coffee at Antonio's.

13

IT HAD BEEN NEARLY AN HOUR SINCE KRISTINA GALBRAITH HAD gone into the hotel and my bladder had long since reached its natural capacity. I used to keep a two-litre Coke bottle cut off at the top in the car for when I was caught short on a stake-out. I replaced it with something fit for purpose with a screw-on lid after an unpleasant incident going too fast round a corner with a bottle of urine I'd forgotten to empty wedged between the passenger seat and the door. The resulting smell had taken several weeks to fade and I still got a whiff when I opened the door on a hot day – it was a bit like entering an elderly care home where the heating was on too high.

Unfortunately, the mobile urinal which I'd replaced the bottle with was sitting in the bottom drawer of my desk in the office where I'd put it after rinsing it. I'd forgotten to bring it back to the car.

I now regretted my sloppiness, although to be fair I hadn't planned a stake-out. If I had I'd have brought food, a book and a flask of coffee. Coffee was the wrong thing to think about. Damn that gratuitous second double-shot Americano at Antonio's. There was no handy shrubbery nearby and the car park was open and in full view of the hotel rooms. There was no getting away from it, I'd have to risk being seen by Kristina and go into the hotel.

I made it without incident to the hotel entrance. Inside the small lobby I couldn't see a sign for any toilets so stepped up to the reception desk where a bored young man forced himself to look up from something behind the counter (I'm guessing his Facebook timeline) and coerced his pasty face into the semblance of a smile.

"Toilets?" I asked, hoping to convey urgency without desperation.

He pointed down a corridor and the sight of an illuminated male figure over a door had not been more welcome than when three kings saw a bright star over Bethlehem. The exquisite relief of emptying a full bladder cannot really be explained so I won't try. Suffice to say I was whistling a happy tune as I washed my hands – it may have been from *Snow White and the Seven Dwarfs*. A handsome grey-templed Asian man in a natty blue suit came in as I put my hands under the noisy dryer. We actively ignored each other as men in toilets do, and I left.

So far so good. Now I just had to get back to my car without being seen. When I got back to the lobby, however, there was Kristina, her back to me, standing by the doors looking at a very large smartphone. Her sunglasses were wedged in her impossibly satiny black hair. I froze, then looked round for an escape. There was none; this was a no-frills place where people came to break their journey. Where were they supposed to get food round here? Thinking about it, the hotel was ideal for an illicit meet-up; out of town, only reachable by car – I was surprised I hadn't been here before in a professional capacity.

"Can I help you, sir?" It was the pasty-faced young bloke, no doubt wondering why I was standing in the lobby looking like a trapped deer. I waved nonchalantly at the bastard and naturally Kristina, alerted by his question at someone else's presence, turned round. Shit. Our eyes met and her mouth opened, either in alarm or possible speech. The man who'd come into the toilets passed me and went up to her. She switched her gaze from mine and smiled awkwardly at him. He placed his left hand, wedding ring and all, on the small of her back. He was fit, tall, and oozed self-confidence, the sort of man who can't get past the fact that he's good-looking. I immediately took a dislike to him. They moved through the doors and I picked up a leaflet describing the delights of punting in Cambridge before following.

Kristina and the man parted ways without making any physical contact as I emerged into the car park. She all but ran to her car as he sauntered off in another direction. I went to my own vehicle, keeping him in view. He was parked in a corner, a sensible low-emission new-model Toyota. Not really the type of car I'd have had him down as driving, not in that suit. I wrote down the licence number as he took off his jacket and put it carefully on a hanger in the back. I watched Kristina speed off; I would no doubt have to deal with her later. Or not, since she might pretend it had never happened.

I stayed with the Toyota, following it out of the car park

towards the city centre and as we did so I saw that there was a burger place behind the hotel, no doubt complete with toilets. But there was no time for regrets as I concentrated on keeping a few cars between me and the Toyota. We headed into the middle of Cambridge, crossing over the river on Elizabeth Way. Did he live this centrally? On the roundabout coming off the bridge the lights changed just as he went through them and I was resigned to sitting there watching him drive up East Road towards Parker's Piece, being ever more obscured by the cars and buses coming from my left until he disappeared.

I considered heading on to the office but didn't really see the point, so when the lights changed I went round the roundabout and headed slowly home in rush-hour traffic.

I got indoors just in time to avoid a downpour. No sooner had I closed the door on it than Linda called on the landline.

"What you up to, Georgie?" She sounded relaxed, like she'd had a little help.

"You coming round?"

"I don't think I can," she drawled. "I'm a teensy weensy bit high."

"I can pick you up."

"Come to my place, you mean?"

"That's what it would involve, yes." The office number on the mobile started to ring. No caller ID.

"I don't have men back to my place. You know that, Georgie."

"Men?"

"I shouldn't need to explain it to you, of all people. Is there a phone ringing at your end or is it mine?"

"Can you hold on a minute, Linda?"

I answered the mobile. "Hello, Cambridge Confidential."

"Mr Kocharyan." It was the pleasingly accented voice of Kristina Galbraith.

"Mrs Galbraith, would you mind holding on a second?"

I put the landline back to my sweaty ear. "Linda?" But Linda had hung up. Good, in a way. I have only ever been able to deal with one woman at a time. Back to the mobile.

"Hello, sorry about that."

"I think we should meet, don't you? In light of, erm, this afternoon."

"I'm sure that's not necessary."

"I would like to meet. If that's acceptable to you, of course."

"Yes, of course. I'm just saying—"

"Perhaps it would be easier to say whatever it is face to face. I would certainly find it easier."

"Of course. When would you like to meet?"

"This evening?"

"Can it wait until tomorrow morning?"

There was quiet at the other end. I couldn't even hear her breathing. The landline started to ring again. It was probably Linda; maybe she'd thought about the benefits of me going round to her place and changed her mind.

"Is tomorrow morning OK, Mrs Galbraith?"

"As long as you aren't planning to mention this afternoon

to anyone else? Or haven't done so already?"

"No, of course not. You needn't worry about that."

"I'll see you tomorrow first thing, at your office."

She hung up without as much as a confirmation or a goodbye. Nice. I picked up the landline as it stopped ringing.

"Linda?" Nothing. She'd given up. The mobile rang again. No caller ID – maybe Kristina was ringing to apologise for being so brusque.

But no, it was a man, sniggering, saying to someone at his end, "Hang on, you wanker, he's answered the fucking phone."

"Who's this?" I asked.

"Is that the Kardashians?" Peals of laughter from him. Great – drunk prank callers.

"Apart from being a fuckwit, who are you?" The laughter stopped.

"Where you hiding that Filipino bitch, you little Armenian shit?" An accent that could match my squat weightlifting friend. Maybe.

I hung up and turned off the mobile – I'd had enough phone calls for one evening. Two things crossed my mind. I hadn't given Mrs Galbraith the office number so she must have got it from her husband somehow – maybe he'd just left the card lying around, maybe she'd asked him for it. The second was that the two clowns who'd rung, assuming there were two of them, had also got the office mobile. Unlike the work landline, the mobile number was only given to people actively taken on as clients.

14

NO FORD FOCUS OUTSIDE THE OFFICE, BUT KRISTINA'S RANGE Rover was there, on the street. I parked on the drive and crossed the road to it. She was sitting in the driver's seat, looking frustrated while fiddling with the radio. I moved to the passenger side on the pavement and her little rat of a dog stuck his head up and looked at me balefully. The window slid down. A heady scent was released, and summarily spoilt by yapping. She snapped at Misha in Russian. The radio was emitting the sound of static with intermittent reception. She switched it off.

"Mrs Galbraith."

"Call me Kristina, please. Mrs Galbraith sounds so... formal."

"Would you like to come up to the office?" I asked, although it wasn't my first choice of place to invite people. She hesitated. "Or I know a place that makes decent coffee, just round the corner?"

She got out of her enormous car with her enormous shoulder bag which she opened and little Misha jumped in.

A minute later, after an awkwardly silent walk except

for her mutterings to Misha to stay in the bag, Antonio was fussing around her like a lovelorn teenager. She was undoubtedly the sort of upmarket customer he yearned for in his café, especially in her expensive-looking tailored trouser suit. I had to make eyes at him to leave and make the coffee. Thankfully it was too early for hipsters so we had the place to ourselves. I grimaced as an American crooners' medley came over the sound system that Antonio had misguidedly installed. At least it offered us some privacy.

I coughed to get things started. She looked me in the eyes and it was an effort to pull myself from their draw. I waited for her to speak.

"Tell me the truth, George. Did my husband hire you to follow me?" she asked in a rush.

"Right, I could see how you might think that, given the, um, circumstances of our meeting yesterday afternoon. I can assure you it was entirely coincidental."

She thought about whether to believe me. I listened to Sinatra fill the silence.

"So what were you doing there?" she asked, just as Antonio arrived with the coffees and biscotti.

"On the house," he insisted, fussing around, reluctant to leave. Annoying, but it gave me time to think of an answer.

"If I was following you, Mrs Galbraith, you wouldn't have seen me," I said, at the risk of sounding pompous. She picked up her coffee and smelled it before taking a tiny sip to check it for heat. She put the cup down and picked up a biscotti which she slipped into her bag. Some frantic chomping could be heard. She fixed me with her eyes.

"I suppose you've come to some conclusion as to what I was doing there?" she said, holding my gaze.

I struggled to keep mine steady. "In my business I have found that it is a mistake to jump to conclusions."

"But most often the simplest explanation is the correct one, no?"

She was right, but I wasn't sure what she was hoping to get out of this conversation. I could only imagine she was worried about one thing.

"Look, this has nothing to do with what I have been hired to do so there is no reason for me to mention it to... Mr Galbraith." I almost said "your husband" but it might have sounded pointed.

She barely nodded and looked down at her coffee. "Things have not been good between me and Bill." Oh dear, she was about to unburden herself.

"You don't have to explain yourself, Mrs... Kristina. It's really none of my business and believe me, I make no judgements."

"It might seem hypocritical of me but I do love my husband, Mr Kocharyan. It's impossible for anyone to know what goes on in my marriage, and why we do the things we do."

She was wrong there. I was perfectly capable of understanding how she might have found herself in her current situation; there are many good reasons why people might find solace elsewhere, without wanting to jeopardise what they have with someone. But I also know that just as often it is simply a matter of lust, and in my experience the more intelligent the person succumbing to physical desire, the more elaborate their rationalisation as to why they did.

Her eyes had welled dangerously. Why did this always have to happen to me? Did I give off some sort of vibe? Mind you, Johnny Mathis and Deniece Williams were warbling about how things were all over and it was all too little, too late, so perhaps I should be giving them the credit. I handed her a napkin. She took it but tears didn't come; instead she blew her nose.

"Bill has been focussed on his surgical career," she said, as if this explained everything.

"And now he has a second career," I said.

She offered me a wry smile. "Yes, he's found a new path, but he couldn't have done it without being a good surgeon." Personally I didn't see the connection: people who are adequate at what they do but have a knack for self-presentation and are pushy are often those who rise to the top of the pile.

"I'm sure you've helped him along the way. Behind every successful man and all that."

She gave me a look and a little smile.

"And you have your own career?" I asked, laying on the praise.

"I run a successful business. Not somewhere you would visit, though," she said.

"Try me."

"A beauty treatment parlour. I'm in the process of opening a second one in London. I have an MBA..." She trailed off, perhaps realising how unnecessary it was to add.

To be fair she was probably tired of being judged on her looks and wanted to be taken seriously; but it made her sound insecure.

"You're right, I don't think I've ever been in one, except as a kid when my mother was getting her hair done."

"Men need to look after themselves too." She took a business card out of her cavernous bag and handed it to me. It was black with cursive writing on it that read "Kristina's Treatment Parlour" with a phone number and physical and web addresses underneath. "It's on Green Street. I can arrange for a manicure and pedicure." She didn't appear to be joking so I smiled politely and pocketed the card.

She slipped Misha another biscotti before draining her coffee.

"Can I ask you something?" I asked. "About Aurora."

She shrugged non-committally.

"Did you know that her daughter is ill?"

She looked at me pitifully. "You believe her?"

I was taken aback; it's true that I had taken Aurora's story at face value. "You think she's lying?"

"She's just a child. She's like a teenager…" tapping her head, "…up here. She does things to get attention." She gathered her bag impatiently. She didn't want to talk about it but I figured she owed me, given my discretion.

"And her passport?"

"What about it?"

"Why do you have it?"

"I told you before, for safekeeping. How long do you think she'd survive out there on her own?"

I shrugged; she'd done alright so far, but I didn't say it. Kristina stood up. I felt obliged to do the same.

"Thank you for seeing me, Mr Kocharyan."

So it was back to formalities. I risked a last look into her eyes before remembering something. "By the way, Aurora is insisting that she didn't take your pearls."

"What, are you working for her now?" she asked with a strained laugh.

"She says she found a single pearl in your husband's study and gave it to him. It's quite a specific lie to come up with."

"Did you ask him about it?"

"Yes, but to be honest he's more concerned with getting his patients' notes back."

"What?"

"The notes in the briefcase she took." She looked puzzled so perhaps she didn't know about the briefcase or the notes, or even both.

I let her walk off. I could have gone with her to the car but I felt that would invite more social awkwardness than either of us wanted to deal with. Instead I sat down again and Antonio came over.

"More coffee?"

I nodded. "Is the *Argus* in?"

"I'll get it."

"And can we turn the music down?"

He gave me a black look and took the used cups away. More customers came in and got out their laptops. Paul Anka came on but was thankfully turned down. Sinatra was one thing, Anka another.

Antonio brought fresh coffee and the newspaper and looked at the half-empty plate of biscotti.

"Did she like?"

"Yes, she loved them," I said. He took the remainder away, because I, a regular paying customer, wasn't worthy of them. I unfurled the *Argus* and the front-page story was by Linda.

YOUNG GIRL FOUND DEAD AT BYRON'S POOL MAY HAVE BEEN MURDERED

THE BODY OF A GIRL FOUND at Byron's Pool last week has yet to be identified. Blond and blue-eyed, she was found by fishermen last Wednesday by the car park at Byron's Pool, a favourite Cambridge nature spot near Grantchester that is popular with walkers and anglers. Following a post-mortem police believe she died from a blow to the head suffered prior to being unceremoniously dumped at the popular dog-walking and fishing spot. Detective Inspector Victoria Stubbing, who is leading the investigation, now suspects foul play and is treating it as a murder investigation.

Coincidentally, Jackie Rowling, from north London, has been reported missing by her parents after visiting Cambridge University. According to her parents, Jackie didn't come home last Tuesday night after taking the first steps to fulfilling her dreams of becoming a doctor by attending the medical school open day at the university and hospital.

DI Stubbing refused to comment on speculation that the body found at Byron's Pool was Jackie Rowling, despite the fact that they are of a similar age and description. We have learnt that Jackie's parents are abroad visiting a sick relative and have therefore been unable to identify the body, but are travelling back to do so. DI Stubbing reiterated that Cambridgeshire police were following all leads, and that they didn't want to jeopardise inquiries at this stage, or to attach undue importance to any one piece of evidence.

Byron's Pool has become an impromptu public shrine to the dead girl…

And so it went on. Linda had seemingly written the piece using a trowel, noting that the missing girl Jackie was of course loved by all her classmates. Her headmaster said she was destined for great things and had her heart set on going to Cambridge to study medicine. There were pictures of flowers at Byron's Pool, where there was already a sizeable shrine created by members of the public.

The whole thing, to be blunt, was a reporter's wet dream of a story, down to the blond and blue-eyed nature of the victim. I don't know whether Stubbing had agreed the piece or even told Linda more than she was letting on but the way Linda had written it made it sound like the police had something that they were withholding.

15

WHEN ANTONIO WASN'T LOOKING I POCKETED THE NEWSPAPER in retaliation for the biscotti and strolled back to the office. I was unsurprised to see the Ford fucking Focus. It was pointing away from me, and as I approached I could see the two heads of Bill and Ben, the blond Bill in the driver's seat and the brown shaven head of Ben in the passenger seat, both looking down at what I presumed to be a phone. Occasionally one of them would glance at my office building. Time to get acquainted with these clowns.

I strode purposefully up to the car and could see through the passenger window that they were engrossed in watching a football clip on a small screen. I rapped hard on the window. Their reaction was priceless, and if I'd owned a smartphone such as the one they were watching, I'd have filmed it and posted it to YouTube, admittedly with a little help from Jason. Bill dropped the phone and his passenger Ben stared at me, mouth agape. He'd sadly missed out on orthodontic treatment as a boy and his current expression would have made an ideal "before" photo for any cosmetic dentistry practice. Bill scrabbled around for his phone in the footwell while the orthodontically challenged Ben urged him to drive off. Bill started the car and pulled out into the path of a slow-moving open-topped tour bus which had to stop with a wince-inducing screech of brakes and surprised shouts of those early-season tourists on the top deck who were trying to save their expensive cameras and selfie-sticks from flying overboard. The Focus also stopped, the driver just inches from the front of the bus.

I felt bad for nearly causing an accident but it quickly passed when the tourists started to lean over the side and photograph the scene. The Focus eventually got away and the bus followed. I crossed the road to see Galbraith's Porsche in the drive. Well, first the wife, then the husband. At least it saved me trying to get hold of him.

Upstairs, I found the office door open and Sandra fawning like a teenage girl over Galbraith, who was sitting in the visitor's chair in front of my desk. I'd not seen this side of her before and it wasn't pretty. Like most people of his background he was holding forth with a confidence and self-assurance that I'd always envied. She was rapt. I mean elbows-on-her-desk, head-in-hands rapt. I thought she was immune to this sort of bullshit. He was talking about some rake-like celebrity with whom he'd done an episode of his show and was describing her ridiculously strict diet.

"She looks gorgeous of course. I mean, I like a thin woman, but is it worth it?" he was asking. I wondered if he'd taken in Sandra's size or whether she just didn't figure on his radar in that way. But Sandra was just nodding as if Galbraith were the Dalai Lama come to impart much-needed wisdom.

I coughed and they both looked up. Sandra sat up, to her credit looking embarrassed.

"Ah, George. I was just about to ring you," she said.

"I was on my way to the hospital," Galbraith said. "I hope you don't mind me dropping by."

"Of course not. I'm assuming Sandra has offered you something?"

"I'm fine. I haven't got long."

Sandra made some excuse, smiled at Bill and winked at me behind his back as she left the office, closing the door behind her.

"So," Galbraith said as I took the *Argus* from my jacket and flung it on my desk before sitting in my chair. "I thought we could sort out this meeting with Aurora. I'm keen to get it done as soon as possible. I have to fly off at the end of the week so, you know…"

"Sure. I did try to contact you yesterday. I'm about to ring Aurora to arrange something."

He leaned forward. "Great, why not ring her now and we can do it while I'm here. Saves you trying to reach me – I'm all over the place at the moment. It'll be done and dusted." He brushed his palms together to illustrate, crossed his legs and sat back expectantly, like he'd just made an incredibly sensible suggestion that I should have thought of myself. He was right that it made sense, but I wasn't jumping up and down at the idea of calling Aurora while he was in the room. I didn't really have much choice, though.

"I only have an intermediary's number, and he might be at work. Like I said, I don't actually know where she is."

His smile was fixed as I dialled Joshua's mobile. I watched Galbraith as it rang interminably. He checked his watch and fiddled with his wedding ring, then absently picked up the newspaper, holding it up to ask permission to unfold it. I nodded and thought of his wife and the other man at the hotel. Did he have even a suspicion? A sleepy voice in my ear replaced the incessant ringing.

"Hello?"

"Hi. This is George Kocharyan. I met with Aurora yesterday, while you were there," I said, avoiding saying his name in front of Galbraith. "I hope I didn't wake you?"

"Yes, you did. Who do you want?"

"I want to speak to Aurora, if I may," I said, in case he thought I'd called him up for tips on basketball dribbling techniques.

"Hang on a minute," he said, not sounding too pleased. There were noises as he got out of bed and opened a door then called out Aurora's name. Galbraith was deeply engrossed in the newspaper. "She'll ring you back," Joshua said.

"She's going to ring us back," I informed Galbraith, who had to be coaxed out of whatever he was reading.

"Oh, erm, right." He looked at his watch, bothered. "Look, George, I'm going to have to dash, I'm afraid. Surgery lined up, have to scrub in, you know how it is."

"What about done and dusted?" I asked, a little tetchily. He stood up, his fists knuckle-white around the newspaper.

"Sorry, but I've just had a text. Complications have set in with a patient, surgery's been brought forward." Now, unless I'm losing my powers of observation, which I'm not ruling out, I did not see him look at his phone. In fact I was pleasantly surprised to see that he wasn't the sort of person who automatically pulls one out whenever they have fifteen seconds to kill.

"When are you free?" I asked.

"Tonight. Let's do it tonight. Just let my medical secretary know what time." He was itching to get off.

"You mentioned compensation, for Aurora. How much are we talking about?"

"I was thinking a thousand."

"Make it fifteen hundred," I said. "She needs to fly home."

"Fine," he said impatiently. He turned on the heel of his pristine trainer and strode out, taking my newspaper with him. The mobile phone rang.

"Mr George?"

"Aurora, how are you? Are you ready to go and see Mr and Mrs Galbraith?"

It was late afternoon when I got back home and I was up for a siesta. I'd agreed with Aurora, via Joshua, that I'd pick her up at seven-thirty from outside the church in Cherry Hinton and we'd go to Fulbourn together. I'd let Galbraith's secretary know we'd be at her boss's house for eight. I'd told Sandra to try to trace the registered owner of the Ford fucking Focus that thankfully had not reappeared. I'd also given her the licence plate of the Toyota that Kristina's mystery man had driven off in. On the way home I'd stopped to part reluctantly with money for a new copy of the Cambridge *Argus*, partly because it had Linda's article on the front page. Although

I wasn't keeping a scrapbook of her cuttings I wanted to show her that I'd read it; I understand it's a big deal to make the front page. But I'd bought it mainly because I thought there was something in it that had spooked our surgeon, and naturally I was curious to know what.

I lay on the sofa and leafed through it, looking for anything beyond the boring small-town ephemera that made up the bulk of its content. At first I thought that he may have been interested in the piece about the body at Byron's Pool but then I came across a one-paragraph story about Addenbrooke's. Nothing earth-shattering – something about the director of medical audit being dismissed for using his computer inappropriately at work, which could only mean one thing. If and how it related to Galbraith I didn't know. There was a connection with something or someone I knew or had met but it eluded me. I let the paper drop to my chest and had a pleasant daydream about Linda and the washing-up before drifting off.

16

I'D BEEN SLOPPY SOMEWHERE ALONG THE LINE BUT I WASN'T
sure how or where; that reckoning would have to happen
later when I did some sort of self-debriefing exercise, as I
was busy braking hard in front of the descending railway
barrier on Cherry Hinton High Street. Companies have
policies and procedures to offset the stupidity of people in
their employ. The best I had were some basic rules. I adhere
to these basic rules even if they seem counterintuitive,
which can compensate for sloppiness. This train of thought,
appropriately enough, swirled round my head as I waited
anxiously and impatiently at the flashing lights of the railway
crossing, my eyes straining to keep visual contact with the
Ford Focus which had just crossed the barrier.

I was thirty minutes early. Indeed one of my basic rules
is Always Be Early. Nothing dents your professionalism
more than being late, and you also never know, like now,
what being early will reveal to you. I'd been driving up the
Cherry Hinton High Street towards the Catholic church
outside which I'd arranged to meet Aurora when I realised
that Bill and Ben were in the FFF in front of me just as

the warning lights on the old-fashioned railway crossing started to flash. They, of course, accelerated across before the barriers started to descend, because it was the sort of idiotic thing they would find fun, even if it put their own and other people's lives at risk in the process. Either that or they'd spotted me, but that seemed beyond them. I thought of joining them in a mad dash across the track, fearing the worst for Aurora, but the red and white gates descended as the sparks came off the bottom of their car scraping the hump created by the railway track.

Now I was waiting desperately for the train to arrive, praying that it wasn't one of those extra-long waits when the gates stayed down after it had passed to allow for another one coming from the other direction. A train eventually trundled past, at a seemingly snail-like pace, and I gripped the steering wheel, hoping that Bill and Ben being here was simply a coincidence and nothing to do with my meeting Aurora. Again, that was for later analysis. The train, which also seemed unusually long, passed by, as I rocked back and forth, praying for the gates to go up. Please let there not be another train.

"Yes!" I shouted, as the barriers started to rise. I accelerated like a joyrider, the gates still rising and lights still flashing and felt a clunk as the bottom of the Golf met the road. Densley would be pleased. I created some distance from the cars behind me and reached the church in time to see Bill and Ben on either side of Aurora, each holding an arm, cajoling her to cross to the Focus parked on the other side. They got her to the kerb, she looking confused, clutching what I took to be Galbraith's briefcase. I blocked their progress by screeching to a halt in front of them. For the second time today they seemed surprised to see me as I came out of the car roadside, the engine still running, and headed quickly towards them.

Another basic rule of mine is that in these situations you need to go in like you mean it. Like you're crazy enough to not care about the consequences of what you're doing. People like that are scary – I should know, they've scared me more than once – so it sort of, sometimes, if you're lucky, makes sense. This approach has a better rate of success if you are bigger than the person or persons you are trying it on. In this case it was true of one of them but not the other, who although shorter, was stockier to compensate.

Luckily it made sense here and now, because Bill, the weedy-looking white guy with the blond hair and beard, let go of Aurora's arm and stepped back. Weight-lifting Ben, he with the crooked teeth and perhaps a little slower on the uptake than his colleague, merely appeared confused by my presence. He looked to Bill for an explanation and I took Aurora's free arm and pulled her towards me.

"Let go," I shouted at him, which surprisingly he did, clearly used to following instructions without thinking. I pulled Aurora towards my car but Bill had recovered enough to realise that this wouldn't do at all. He took a step towards me as I pushed Aurora towards the passenger door, hoping she would be proactive and get in. Ben reached for something in his back pocket. I didn't wait to see whether it was a business card he was retrieving to give me, but instead kicked him where his tracksuit bottoms met in the middle. He groaned and buckled satisfyingly. I glanced back at Aurora who was standing there, mouth open.

"Get in the car," I urged.

She opened the door and Bill took the opportunity of my distraction to take a swing at my head. I only managed to escape the worst of the impact by jerking back. He caught me a glancing blow on the cheek and it was enough to get me off balance. I could see in my peripheral vision that he was coming for me again but the brass corner of Galbraith's briefcase caught him on the side of the head and he slammed into Ben who was on his feet but bent over, still unable to stand upright. Their collision bought me enough time to run round to the driver's side.

"Get in," I shouted to Aurora, who was standing legs apart, clutching the briefcase handle with both hands, perhaps surprised at what she'd just done. This time she obeyed.

Ben was coming towards me, a butterfly knife in hand, murder in his face. I slipped in to the well-worn seat as he grabbed the passenger door handle and pulled. His other hand held the now open butterfly knife. As it was opening I put the car in gear and accelerated without closing my door, narrowly missing a cyclist on my outside who swerved onto the other side of the road, causing an oncoming taxi to take evasive action and crash into the parked Ford Focus. Ben had let go of the door handle so I slowed down.

"Close your door, Aurora," I said, shutting my own. She just sat there, looking forward, probably in shock. I reached over her and pulled her door closed, my eyes on the road.

When I put my left hand back on the steering wheel I saw blood on the cuff of my shirt. I glanced at Aurora.

"Are you injured?"

She looked at me, confused.

"Are you hurt, Aurora? Your left arm."

She checked her bare arm and touched it with her right hand. She showed me the bloody hand. Shit. I wasn't prepared to stop this close to Cherry Hinton, even though Bill and Ben were probably busy politely exchanging insurance details with the taxi driver. I reached to the glove box and pulled out a small first-aid kit. Let it not be said that I'm not health and safety conscious. I gave it to Aurora who nodded and, using the briefcase as a lap-desk, took out a bandage and proceeded to use it on her wrist.

Driving aimlessly, I pondered what to do next. The Galbraiths' was out of the question until I had figured out what had just happened. First I had to make sure Aurora was OK and not seriously injured.

"Is it bad?" I asked her.

She shook her head. Good, but I would still need to get it checked. Her mate Dolores lived in Cherry Hinton and I wasn't going back there in case the men turned up again.

Sometimes there is really only one place you can take a woman in trouble, and that's to another woman. So that's where I steered my car.

17

"WHAT AM I SUPPOSED TO DO WITH HER?" SANDRA SAID AT the front door of her terraced house in north Cambridge, looking beyond me to the car where Aurora stood clutching the briefcase which she hadn't let go of since getting in the car. I hoped she appeared vulnerable and forlorn enough to summon Sandra's pity.

"It's just for the night, Sandra." She huffed and puffed and relented, as I knew she would, and I gestured to Aurora who came forward tentatively.

"What's with the briefcase?" Sandra asked.

"It's her bargaining chip," I said, although I was beginning to think there was more in it than just patients' notes. For the moment though, I needed to talk to Galbraith and told Sandra so as we all went inside.

"He rang after you'd gone."

"What? Why didn't you bloody tell me?"

"Behave. I'm telling you now."

"Well? What did he want?"

"He wanted to ask me out, of course."

"Come on, Sandra, I'm not in the mood right now."

"Oh, it's so hard to believe is it, that he might be interested in me? I know men are brainwashed with images of thin women—"

I put my hand up; this wasn't the time for a lecture on the social construct of male sexuality.

"Sandra, Aurora here was almost kidnapped by some hoodlums and cut in the process. The reason for which is beyond my grasp at the moment. Galbraith is likely the only person who somehow, but I'm not sure how, knew I was going to meet her there." A horrible thought struck me: maybe he had asked Sandra out, distracting her with his oily smarm, and teased the information out of her? Perhaps I was being paranoid, but Bill and Ben hadn't followed me there – they'd arrived before me.

"Did he ask about me picking her up when he rang?" I asked her.

A vein in Sandra's temple started to throb dangerously. Her eyes were like needles in mine.

"He just wanted to speak to you," she said, very controlled. "I would never give out your whereabouts or movements to anyone."

We locked eyes for a few seconds.

"What did he want to talk about?" I asked.

"I don't know. He wouldn't say."

I noticed that Aurora was looking distressed at our exchange.

"What's happening?" she asked. Sandra, finally appreciating the situation Aurora was in, adopted a mollifying tone lacking in our exchange.

"Nothing, Mummy and Daddy are having a fight. Let's have a look at that arm."

"Just a minute," I said, as Sandra started to lead Aurora into the kitchen. They stopped. I pointed to the briefcase.

"Aurora, why don't I take that to Mr Galbraith and get your passport, and the money? Then this will all be over."

She thought about it but shook her head, pulling the case to her chest.

"Maybe try tomorrow, George. She's been through enough for one night." Well, I tried, and to be honest I didn't blame her – it was her one bargaining chip. "By the way," Sandra said, "I checked those number plates you gave me. One of them, anyway. I could only ask my contact for one favour at a time."

"And?"

"It's registered with a lease company. That's the most I can get at the moment."

"Which car was that, Sandra?"

"The Toyota. I'll try the lease company tomorrow, see if I can blag any more info, although you are aware that once you're licenced blagging becomes illegal?"

She was right: once the regulation of private investigators came in, engaging in that sort of dubious practice would make getting a licence impossible. "Better make the most of it then," I said. She led Aurora away. Jason appeared, eating an apple.

"Boss. What's the rumpus?" he asked, mouth full.

"Nothing."

"OK…" he said, unconvinced. "Oh, I've had a trawl

online looking at the Galbraiths, like you asked." He waved the apple at me. "Do you want to see what I've got so far?"

"Not now, I have to go. Keep digging."

I drove over to Fulbourn as it got dark, trying to make sense of what had happened earlier. Why hadn't Bill and Ben just snatched the briefcase from Aurora if that's what they wanted? It would have been easy enough between them; she wasn't exactly built for fighting, although I liked the way she'd swung the briefcase at Bill (or was it Ben?).

Why try to take her?

The Galbraiths' house was the centre of activity when I arrived. Five or six cars filled the drive and a Bentley with privacy windows was parked in front of the open gates. I turned the car round and parked in the pub car park down the road again. I thought about fortifying myself with some Dutch courage but it remained a thought.

I checked the cars on the drive, just to make sure the FFF wasn't there, but they were all high-end cars one or two years old: Mercs, Beamers and Audis, apart from Bill Galbraith's Porsche which was, of course, a classic. As I approached the house I could see people milling around on the upper floor. Galbraith, unless he was trying to break down class barriers, had not intended for us to attend a dinner party. Perhaps he had anticipated that we would conclude our business quickly in the scullery, or perhaps, I speculated, pressing the bell, he wasn't expecting us at all. To give him the benefit of the doubt maybe his secretary hadn't passed on my message.

"You're here," Galbraith said, slightly taken aback. Then, "Where's Aurora? Is she in your car?"

"Really?" I asked. "You're going to play it like that?"

"Play what like what? What are you on about? Where the hell is she?" He lowered his voice and leaned into me. "We had a fucking arrangement." His breath smelled of wine and cured meats.

"Someone tried to kidnap her and the briefcase," I said. "Someone who knew where we were meeting."

To be fair, he looked genuinely shocked, but that could be because he'd been rumbled.

"Bill? Who is it, my darling?" Kristina asked from the top of the stairs, her voice falsely bright. I couldn't see her from the door, but imagined her dressed for dinner.

Bill stepped outside, sliding the door to. "What on earth are you talking about?" he said.

"Why did you ring the office this afternoon?"

"I wanted to—" He looked over my shoulder, his eyes widening. "Who the hell are you?" he demanded. I turned. Bill and Ben were a good stride back from me, slightly in the shadows. Blond Bill looked past me at Galbraith.

"Mr Badem says to go inside, Mr Galbraith, and that he'll join you shortly," he said in a softer, more educated voice than I'd had him down for. "Everything will be fine." He held his hands together loosely in front of him. They contained something too big to be a knife but I couldn't make it out.

I turned to Galbraith. "Might be a good time to invite me in for dinner," I suggested. He looked over my shoulder and reached behind him to open the door just enough to back into the house. It slid closed after him. No dinner for me.

Before I could turn, arms gripped mine. Something metallic was placed against the back of my neck; it felt like two points. Bill and Ben were either side of me. Blondie Bill was at my right. He was holding whatever it was with his left hand, his right clamped to my wrist. Ben had both his hands on my left arm. Whatever was pressed against me didn't feel like a firearm, or a knife.

"That's a Taser at your neck," Bill gently explained, a bit like a doctor talking through a procedure he's about to perform. "It's set to what they call 'drive stun' mode, or 'contact' mode, which is used for pain compliance rather than disabling at a distance. Do you understand?" Ben sniggered, a noise familiar from the hilarious Kardashian call last night. Since I'd kicked Bill in the nuts earlier in the evening, I deduced he was itching for an excuse to administer some pain compliance.

"I'm cool," I said. "What's the plan?"

"We're going to turn round and walk to the gates. Mr Badem is waiting."

"I'm dying to meet Mr Badem," I said, as we turned round. The Taser was pressed harder into my neck and Bill's mouth was at my ear.

"I've never used this on someone's neck before, so dying could be a distinct possibility. Shall we go?"

I decided it was best to shut up.

18

WE WALKED DOWN THE DRIVE TO THE BENTLEY WITH THE
tinted privacy windows parked outside the gate. Crooks
and celebrities always have tinted windows. Ben knocked
on the rear-door window and opened the door, releasing a
great cloud of cigar smoke from inside. He gestured for me
to enter, with Bill placing his hand on the top of my head to
guide me in. He followed, the Taser moving to the side of my
neck. Inside, a very large man, whom I took to be Mr Badem,
was doing a Sudoku puzzle in a big book of Sudoku puzzles.
He had a fountain pen in one hand, cigar in the other, double
chin supporting his fat head. The door thunked satisfyingly
behind us and I was wedged between the two on the pale
soft leather. The heady smell of spicy aftershave battled for
olfactory supremacy with the cigar smoke.

"Put that away, Leonard, it's unnecessary," the fat man
told Bill. Disappointed though I was to learn Bill's real name,
I was pleased when he removed the Taser from my neck. I
waited, focussing on my breathing, not wanting to advertise
my fear. Badem looked at me with green eyes topped with
free-range eyebrows and ear hair to match. Badem was a

Turkish name, I knew that much, and historically the Turks were no great friends of my ancestors. Ben, I realised, had got into the driver's seat. He grinned at me through the rear-view mirror, remarkably unselfconscious about his teeth, which oddly enough I found endearing. Mr Badem cracked a window and chucked out the remainder of the cigar. Smoke was thankfully sucked out.

"I shouldn't be smoking those, Mr Kocharyan. Not at all. Doctor's orders." He had an accent to him, not strong, one he had worked on to suppress, along with the verbiage to impress.

"We all have our vices."

"I took up Sudoku to help me stop smoking. Now I do both. Do you do Sudoku?"

I shook my head. "I'm a chess problem type of guy. I take it you must be Mr Badem."

He put his pen inside his jacket and handed the Sudoku book to Ben, then stuck out a giant hairy hand. "Apologies for this most unsatisfactory way of meeting." I let my left hand be engulfed in his moist flipper.

"I feel, Mr Badem, that some sort of explanation is in order."

He laughed, using his stomach, which undulated beneath a black silk shirt. The laugh turned into a wheeze, then a full-blown coughing fit. Neither Leonard nor Ben seemed concerned. Badem, incapacitated, reached out blindly to the front and Ben put a cotton handkerchief in his grasping hand, obviously practised at this. Badem wiped his eyes with it before handing it back.

"An explanation. Yes, of course," he said, finding his breath. To my surprise and alarm he slowly unbuttoned his shirt, his big fingers struggling with the tiny buttons. I looked at Leonard who was staring longingly at his still fully charged Taser. Ben just grinned at me in the mirror. Eventually Badem tried to turn to me, his shirt undone. I looked at his exposed chest and stomach, heaving with each breath. Between his pendulous breasts ran a long, still-red scar. He looked at me expectantly. I wasn't sure whether commiserations or congratulations were in order. Then, masterful detective that I am, I remembered whose house we were parked outside.

"Galbraith was your surgeon," I said.

"He saved my life. He and a young man on a motorbike. Do you know what surgeons call motorcyclists?"

I shook my head.

"Organ donors." He chuckled and tried to rebutton his shirt but struggled; getting the buttons back through their holes was harder than undoing them. "He's a great man," Badem said, gesturing at the house behind the willow trees.

"So…?" I prompted.

"So? I owe him my life. So, when I go to the follow-up clinic and he tells me that my medical notes are missing because his maid has run off with them, I decide to help him out, such a great man is he."

"By following me?"

"You were withholding. You wouldn't divulge the location of the maid."

"I didn't know where she was," I said.

"Maybe you didn't at that time." He shifted his head to study me more closely. "But you do now." It wasn't a question. He stared at me so I could grasp the significance of his statement. I wasn't happy about the direction things were headed, and they hadn't started from anywhere good. I needed to buy time.

"May I ask a question?"

"Of course, but I am late to dinner at the house, so…"

"Why didn't your men here just take the briefcase with your notes in it? Why were they trying to kidnap the woman?"

He smiled and pointed a sausage finger at me. "That's a good question, Mr Kocharyan… Armenian, if I'm not mistaken." Another statement that didn't need an answer. "I'm Turkish, you know," he said, allowing history's baggage to settle heavily on our already imbalanced relationship.

"I'd worked that out, Mr Badem." He smiled, but his demeanour had hardened.

"You asked why Leonard and Derin here didn't just take the case from the girl, although I disagree profoundly with your description of their effort to persuade her to accompany them as a kidnap." Ben, now revealed as Derin, was busy digging something out of his nose. "If you take something from a great man such as Mr Galbraith…" Badem was saying, "…then there should be consequences. Returning the case is a given. Getting my notes back is a given; they are needed for my personal care. But I strongly believe more is required of her than that. She owes her employer a grovelling apology. I think that's what he is expecting, at the very least. Then there is the matter of a fitting punishment. It's a question of honour, you see. She is in his employ."

"Yes, the employ of a great man," I said. Leonard, perhaps the only person to catch my tone, tapped my thigh with the Taser. "Mr Badem," I continued. "The irony is that I was in the process of bringing the domestic – she's called Aurora – to meet with Mr Galbraith, to come to an arrangement, when I found your men manhandling – sorry, persuading her to accompany them."

"I concede that it is an unfortunate coincidence, Kocharyan." What happened to Mister? "But the problem presenting itself to us right now is that you know where she is and we don't."

I felt trapped. Badem absently caressed his left breast and I felt nauseous, what with the smell of aftershave and cigar, Leonard fondling his Taser and Derin feeding himself with whatever he had found in his nose. I closed my eyes and tried to breathe through my mouth.

"How did you know she'd be there?" I asked.

"You ask many questions, but provide very few answers." Giving up on his buttons, he said something to Derin in Turkish who turned in his seat and leaned into the back to button up Badem's shirt. "Derin is my sister's boy," he told me, like I gave a shit. Then I realised that he felt it necessary to explain Derin.

I thought of making a dash over Derin onto the front passenger seat and then out of the door but all Leonard had to do was press that thing against me. My best bet would be going through Leonard himself, but up close he looked more canny than I'd initially stereotyped him as. He was resting against the door at an angle, so he was turned towards me slightly, and although he seemed to be occupied with his own thoughts there would be no element of surprise. I thought about using my witty banter to induce another coughing fit in Badem, but even if possible, the idea of trying to get over or past him to open his door and jump out was more fantasy than plan.

"So," Badem said, now fully buttoned. "I must go to dinner with my surgeon and his lovely wife and the other interesting guests while you tell Leonard and Derin here where the girl is."

Leonard, who hitherto had perhaps been meditating on life's injustices, came alive. Derin got out and opened the door for his uncle.

"It's been a pleasure to meet you, Mr Kocharyan." He started to slide out. The Taser was reapplied to my neck. "I like you," Badem continued. "So I hope that you will be sensible and not cause yourself too much pain. I feel your people have suffered enough." Once out he leaned back in, huffing and puffing. "Leonard, please don't activate that infernal contraption inside the car. Last time you used it I seem to remember the consequences being involuntary urination and defecation."

"Right you are, Mr Badem," said Leonard, smiling at me. "Not in the car."

19

I'M NOT VERY GOOD WITH PAIN, AND WOULDN'T DESCRIBE myself as stoic. So I went to my happy place, and visualised myself in the pub down the road, sipping a pint of the guest beer and perhaps indulging in a game of darts with an eccentric local. Imagine my surprise, therefore, when we disembarked from the luscious yet cloying interior of the Bentley and started walking towards the pub along the road. Perhaps positive thinking worked after all, and merely imagining a good outcome could make it happen. Of course Leonard and Derin were either side of me, close, gripping my arms as before, so that took the shine off things. To allow for the fact that we could be seen like this on the road by passing motorists, Leonard had moved the Taser from my neck to the base of my spine, where it was less obvious, although he made sure to explain, in his kindly doctor's voice, the risks of permanent paralysis if ten thousand volts were applied for too long a period.

"I've disabled the five-second safety override," he explained. I didn't know what he meant or whether paralysis was actually possible but it wasn't something I wanted to put to the test, especially since sweat was running down my spine into the small of my back. According to my basic knowledge of physics that would only increase conductivity, right?

Unfortunately nobody drove past us, so any ideas I had of leaping into the path of an oncoming car were unrealisable. But we were walking towards the pub, and therefore people. Leonard and Derin too must have parked their car there; I hadn't thought to look for it when I was there.

"Electrocution and paralysis aside, what's the plan, fellas?" I asked as cheerily as I could muster. There was no answer but the lights of the pub were a welcome sight. Lights meant people and that offered some hope. I presumed they wanted to know where Aurora was, and it seemed to me that this was all a bit OTT for some twisted concept of honour that didn't really affect the person orchestrating it, namely Badem. But then a lot of people get killed in the name of honour so who was I to question its pernicious hold?

We turned into the pub car park which was only half full as it was a weekday.

"How about we talk about this over a drink?" I could see the Ford Focus in the corner, previously obscured by a since-departed plumber's van. To get to it we were going to pass my car. Derin, to my left, spoke up for the very first time.

"A drink sounds really good right now," he said, leaning forward to look across me at Leonard.

"Shut up, Derin. We get the bitch, then you get a drink."

A group of four burly men tumbled out of the pub, laughing and joshing loudly. From the rugby club, by the look of them. All the better. One of them had his mate in a mock headlock, rubbing his bald head.

"Easy now," Leonard said softly, pressing the Taser anew into my sore flesh. "No funny ideas." Leonard was wary about attracting attention, which offered a glimmer of hope.

"I need to get something from my car," I said, as we drew level with it.

"We're going in your car," Leonard said. "You're going to drive." At that moment I realised that Leonard was sensible and would not take unnecessary risks, which is why I decided to do what I did next.

"My keys are in my trouser pocket," I said to him, jiggling my arm to let him know I meant his side. He relaxed his grip.

"OK. Slowly mind," he said.

I nodded, lifted my head towards the group of men and shouted at the top of my voice, "YOU FUCKING CUNTS!"

"Shut up!" Derin hissed, sounding terrified. "What are you doing?"

The men went silent and looked at us, not believing what they'd heard. No pain shot through me. Nothing happened. The Taser dropped from my back – Leonard, as I'd hoped, wouldn't do anything stupid in public that would attract attention.

The men were striding towards us, angry. "What did you say?"

"He's drunk, mate," Leonard said, trying to laugh it off. "No offence meant."

"WE'VE JUST BEEN FUCKING YOUR MOTHER," I shouted, in case my first provocation was attributed to high spirits. "SHE LIKES TO TAKE IT UP THE ARSE!"

They charged, from just twenty feet away. Leonard and Derin instinctively let go of my arms, Leonard's Taser now held out in defence at the incoming herd. Derin turned and high-tailed it out of the car park, back to his uncle no doubt. I felt for my keys and scrambled over the bonnet of my car with all the grace of a shot-putter. It didn't go well – my head and shoulder met the hard ground the other side of the car just as Leonard's Taser met three hundred pounds of rugby prop, judging by the scream. Although I was away from the action I was now on the passenger's side and unfortunately my car is too old to have remote locking so I had to actually fit the key into the lock. I focussed on this normally simple task, trying to ignore one of the guys heading to my side. I opened, slid into the car, shutting and locking the door just as he arrived and started pulling on the handle. I moved over the handbrake to the driver's seat, the key slippery in my sweaty fingers. Leonard was pressed against the window, the Taser pinned uselessly between his chest and the glass. The guy on the passenger side gave up trying to open the door and began to rock the car instead. Leonard was pulled from the window and held in a bear hug, the guy he'd Tasered still stunned, sitting on the ground. Now two of them were rocking the bloody car, one each side, and it was listing alarmingly, first one way, then the other. These guys would have no problem tipping it over, given there were no cars parked either side – it was exactly the sort of challenge drunken rugby players would rise to.

I don't know if you've tried getting your car key in the ignition while two very strong men rock it in ever-increasing arcs and your sweaty hands are trembling with adrenalin. It took a couple of hit-and-miss stabs until the key finally found its home and I turned it. The money I'd paid Densley was suddenly worth every penny as the 1.6 GTi roared to life. I gave her some extra fuel and put her in gear as my horizon shifted like the captain's on the bridge of a rolling ship in a force 10 gale.

The Golf took off, wheels spitting gravel, people kicking the car. Something smashed through the rear window. I caught sight of Leonard managing to administer ten thousand volts to the thigh of the guy holding him, who went rigid and tipped onto his arse. I nearly ran Leonard down as he bolted and headed across my path for the exit onto the road. Our eyes met for a second through the windscreen before he disappeared into the dark. A quick glance in the rear-view showed the two rugby players who'd been trying to tip my car helping up their fallen comrades. I accelerated onto the road and headed for the relative civilisation of Cambridge.

Not running Leonard over when I had the chance was probably the worst mistake of the many that I made that night.

20

WITH THE BENEFIT OF THE FOLLOWING MORNING'S DAYLIGHT I surveyed my car on my drive, coffee in hand, in my pyjamas. There were dents in the bonnet, created by my attempt to skim across it, and in the doors, where I recalled the car got a kicking as I'd made my escape. The hatchback window was smashed, and a large stone, half painted white, was sitting on the back seat. I recognised it as one used in the pub car park to mark out parking spaces. Expensive fixes. I wondered whether it could be legitimately charged to Galbraith. I mean, I assumed this was his fault, directly or indirectly. I still hadn't figured out how Badem's Leonard and Derin had known that Aurora would be outside the church in Cherry Hinton, or that she'd be early. I hadn't known that she was going to be early. Galbraith couldn't have known from my call in the office.

Mothers on my street walking their kids to school gave me a forced smile and the minimum acceptable nod as they passed me. I would probably now be that creepy guy who lived on his own with the overgrown garden and stood outside his house in his pyjamas watching the kids go to school.

I went inside and called Sandra. She's not very good in the morning, so I was passed to Aurora without much preamble.

"How are you, Aurora? How is your arm?"

"Very good, Mr George. It's not serious."

"You can just call me George, Aurora." She remained silent so I got to the reason I'd called. "Who did you tell about our meeting yesterday, Aurora?"

"I told nobody, Mr George."

"What about Joshua? He was there when you called because you used his phone."

"Yes, of course Joshua know. He call me after to make the meeting time early. You told him."

I stopped myself from reacting to this news out loud; I didn't want to alarm Aurora.

"You haven't called him, or anyone, since you've been at Sandra's?"

"No, not yet. I am going to call now. They will be worried."

"Please don't call them, Aurora. I'm going to ring Joshua now and tell him you are alright."

"You don't want me to call?"

"No, it's very important. You just stay there today and relax."

"OK. I clean house," she said.

"Right… Can I talk to Sandra?"

The phone passed hands.

"What's up, George?"

"Can you make sure she doesn't call anyone? I don't think all her Filipino friends are as loyal as they might be."

"Sure, but I'll be going to the office soon and short of unplugging the phone…"

"I don't think you should go to the office. Just in case Bill and Ben are back."

"Who?"

"They've been following me around and hanging outside the office. They tried to pick Aurora up yesterday and I don't want them to associate you with me."

"That's sweet of you, George, but I can take care of myself."

"I couldn't take care of myself last night and neither could four rugby players so please stay away from the office."

"OK, OK. I can make some calls from here. I'll chase up those number plates."

"You can forget about the Ford Focus – it belongs to Leonard and Derin who I met last night – just the Toyota."

"Fine. Are you alright?"

I looked at myself in the hall mirror. I had two bruises on my neck, like a vampire bite, and the small of my back was bruised. I'd hurt my shoulder after landing on it doing stunts over the bonnet of my car but otherwise I was intact.

"Mostly ego damage, and dents to the car, which I've just spent a fortune on. By the way, you're not making Aurora clean your house, are you?"

"Yes, that's the first thing I did when I woke her at five a.m. No, she's adamant she wants to do it. I think it's her way of thanking me for letting her stay here. She's never had a day off so she doesn't know what to do with herself. To be honest it's too early in the morning to argue with her so I'm just going to let her do it and be happy. Besides, the place could do with a clean, I'll be the first to admit. She's just relieved that we don't have a dog."

"She doesn't like dogs?"

"That ex-beauty queen of a boss has a dog, apparently lets it shit anywhere in the house. Guess whose job it was to clean it up?"

I rang Joshua from the office mobile but he didn't answer and I declined to leave a message. I ran a bath and, as I soaked my shoulder, worked through the events of yesterday, which now felt like a surreal dream. It looked like Galbraith had increased the odds of finding Aurora and his briefcase by roping in this Badem fellow, an ex-patient he had befriended. It was also clear that Galbraith wanted to speak to Aurora, not just retrieve the briefcase, but was it, as Badem had intimated, just to give her a telling off? Or would he have sanctioned a stronger punishment, as Badem seemed keen to administer? Kristina seemed less bothered about seeing Aurora again, or even the pearls, but then she had other things to worry about, like managing a lover on the side.

I remembered that Joshua worked as a theatre orderly at the hospital, and it was entirely possible he had access to Galbraith. Joshua was probably on minimum wage, Galbraith drove a Porsche and was on TV – it wasn't beyond the realms of possibility that he'd tried to earn a bit of extra cash by telling Galbraith he knew where Aurora was going to be. After all, Joshua knew that she worked for him. If Galbraith had then told Badem, Badem might have suggested getting

Joshua to tell her to be there early so I wouldn't be around when they picked her up. Luckily I'd arrived early myself, otherwise who knows what might have happened to her. Galbraith was behaving like a man on the edge, not a TV-appearing surgeon who had it all – the job, the attractive wife, the classic car, the nice house, the prestige.

I got out of the bath and put yesterday's clothes in to wash. The work number rang as I set the machine going.

"George?" Speak of the devil.

"Mr Galbraith. How was your dinner party?" I asked, keeping it light and breezy.

There was a long sigh at the other end. "I'm ringing to apologise about last night. I was somewhat taken aback by events. I take it that you're OK?"

"As well as could be expected in the circumstances."

"I see. I understand that you had a conversation with Badem?"

"More of a verbal tirade and promised electrocution, which I narrowly avoided."

"Gosh, I'm very sorry to hear that. As it happens it's entirely my fault. I made the mistake of explaining why his notes were missing. Despite being a cultured person Iskender is a man of great emotion. He is, shall we say, exceedingly grateful for his surgery."

"That he is," I said.

"He's Turkish, you see," Galbraith said, as if that explained everything.

"A temperamental lot, people from that part of the world," I said, wondering if he'd get the irony.

"Quite. Now, the thing is, George, I'm supposed to be flying off tomorrow for the US to do some blasted filming, and I was hoping we could conclude our business before then. I would actually like to travel with my briefcase," he said with a fake chortle.

"What about Badem?"

"I've told him that I no longer need his help since you are obviously on the case, as it were."

"And he'll back off, will he? Him and his minions."

"He assures me that you will be left alone. I told him last night that he'd taken things too far and from what you're saying perhaps even further than I realised. Anyway, he agrees that he may have, um, overstepped the mark. I do have a reputation to uphold, after all; I mean I can't afford these things coming back on me. It would be disastrous. Can you imagine the headline…" he chuckled, "…'Top Surgeon Hires Thugs to Recover Patient Notes'."

I laughed with him, as it did all seem rather funny in the light of day. He was being reasonable – maybe too reasonable.

"There will be adequate compensation for you, obviously," he added. "In light of what happened. As I said, I do feel completely responsible."

He was very good, I'll give him that. Convincing. You could see why he was on TV. No mention of Joshua, or passing on the whereabouts of Aurora to Badem. No, it was all a terrible misunderstanding due to hot-tempered people from the Middle East. The more I thought about it, the more I wanted to look inside this bloody briefcase of his.

"Great," I said. "So how do we put this matter to bed?"

21

GALBRAITH AND I DISCUSSED WHERE WE WOULD MEET THAT night. I wasn't keen on going back to Fulbourn so soon after my run-in with both Badem's people and the rugby players, who might recognise me, and besides, Aurora didn't want to go there. We eventually agreed to meet at my office at ten that night, since he had evening surgery.

I rang Sandra back and told her I'd be round later and, now that I had his full name, asked her to look up Iskender Badem, just out of curiosity.

I took the white painted rock from the pub car park off the back seat, brushed out the small cubes of glass and drove over to Densley's in my beat-up car. He was standing on the forecourt with his staff as I drove in. They stared at the car as I got out, my shoulder twinging with pain as I closed the door.

"Looks like she's been in a fight," was all Densley said.

"Not far off."

He gestured to the sign over his garage. "I'm a mechanic, not a body repair shop, George."

"I know that," I lied. I'd assumed he just did all things car related. "I was wondering if you could recommend someone?"

He nodded and looked at the sky. "Looks like rain. We can rig something temporary up for the back window?"

"That would be great." We went into his office and it was a mess. Filing cabinet forced open, papers scattered everywhere.

"What the hell?" I said.

"Yep, someone broke in last night. Junkies looking for cash, I'm guessing."

"Have you called the police?"

He snorted, retrieved a business card from the pin board and gave it to me. "What's the point? Nothing missing anyway. If the buggers knew what they were doing they'd have taken some of the tools. We might know them if they're local. My son's coming later to check the CCTV; I don't know how to do it."

"The young 'uns can be useful occasionally," I said.

"That they can, although I hate the way they think they know it all, when they know nothing."

"Amen to that."

"Can you leave the car with us for an hour?"

Since I was off Mill Road I walked over to Kamal's, texting him on the way. He replied, asking me to bring some breakfast. I picked up some croissants and a couple of coffees and soon we were sitting at his small table overlooking the road.

"Late shift last night?"

"Yes, but writing, not work. When the muse grabs you…"

"…she grabs you by the balls," I said.

He laughed. "Something like that. By the way, I did a little more digging and got a titbit on Mr Galbraith, or at least about his senior registrar."

I ripped a croissant and dipped it in coffee. "What about him?"

"Her, not him. The talk among nurses is that she's taking up the slack resulting from his focus on TV and starting to feel the load. Might be getting help to focus and stay awake."

"You mean pharmaceuticals? You know that for sure?"

"No, it's just speculation."

"Hopefully it will be over tonight, the case, so it's probably academic."

"Not to the patients," he said. We finished our croissants and I remembered something.

"Have you got yesterday's *Argus*?"

"It's in the recycling bin. Why?"

"Fish it out and I'll tell you."

I watched the street while Kamal went into the kitchen. He came back unfolding it.

"You mean your girlfriend's story on the murdered girl? A little flowery and clichéd, don't you think?"

"No, not that, although I agree with you about the writing. Something in the paper spooked Galbraith, and there was only one story about Addenbrooke's."

He flicked through it, saying, "I thought you were going to be done with the case tonight?"

"Indulge me, I'm curious. It comes with the territory."

He stopped turning pages and folded the paper to make it manageable. "You mean this story about the director?"

I nodded.

"Yes, it's a juicy one. What it doesn't say here is that

porn was found on his computer at work. Apparently he was asked to leave without as much as a farewell to his staff. One minute he's there, the next he's escorted from the building. I only know about it because Chris, my lodger, works in the department he heads up, or did head up. But why would the story spook Galbraith?"

"I've no clue. Maybe they were pals?"

"I could ask Chris later what he knows. If you want."

"As you say, it's all a bit academic."

"Yeah, but it leaves you feeling dissatisfied, right? Like a gnawing in your gut. I know you, George, you're like a dog with a bone."

"Now who's using clichés?"

"Touché."

One of Densley's men had duct-taped some plastic sheeting to the rear windscreen which he said would only hold for a few days. Densley was busy with his son going through CCTV footage so I offered the guy some cash-in-hand for sorting it out but he told me Densley had said it was on the house.

I could see through the plastic well enough to see whether something was looming behind me but it was going to be difficult to know if I was being followed from a distance. Plus it was only a matter of time before either I got stopped by the police or it started leaking.

It flapped noisily when I got up to speed, driving to Sandra's. I parked a few streets away and took a little walk to make sure I wasn't being followed. I didn't trust Galbraith's assurance about Badem; he didn't strike me as the sort of person who would laugh off what had happened last night. His men had been humiliated, which he would no doubt take personally.

Sandra answered the door in an apron, something I'd never seen her wear before. Aurora was shouting in Tagalog to someone in the living room.

"What's going on?" I asked, alarmed that perhaps Joshua had turned up.

Sandra smiled and any tension lingering between us from yesterday was gone in an instant. "She's on Skype with her daughter," Sandra said. "From the few English words being thrown in I think she's got leukaemia." So much for Kristina telling me Aurora was lying about it. Sandra grabbed my arm and led me to the small but now spotless and sparkling kitchen. "When can you get her passport? It doesn't sound like her daughter has that long, to be honest."

"Tonight, hopefully. But I want to have a look in the briefcase beforehand if she'll let me."

"While she's busy, let me tell you about Mr Badem." She lifted a sheet of paper from the table. "He's Turkish but with German nationality. He's a property tycoon, owns nearly two hundred properties. Rents them out and doesn't maintain them. Kicks people out if they complain about damp or rats."

"A good old-fashioned slum landlord."

"Exactly; there seem to be a lot more of them about nowadays. He's strong-armed people into dropping legal cases against him. Nothing proven, of course."

"And he has properties in Cambridge?"

"A few. Mostly London and Cologne. Apparently he has a

house and family just outside Cambridge. A wife and daughter."

Aurora had gone quiet so we went into the living room which was dominated by a large flat-screen TV fixed to the wall on which some daytime soap was playing with the sound muted. Aurora was on the sofa, hunched over a laptop on the coffee table, her face in her hands and her small shoulders shuddering as she tried to cry quietly. Sandra sat next to her and put her arm around her.

"It's OK, sweetheart. It's OK," she said. Aurora looked like a child next to Sandra, who pulled her gently to her chest.

Rather than be a useless voyeur I went into the kitchen and put the kettle on. Making tea during emotional situations is always a good idea; it provides a useful displacement activity and everyone needs tea at a time like this.

22

I TURNED THE TV OFF AND SAT WITH AURORA IN SANDRA'S living room to examine Galbraith's briefcase which she had just brought in. It was more of an attaché case, really, something a pilot might be expected to carry. This was not a case you could pick up on the high street. An oil-coloured soft leather affair reinforced with brass corners (which must have given Derin a nice bruise), it was pleasingly scuffed with use. Monogrammed with the initials W.H.G. (Henry? Horatio? Harpo?) it had two heavy-duty four-digit combination locks on the top. I tried them, just in case I got lucky.

"Why you want to open, Mr George?"

I had to think about that. I didn't really have a good reason to open it, except inherent curiosity about its contents, the desperation Galbraith was exhibiting about getting it back and the malign effect it was having on my life. The trouble is, although I can pick locks, there's nothing to pick with a combination lock, just four wheels with numbers on, which meant over ten thousand different combinations and I didn't have the time. And Aurora, bless her, was adamant that it shouldn't be damaged. She was right. I didn't really want to hand it over obviously tampered with. I picked it up by the sides. It was heavy, and lifting it triggered a sharp pain in my shoulder. I tilted it from side to side and listened. Something, more than one thing, slid from one end to the other. I repeated the motion, listening for clues. Something travelling more quickly than the other, heavier thing, which didn't make a sound when it hit the side. When the lighter thing hit the side it made a sort of clunking sound. Aurora looked at me curiously and shrugged, as did I. I went through the outside zippered pockets and found some corporate branded tat, cheap pens and notepads, with what I took to be pharmaceutical logos on them, which I put back. There was a week-old receipt for the dry cleaner's on the concourse at Addenbrooke's, which I also put back. Short of prising the case open, that would have to do for now.

"I'll come back tonight at nine, Aurora, so we can go and meet Galbraith."

"We go together, yes?"

"Of course. We leave from here together. No standing on the street this time."

She looked at her hands. "Those men. They worked for Mr Galbraith?"

"Indirectly."

She looked blank.

"They work for somebody who knows Mr Galbraith," I said. This provided a good segue into my next question.

"Why do you think they wanted you to go with them, Aurora?"

She shrugged. "Maybe work somewhere else? Dolores

say sometimes foreign girls sold to new boss."

Jesus, that hadn't even crossed my mind. Was it possible Badem was taking Aurora off Galbraith's hands, for something a lot worse than cleaning?

"Did Joshua tell them where I was?" she asked.

"Yes, you worked it out."

"He works in operating room. Mr Galbraith works in operating room. Maybe they friends?"

I shook my head. "Unlikely. I think he did it for money. Or for a better job at the hospital."

"Yes, he send money home to family," she said, looking at her hands, prematurely wrinkled from cleaning. "Everybody send money home."

As Sandra was staying at home I decided to head to the office, to check the post and any messages; I had a business to run, after all. There was no Ford Focus, no Range Rover and no Porsche outside, much to my relief. Maggie was standing by the bike rack, smoking. An act she obviously wasn't used to.

"That can't send a positive message to clients," I said, pointing at her awkwardly held cigarette.

"I'm done for the day. Anyway, fuck 'em, the whiny entitled lot of them."

"Oh dear. Bad morning?"

"You could say that."

"You want to talk about it?"

She ground out the half-smoked cigarette and smiled.

"You going to counsel me, George?" she asked, putting on her cycle helmet.

"Maybe. How does that make you feel?"

"Ha ha. Very funny."

"What I can do is provide coffee and listen. If there's anything I've learnt how to do it's listen."

"That's sweet of you. I'll bear that in mind."

I trudged up to the top floor, through the pleasant smell of aromatherapy oils lingering on the stairs. I bumped into Stubbing in her cheap work suit coming down the other way. We stopped; the stairs in this old house are narrow and someone has to give way.

"Been having your chakras realigned, Stubbing?"

"I doubt I have any chakras left. You got a minute?"

"Lead the way."

Upstairs in my office she looked around, appraising the tired paintwork and grimy windows. I kept trying to get Jason to clean them but he thought the task beneath him.

"Last time I was in here you'd been burgled. Remember that?" She sat in the chair opposite my desk.

"How could I forget? You didn't want me to report it to the police. Remember that?"

Disappointingly, she didn't rise to the bait but looked pensive, retightening her ponytail.

"How well do you know Linda?" she asked, finally looking at me, wearing her cop's face.

"Is this a police business question, or personal?"

She thought about it. "A little of both, I guess."

The landline rang but I pressed a button that sent the caller to voicemail.

"Judging by how you two were getting on at my place I'd say you know her better than I do," I said. "So you're either trying to tell me something or there's a real question lurking beneath your non-question." The mobile vibrated in my jacket. I reached in, silenced it and put it in my desk drawer.

She gave me her thin-lipped smile. "Someone's in demand."

"What can I say, I'm a popular guy."

"That's what I want to talk to you about. How popular you are – with certain ladies."

"What the hell are you on about?"

Stubbing glowered at me, not a look many people can take without being psychologically scarred. It was a scar I already bore, so it didn't affect me like it once had. It was more like an old wound that played up in cold weather.

"Linda's a big girl and can take care of herself, obviously," Stubbing said. "But I'm fond of her and, as you know, she's been put through the ringer once already."

"You don't need to tell me her history."

She smirked. "You two wouldn't be together if it weren't for me, did you know that?" She sat back and crossed her legs, enjoying my surprised reaction. "Linda and I went to sixth form together in Cambridge, she went on to uni, we lost touch for a few years then reconnected after she ended up back here. I told her to contact you when she was having that problem with her prick of a husband who hired you to do his stalking for him."

"She told me she got my name through her husband."

"She did, but she came to me for help when she found out he'd hired you. I couldn't really do anything, no actual crime had been committed, but I suggested she come and see you. I told her you weren't such a terrible person and might be able to help."

"I'm welling up here."

She responded with a withering look. "So what's the situation with you two?"

"What business is it of yours?"

"Just fuck buddies then?" There she was, the old Stubbing I knew and loathed.

"What do you want, Stubbing? Come out with it or piss off."

She hesitated, thinking about how to put whatever it was she was trying to say.

"I'm here as a courtesy to her, because I like her. Otherwise you'd be down at the station."

"Yes, I get it, you like her. Just spit it out, already."

"OK. Someone reported that a woman was forced... 'bundled' is the term they used, into a car yesterday evening. Outside the Catholic church in Cherry Hinton," she said, studying my face for a reaction. "Know anything about it?"

I put my elbows on the desk and winced with pain. Since Aurora hadn't been anywhere near Bill and Ben's Ford Fucking Focus, which had been on the other side of the road, whoever had reported it must have seen her get into my car, which after all had been parked illegally on double-yellows. I suppose it might have looked like she was being bundled into the car if someone had just caught a quick glimpse of what had happened; Bill and Ben had been taking her towards their FFF before I intervened and it had all happened quite quickly. I remember shouting at her to get in the car.

I kept my counsel, however, while considering the implications of saying something in front of a police detective. Another basic rule I like to follow.

"Even you…" Stubbing continued when I didn't speak, "…with your limited deductive capacity, have probably already worked out that the concerned citizen took down a number plate. Guess whose name should pop up when we did a check?"

"And it gets flagged to you, why? Aren't you busy solving the murder of a young girl?"

"Because, Kocky, someone has the hots for you at the station." I couldn't tell if she was pulling my leg or not. She leant forward over my desk and fixed me with a gaze of steel. "So, why don't you tell me what happened, in a nice, friendly off-the-record heart-to-heart manner, just a guy talking to his main squeeze's girlfriend?"

I stared at her, thinking about how much to tell her.

"Or," she said, flicking something off my desk, "we can do this on my turf at the factory, using my rules."

23

SO I CAME UP WITH A NARRATIVE TO GET STUBBING OUT OF MY office: I'd arranged to meet a client – for the purposes of my story this was an unnamed Aurora – and arrived to find her being harassed by two men in the street, outside a church of all places. I mean what was Cambridge coming to? I then "bundled" her into my car and we drove off.

"So she's not a prostitute, or some woman you were just picking up?"

I stared at Stubbing like she was demented, which in truth she may well be. I cringed at the sudden thought that she might be sex-starved and all this was just her way of releasing tension.

"And these two men," she said. "Assuming they weren't her pimps and you weren't arguing over the price, what did they want?"

"They were trying to steal my client's briefcase," I said, on the off-chance that Aurora had been described with one by the concerned citizen.

She took out a notebook and flipped through it until she reached a page that she read impassively.

"Can anyone corroborate this, like your so-called client?"

I shook my head slowly. "Stubbing, Stubbing, Stubbing." I made a show of pulling out my own notebook. "Ye of little faith. I don't believe that even you really believe that I'm the sort of person you like to think I am."

"I don't believe things, Kocky. I'm just interested in the facts."

I found the licence plate number of the Ford Fucking Focus and wrote it down on a scrap. "Here's a fact for you," I said, handing it to her.

She took it, looking displeased at my co-operation.

I remembered something more she could use. "Oh, and if there's a video camera on the Cherry Hinton railway crossing that comes on when the warning lights do, you might even get confirmation that the car in question was there at the time of the report. Maybe there's even a nice clear mugshot of the two of them sneaking under the barrier in the car."

With Stubbing gone I felt rather pleased with myself. If it happened – and it wasn't guaranteed, given recent cuts to police resources – a little visit by the plod wouldn't do Leonard and Derin any harm. Despite what assurances Galbraith might make, even if I believed them, I was pretty sure they hadn't forgotten our little run-in last night and would come a-calling on their own initiative when they had the chance.

Thinking about them prompted me to go and have a look out the window at the road below. No sign of their car, but Kristina's Range Rover was there. I could see her sitting in the driver's seat, her phone in her hands, either texting or Facebooking or whatever. Her face wasn't visible at this angle but little Misha was scampering around on the dashboard, yapping at passers-by. I noticed that the roof of her car had been scraped and I could see where the antenna had come off at the back, which would explain why she was having trouble with reception. I waited for her to get out, but she didn't, so I went back to my desk to check the voicemail for whoever's call I had diverted when Stubbing was here.

It was Kristina; she'd called both numbers. She wanted to see me "as soon as". I hung up and went back to the window only to catch her pulling away.

"Afternoon, boss."

I jumped, turning to see Jason sitting at his mother's desk.

"Shit. You almost gave me a heart attack."

"I guess that's a worry at your age," he said, switching on the computer. There was a time when the young respected their elders, even though that respect was often misplaced and undeserved. Still, a pretence of it would be nice.

"You were going to tell me what you had on the Galbraiths, boy," I said.

"Can't remember, but I can bring it up on the computer."

"Let me just make a call." I picked up the office mobile from the desk drawer and selected the last incoming number. It went through to Kristina's voicemail. I decided not to leave a message, thinking I might wander down to her salon later. I turned to Jason who was finishing combing his hair.

"So, whatcha got?" I put my feet up on the desk and leaned back, my hands behind my head.

"OK, William Hamish Galbraith first." Hamish, of

course. "He's not personally active online. He has a Twitter account relating to his TV programme but it's just PR fluff about it, probably posted by an intern. He's got a fan base, believe it or not, mostly women but also a bit of a gay following. There's a Facebook page that looks genuine, rather than PR-created, where people post selfies of their encounters with him, which he seems game enough to go along with." We live in a doomed culture, I thought, but let him continue. "Nothing unusual there, nothing negative, just testimonials on forums from ex-patients who he operated on. But I'm guessing they're the ones who lived, the others don't get to post on forums."

"What sort of forums are these?"

"Like for people with heart disease, or failing lungs, who are waiting for surgery. There are forums for everyone, whatever their interest or problem, boss. Even you might find something out there."

I tried a Stubbing-like glower on him but, judging by his concerned look, I'm guessing he thought I was having a stroke.

"Shall I carry on?" he asked.

I nodded.

"As far as I can tell, he doesn't do any private surgery, which is unusual for a consultant, but I'm guessing his TV stuff takes up all his non-surgery time and is just as lucrative."

"Nice work if you can get it. He told me he was off to the US tomorrow to do some filming."

"Yep. They've sold the series to a US network. They'll love him over there; the looks, the hair, the British accent."

"The right hair is important," I said, but he ignored me.

"So, moving on to Kristina Galbraith—"

"Now there is someone with hair," I said.

"Right. So, Russian beauty queen back in the day. Bit of controversy because of her dark hair and eyes; some didn't consider her Russian enough. Did an MBA after her win then left Russia for Dubai, of all places. It's the most expensive city in the world, did you know that?"

I shook my head but he was looking at the screen. "Did some advertising on the back of her win – perfumes, etcetera. Set up a chain of beauty salons. She met Bill out there—"

"What was he doing there?"

"Working as a surgeon. It's tax-free income. You do it for a year and earn enough so you can build an architect-designed house outside Cambridge. Anyway, they got married in Dubai and she sold her business and followed him a year later. She started up a nail bar here in Cambridge—"

"She called it a treatment parlour, something like that."

"Yeah, that comes later, first comes the juicy bit. The nail bar had to close down because she was caught hiring illegal immigrants from Vietnam. They were living over the shop, four to a room. They, poor buggers, were arrested. She blamed the shop manager but as the owner she was responsible and got fined ten grand. Anyway, she sold the premises and bought somewhere more central. Rebranded under a different name. Her new place gets good reviews even though it's considered to be overpriced." He sat back and looked at me.

"Good job."

"Useful?"

"As you know, Jason, you never know what is going to be useful until it becomes so. But not knowing a thing automatically renders it forever useless."

"Should I be writing this shit down?"

"Definitely."

He turned off the computer and stood up.

"You going to help me lug that fax machine downstairs?" I asked, pointing to it.

"Nah, got to get to my punting job, the one that actually pays properly." He winked at me and left, the ingrate.

24

I WALKED DOWN TO TRUMPINGTON STREET AND BOUGHT A sandwich which I ate as I continued into town, past the Fitzwilliam Museum on my left, where Olivia had taken me several times. I haven't been in it since she left. I walked past Kings College on my left and Market Square on my right. It wasn't yet peak tourist season but the place was thick with a large group of teenagers milling around with matching rucksacks. I checked the address on Kristina's card and turned onto Green Street.

Her salon looked a high-class joint, with frosted-glass front and a swinging black sign on chains with cursive gold lettering that read "Kristina's Beauty Treatment Parlour". I walked in, tinkling a bell in the process. A young woman came to life behind a marble-top counter. Classical music played softly from hidden speakers. Behind the counter there were curtained-off cubicles on either side of a central hallway that led to a door at the end. One opened and a young woman in a white coat emerged carrying a bowl. Unlike the painted Caucasian woman beaming unnaturally at me from behind the counter, she was from Southeast Asia, as was another woman in a white coat who came out of a different cubicle with towels. This was obviously not the sort of salon where the women gossiped and read trashy celebrity magazines, like when my mum had gone to get her hair done once a month. Here everyone sat insulated, getting their treatment. I was being addressed.

"Are you waiting for your wife?" An Eastern-European accent.

"Maybe I'm here for a facial," I said, deadpan. I wasn't sure what a facial entailed beyond it having something to do with the face. Somehow she managed to blush through her foundation and her smile faltered but she rallied.

"You want a facial?"

"Not really," I said.

"Usually men come in here for waxing." I wanted to ask what they came in to have waxed but I didn't really want to have that conversation with a young woman who was easy to make blush.

"Is the boss in?" I asked her.

"She is expecting you?"

"Not really, but I think she'll be pleased to see me."

She shrugged to let me know what she thought of my humour but picked up the phone. I told her my name and she tried to ring through, but had trouble with the phone.

"I'm new here," she said, by way of explanation. Eventually she managed it, turning her head and cupping her mouth like it would stop me hearing. After a conversation brief enough for the purpose, with the word "sorry" being repeatedly uttered, she led me through between the cubicles.

I glimpsed, through a gap in a curtain, another Southeast Asian woman on a stool painting toenails on some fat toes separated with cotton wool. The owner, wrapped in a white bathrobe, was hidden behind a TV soaps magazine, proving me wrong yet again.

We stopped at a door and my escort knocked. There was a tinkle from the street door and she rushed off in pursuit of an actual customer. The knocked-on door opened and Kristina stood there in a high-waisted trouser suit flared at the ankles. She gestured with her head for me to come in and closed the door behind me.

This was the sort of office I should have. Plush leather armchairs, a large antique desk, soft lighting provided by brass lamps, the faint smell of incense. Misha, lying on a small embroidered cushion in the corner of the room, stared at me malevolently and decided I wasn't worth getting up for. The dog would be a worthy adversary for Stubbing in a staring competition.

I gestured around the room. "Do you do interior design as well?"

"No, but I can give you a name," she said distractedly, pointing to a chair.

I shook my head but she didn't see it. I sat where instructed. She sat behind the wooden desk. "I got your message," I said. "Thought it easier to talk face to face."

She nodded and clasped her hands. "I'm worried about Bill," she said, getting straight to it.

"How so?"

"He's stressed, distracted."

"He's a surgeon and has a TV show so I—"

"No, it's not that."

I waited for her to put some flesh on it but she left it there, bony and insubstantial. Prodding was needed.

"Well, there's Aurora's leaving."

She flashed her eyes dangerously. "Why would that upset him? Has he said something to you?" she asked, sweeping her hair back with both hands and baring her teeth.

I left that question hanging. Missing patient notes aside there were several answers and one obvious one, but maybe she just needed me present to have a conversation with herself.

"No," she continued, jabbing a finger at me. "There was nothing like that going on and I don't like what you are suggesting." As I hadn't actually suggested anything, I kept quiet. I could have told her that she might be the last person to know if something was going on between Bill and Aurora but thought better of it. I was spared further finger-jabbing by her phone ringing. She picked up and impatiently replied to questions with "yes" and "no" answers.

Although the idea of Bill and Aurora had occurred to me, I was unable to convince myself that they'd been exchanging Valentine cards and love poetry. I could see that he may have coerced her into something sexual, given he was in a position of power as her employer. It happens all the time and it would explain Aurora's antipathy to returning to the house. The other possibility was that he genuinely thought he was in love with her, but that it was unrequited, which might explain why he wanted to speak to her – maybe he was planning to tell her that he was going to leave his wife.

"I know you're new," Kristina was saying, annoyed. "But try a little bit harder, please." She hung up, took a breath and forced a smile at me.

"Staffing problems?" I asked.

"It's difficult finding people at short notice."

"Is that why you hire foreigners?"

She stared at me then waved my question away. "We're getting off the subject," she said. "Perhaps Bill has somehow learnt of my own… situation?" She stared at me meaningfully until I realised what she was asking.

"We've already had this conversation. If he knows, then it wasn't from me; it's not what I was hired to look into."

"So you say. You didn't really explain why you were at the hotel."

"I often work on more than one case at a time. That's a popular hotel for couples to meet, so…" Of course I didn't know that, but having seen the place it seemed fit for purpose.

"So when you watch people you actually go into the hotel they are in?"

"Is this why you asked me here, to quiz me about my working methods?"

"Something is bothering Bill and I want to make sure it isn't… this."

"Did you know that sometimes people learn that their spouse is having an affair from the person they are having an affair with?"

She flinched and paled and I guess she hadn't considered the possibility. Or maybe she just didn't like me saying "affair" out loud.

She shook her head dismissively and the phone rang again. She snatched it up and for something to do I clicked my fingers at Misha who was curled up half-asleep on his cushion, a paw over one eye. He ignored me with a disdain I didn't think dogs were capable of.

"So why did he hire you?" Kristina asked, after hanging up and disturbing my bonding with Misha.

"You know why, you were there."

"So have you found her, Aurora?"

"Yes, as it happens."

"Has she said anything to you?"

"About what?"

She shrugged and pursed her lips. "About Bill," she said. "Or me?"

"What are your concerns?"

She shook her head as if she didn't really have any. "Did she tell you why she left?"

"You don't know? Have a suspicion?" I asked.

She swept some imaginary debris from her desk.

"Maybe she just wants to get her passport back and see her daughter," I said.

"Yes, yes of course," she said. "Since you've found Aurora is your work over?"

"I hope to conclude business with your husband tonight."

"What's happening tonight?" she asked.

"He gets his briefcase. Aurora gets her passport." The money was none of her business and, given her view of Aurora, she might convince Bill not to hand any over.

"That's interesting," she said, standing up.

"What do you mean?"

She looked at a bracelet on her wrist, then I realised it was a watch. "Because he won't be handing over any passport unless I give it to him." She walked to the door and opened it expectantly, her face set in polite stone. I walked out and heard the door close behind me. The woman wasn't big on hellos and goodbyes.

25

STEPPING OUT INTO THE CAMBRIDGE AFTERNOON SUNSHINE, I reflected on what I'd learnt, if anything. She was fishing, that's for sure. Maybe I'd put my foot in it about the passport. Maybe he'd planned to acquire it from her without her knowledge, and now she was alerted would take steps to make things difficult. Also, if she had the passport, then what had he been planning to give us at the last aborted meeting? The only definitive conclusion I reached was that the sooner the Galbraiths were out of my life the happier I'd be.

I walked on to Market Square to buy some things for dinner from the food stalls. I felt like I hadn't seen Linda in ages and wanted to entice her over before the briefcase-passport exchange, if it was still going ahead. I now had my doubts after what Kristina had just said.

I rang Sandra and asked her to see if she could establish, woman to woman, whether Aurora had had any relationship with Galbraith.

"You want me to ask her if she had sex with him?" she asked.

"Erm, yes, but perhaps not that directly. And if she did,

was it consensual or not? She has a problem with going back to the house."

Sandra agreed to see what she could get out of Aurora and ended the call. Having bought a couple of steaks and salad, I was choosing some olives when I saw Kristina striding across the square, Misha's head sticking out of her large bag. I quickly paid for the olives as she walked by the council building that dominates one side of the square and turned towards the multi-storey car park. As she was going in the general direction of my office I decided to follow.

I thought I might lose her going into the car park as there'd be little point me following, but she went through the Grand Arcade, Cambridge's temple of upmarket consumerism. She wasn't shopping, though. We went quickly through it and emerged onto St Andrew's Street, where she turned right. She skipped across the junction of Downing Street just as the lights were changing and I had to run so I wasn't left behind. That meant I ended up fairly close behind her. Misha spotted me and started yapping. Kristina addressed him without stopping which quieted him, although his large ears were pricked in high alert as he watched me drop back. She ducked into a bar and I looked through the large windows as I passed.

I caught her in a quick clinch with Mr Suave Suit from the hotel before they sat at a table towards the back. The pavement was too narrow here to hang around unobtrusively and opposite the bar was Emmanuel College, so no shops to lurk in. I decided to try to take a photo with the mobile phone. I brought up the camera app and walked back past the bar, holding the phone up and pressing what I hoped was the right button. I repeated the process going the other way then I had a quick look at the photos: selfies of me reflected in the window.

I went into the arts cinema two up from the bar they were in and headed upstairs. The cinema has a bar-cum-café that overlooks the street although I realised it might be difficult to see the pavement directly below to spot them leaving. There was only one way to find out.

The place was full of young mothers with babies. I made my way through the pushchairs to the one empty seat near a window and peered out. Yes, by leaning close to the glass I could make out the pavement and see the tops of people. There was a cough behind me and I turned to see a young woman in a black apron and T-shirt with tattooed arms. She looked embarrassed.

"I was just about to come and order something," I said. They weren't usually this anal about people sitting here without food or drink.

"Erm, it's a mothers-and-babies-only screening this afternoon," she said, sweeping an arm over the scene in case it had escaped me. I became aware that the level of chatter had dropped and I was being scrutinised by bemused women, some of whom were breastfeeding. A few scowls greeted my transgression, but mainly smiles.

"Ah. And I am neither mother nor baby."

She nodded and I slunk out.

Back on the street I looked in the bar window again but Kristina and her fancy man had gone. I headed back to the office.

It was after three when I got behind my desk. I left a message for Linda, asking if she wanted to come round to eat later. I told her I would have to go out again afterwards on business for a couple of hours at most.

I received a text on my personal number from Kamal:

I think you should come talk to my lodger.

Can't do tonight. Tomorrow? I replied.

Now is good if you're free…

Better be worth it.

There are known unknowns & there are unknown unknowns…

See you in 15!

Kamal's lodger Chris was biting his nails and jigging his knee up and down as he sat at the small table in Kamal's room. Kamal had told me that Chris had come home after lunch feeling ill and that he was a little jittery. He didn't look ill to me, just jittery.

"It's about that story in the paper about the sacked director," Kamal said as he sat on his bed and I sat opposite Chris. Chris wasn't much older than Jason. Freckle-faced with flyaway brown hair, he was still in his work suit with his tie undone.

"Tell George here what you told me," Kamal prompted.

"I'm not sure. Feels a bit disloyal to me."

"I work by a strict code of confidentiality," I told him. "What's your area of work?"

"Clinical audit."

"Which means?"

"We analyse the quality of clinical care, you know, patient outcomes, complication rates, things like that, and compare them to the national figures, to see if there are any outliers. We also monitor critical incidents to make sure procedures are tightened if they're a result of poor processes." It sounded terribly dull.

"That sounds like important stuff," I said. "Right, Kamal?"

"Absolutely. It's about putting patients first. Holding clinicians accountable," he said, winking at me. Kamal had obviously picked up some jargon while wheeling people around the hospital.

"So I imagine that you're careful to make sure patients' names aren't used, that sort of thing?" I said to Chris, who was removing a hangnail with his teeth.

"Confidentiality is very important," he said.

I nodded vigorously. "Exactly, it's the same for me. As professionals we have to make sure that people can trust us with information, right?"

Chris nodded and turned to Kamal. "And you're sure it could be important to whatever this case is?"

Kamal leant forward, elbows on knees. "It might also help exonerate your boss, if you really think he's innocent."

"There's no way he downloaded that stuff. He's married with young kids, why would he be interested in that sort of porn?"

I looked at Kamal questioningly.

"Yes," he said. "It's worse than I was originally led to

believe. The police have taken the computer away."

I turned to Chris. "The truth is he could be a devout Christian volunteering his spare time in a hospice, giving blood regularly, being a loving father and devoted husband and still look at that stuff."

Chris just shook his head. "It's just a bit of a coincidence."

"What is?"

He glanced at Kamal who gave him an encouraging nod. "There was this confidential audit meeting set for Monday. It was arranged by my boss, who is... was the director of information, and involved just the clinical director and the chief executive. Just those three. The meeting's now been called off, obviously."

"What are you telling me?" I asked.

"They were going to discuss an audit the director had been preparing. I know because I helped analyse some of the data, although what I was given was anonymised, so nobody was named in it. He'd been working on it for weeks, which is unusual. I mean, he's the director, doesn't usually get his hands dirty with this sort of thing. Told me it was dynamite. Then, lo and behold, child pornography is found on his computer and he's sacked? Too much of a coincidence. Too convenient."

"Have you seen this report?"

"No, of course not."

"And you think your boss was set up?"

"I know what you're saying about appearances being deceptive but I'd have been less surprised had he been all those things you mentioned. Even if it was true, he was the director of information, for Christ's sake, he would know better than to look at that stuff at work, never mind actually download it. Besides, you'd have to bypass the Internet filters set up by IT."

I sat back and studied Chris, whose pale face had reddened at his own outburst.

"So what was he looking into?" I asked him.

"Well, it started with all the surgeons, doing a comparative study of complications and readmission rates, which is quite normal, then that threw up something which meant the director focussed on one firm."

"Firm?"

"Yes, a consultant's team of doctors is called a firm, and although you might be admitted under a particular consultant, you'd most likely be seen or operated on by one of his or her team. I mean that's how they learn, doctors. Anyway, that's when things got all weird, became hush-hush, meetings held that weren't in the calendar, no minutes taken."

"I see. And which consultant did the study focus on?" I asked, already knowing the answer. Here Chris faltered; this is where he felt like he was about to give away too much.

"Mr Galbraith."

"So how did they discover what your boss was doing? Allegedly doing."

"I don't know. I mean, there are filters on Internet access so it would be difficult to actually do it, I'm guessing." I knew from my work with companies that Web access was sometimes limited for most staff, but often unrestricted for senior staff.

"Did he leave his computer unattended at all?"

"Yes of course, he was in meetings all the time, but they're all password protected. Why, do you think someone could have put something on his computer?"

"You're the one who doubts he did it. How would you frame him?"

26

I DIDN'T REALLY KNOW WHAT TO MAKE OF CHRIS'S STORY. IT didn't really explain why Galbraith had freaked out when he'd seen the newspaper article about the director being summarily dismissed. If he'd engineered the porn downloads to get rid of him, surely he'd have been pleased, not upset.

But I had more pressing issues. I drove home, had a shower and changed. In the kitchen I took the steaks out of the bag, patted them dry with paper towel, oiled and seasoned them, then opened a bottle of red. I washed the salad leaves and made a dressing ready to pour over it.

"What happened to your car?" Linda asked, when I opened the door to her. She was in a dark work suit.

"She got caught in the middle of something," I said.

"She, is it?"

"I know, crazy to think of a car as a she."

She gave me a friendly pat on the cheek. "Men and their cars." We went into the kitchen where I poured her some wine.

"I saw you made the front page," I said, raising a glass.

"Thanks, although it's now a load of shit." She drank deeply.

"What?"

"The missing girl, she's no longer missing. She turned up."

"Oh dear. I mean, good, obviously, but I could see how that blows your story out of the water."

"Yeah, thanks for putting it in such stark terms."

"Sorry. Where was she?"

"Camping with her boyfriend. She did go home after the open day for one night; her parents happened to be away at her grandmother's for the night. The next day she and her boyfriend buggered off to Wales. She claims she left her parents a note."

I fired up the gas under the frying pan to get it up to temperature. You don't want to put a steak in a cold pan, I know that much.

"So what leads do they have on the identity of the dead girl, then?" I asked.

"None, except she's not a girl, she's a woman in her early twenties. Just looks young for her age. I guess I wanted her to be the same woman. I was looking at the story rather than the facts."

"I've done the same thing. We look for things that confirm our beliefs rather than the other way round."

She pulled a face and poured herself more wine. "I thought I was better than that. It's a sign of my desperation."

I cut a clove of garlic in half and rubbed it over the steaks, a little trick I'd picked up from Olivia.

"Speaking of desperation, Stubbing came to see me today," I said.

"Oh yeah? She still got feelings for you?"

I laughed. "Feelings, yes, but not warm and fuzzy ones, I can assure you."

"What did she want?"

"Beyond harassing me I'm not sure. She did tell me that she was responsible for us getting together. Said she recommended me to you." I laid the steaks together side by side in the hot frying pan. They sizzled and I let them be. I turned to look at Linda. "You didn't tell me that."

She shrugged. "Didn't think it was relevant. I think I asked her about you when I found out that my ex had hired you, thinking I could take out a restraining order against him. But she counselled against it, said it would just make him worse, which is what you told me." She smiled and placed her hand on my arm. "Does it bother you that she brought us together?"

"I guess I don't want her, of all people, to be responsible for my happiness."

"Is this your tortuous way of saying that you're happy?"

"At this very moment I am," I conceded, kissing her lips.

"Don't overcook my steak," she said, pushing me away and laughing. "I like it pink in the middle."

"Don't you worry, I know what you like," I said, flipping the sirloin.

Later, I left Linda asleep in my bed, had another shower and drove to Sandra's.

Sandra took me into the kitchen when I arrived. Jason and Aurora were watching TV, some dreadful soap opera judging by the sound of the hammy arguments coming from the screen. Sandra had her youngest, Ashley, in his pyjamas on her hip, and he looked at me with half-closed eyes, his head on her shoulder as he absentmindedly fiddled with her hair.

"I spoke to you know who..." Sandra said, pointing to the living room, "... about her and her boss. You know, like you asked?"

"And?"

"And nothing. She found the idea laughable, to be honest."

"But there's something she's keeping to herself, don't you think?"

"I agree. She's afraid of something, either talking about it or whatever, but all I know is that it's not what you thought."

Aurora, who'd started biting her lower lip ever since we'd got ready to leave Sandra's house, couldn't have been reassured by the state of the Golf when she saw it. She locked the passenger door as soon as she got in, unsurprising given her last experience in it, and when I sat next to her she had the briefcase on her knees and her hands screwed together tightly on top.

I drove to the office with the aim of getting there half an hour early and I kept a wary eye out as best I could with the plastic sheet flapping in the window. I backed onto the office drive, the only car there. Once inside the building I locked the main door and we headed upstairs. I sat Aurora at Sandra's desk and looked out of the window.

"Can I have water, please?" Aurora asked, fidgeting in her chair. I went to the shared kitchen and drank a glass myself before filling one for her. She sipped at it repeatedly, the briefcase flat on the desk in front of her. I went back to the window and looked out. This was the only way into the building, the back door having been converted into a fire exit to meet building regulations, and that was alarmed.

At ten minutes to ten Galbraith pulled into the drive in his Porsche and parked underneath my window. He had the soft top down so I could see that he was alone. I looked to the street for a black Ford Focus but could see nothing, no cars parking after he'd arrived, nobody sitting in cars already parked. He disappeared from view and the buzzer went at the intercom near the door. Aurora knocked over her nearly empty glass and the remaining water dripped onto the floor from the desk. I put the glass upright out of her reach and went to the intercom.

"Yes?" I said, pressing the speak button.

"It's Bill," Galbraith said.

"Are you alone?" I asked pointlessly, because it seemed like the thing to do.

"Yes, of course." I buzzed him in. Aurora looked like a deer caught in headlights. I opened the office door and smiled at her.

"Aurora, it's going to be fine. It will all be over soon. OK?"

"Don't go."

"OK, don't worry, I'll be right here."

I could hear Galbraith on the stairs and then on the landing. I propped myself against the front of Sandra's desk, adopting a relaxed pose, facing the door, with Aurora sitting the other side of the desk behind me.

Galbraith appeared, smiling a little too hard. He had an envelope in his hand and was dressed in a blue linen suit and open shirt with a scarf around his neck with matching cloth cap. His gaze flitted between me and Aurora and then settled on the briefcase.

"Hello," I said, as if he'd come to join us for a cup of tea.

"Jolly good," he said, which he followed with his pony-like whinny. I wasn't sure what he had to be nervous about but between him and Aurora it was becoming contagious.

"Right," I said. "Aurora has got the briefcase here, as you can see. I'm assuming you have her passport and the severance pay we talked about?"

"I have more than that," he said. He held out a sealed envelope which I reached forward to take. Keeping my eyes on him I ripped it open and had a quick glance. It contained a printout with something handwritten on it and a wad of twenties thick enough to be one and a half thousand quid.

"Where's the passport?"

He reached into his jacket and pulled it out, showed it to me then put it back. I wondered how he'd got the passport from his wife.

"She can have the passport at the airport. That piece of paper in there is an e-ticket for a flight to Manila via Hong Kong. It leaves at two-thirty tomorrow afternoon from Heathrow, just forty minutes before my own flight to New York."

I checked the printout in the envelope. The details were as he stated. I passed the envelope to Aurora and she looked inside, awestruck; no doubt she'd never seen so much money.

"How do we know that's genuine?"

"I've written the login and password on the printout. So you can log on to the Cathay Pacific website and check it yourself. I've entered her passport number as well."

I moved round to Aurora's side of the desk and switched on the computer, then asked Aurora if I could look at the printout from the envelope again. I logged on to the computer and brought up the website. There were her details on the flight, seven hundred and sixty pounds' worth. A passport number had been entered as ID.

"Can I check her passport number against what's in here?" I asked, holding out my hand.

He smiled. "I gave you a photocopy of the passport, use that." I went to my desk to retrieve it, then checked the number on it against what was on the website. It was the same.

"Now, if I could have my attaché case," he said.

27

"WHOA, LET'S HOLD ON A SECOND," I SAID TO GALBRAITH, who had removed his cap and was smoothing down his hair. "You want to have the case back but don't want to give Aurora her passport until tomorrow? You don't think that's unreasonable?"

He thought about it. "Fine, she'll get it as soon as I've had a private word with her," he said, as if she weren't in the room. "Now if you don't mind giving us a minute, George."

Behind me, I heard Aurora take a breath.

I smiled to keep things nice and friendly, saying, "That's fine, but if you don't mind you'll have to do it with me here."

Galbraith pursed his lips and shook his head ever so slightly.

"It's personal. I just need to ask her a question," he said.

"Anything you say here stays in this room," I said. Galbraith sucked air through his teeth and stared at Aurora.

"Aurora," he said softly. "I was good to you, wasn't I? I helped you when Mrs Galbraith was sometimes too strict?"

"Yes, Mr Bill," she said so quietly I wasn't sure he could hear her.

"As well as a ticket to go and see your daughter I've

given you a lot of money there, Aurora." I heard her rustling through the envelope behind me.

"Too much, Mr Bill. Thank you."

"I just want two minutes, Aurora. Mr Kocharyan will be outside the door." He was almost pleading with her.

"OK," she said.

I turned to her. "Are you sure?"

"Yes, it's fine, Mr George."

I picked up the briefcase. "I'll take this outside with me, if you don't mind, since we haven't completed the trade."

Galbraith nodded and made room for me to step out. "Two minutes," I said, closing the door behind me. I put my ear against it but could hear nothing so stood against the wall, looking at my watch.

Less than a minute later the door opened and Aurora was there.

"He wants me to go with him," she said, sounding scared.

I stepped in and closed the door. Galbraith was standing by the desk looking determined. I moved so I was standing nearer him than Aurora.

"I'll take you to a hotel near the airport," he said to her. "Mr Kocharyan has finished his business, he doesn't want to look after you any more."

I put my hand up to silence Galbraith, saying to Aurora, "It's fine. You don't need to go with him."

"I have your things in the car," Galbraith said. "Your clothes, the photos of your family from your room. I will take you to a hotel near the airport tonight and make sure you catch the flight tomorrow. I have to go there anyway." His unctuous voice was like thick oil filling the room, making everything sticky and difficult to navigate.

"I can go down and get your things for you," I told her. "You don't need to go with him. I will take you to the airport tomorrow." I was suddenly aware of her as a young woman caught between the wishes of two middle-aged men. I couldn't really tell Aurora what to do – she was an adult. But on the other hand this guy, who'd kept her isolated from any other influence, was clever and manipulative and I didn't trust him one bit. I wished Sandra were here but she wasn't so I decided to reach for a large dose of truth.

"Aurora, Joshua told Mr Galbraith about where we were going to meet, and Mr Galbraith told the men that came to get you. Do you understand?" I pointed to him. "He told Joshua to call you and tell you to go early so those two men could find you." She looked at Galbraith whose rictus face said it all. Then he exhaled a long breath and his face relaxed, leaving only fatigue visible.

"You need to think hard about this," he said. "Believe me when I tell you it's best for both of you if she leaves with me now. I'm imploring you." His tone seemed genuinely urgent.

"Or what?" I asked. "What will happen if she doesn't leave?"

He just stood there looking as if he was about to burst into tears and said, "I'm sorry."

He took out the passport and handed it to me. I passed it to Aurora. I handed the case to Galbraith. He took it distractedly, like it was something not very important he might have easily left behind had I not reminded him of it.

"I tried," he said, his voice low with exhaustion.

"Tried what?" I asked, but he walked past me and Aurora and left the office. What the hell was he on about? A horrible thought crossed my mind. I strode to the window. I was relieved that I couldn't see the black Ford Focus but then caught sight of a couple of glowing red lights below me, near the bike rack. Smokers. Then a smartphone screen lit up Leonard and Derin's faces. Leonard put the phone to his ear and looked to the building.

Galbraith was about to let them in and it was too late to catch up with him.

My eye caught the lump of redundant fax machine under the window. I raised the bottom section of the sash window and picked it up, the pain in my shoulder shooting down my arm. I hefted it onto the window ledge and rested it there for a second, checking the anticipated trajectory. Then, just as the scene was lit by Galbraith opening the front door of the building, I launched the machine down onto the parked Porsche. For three long seconds my heart was in my mouth as I thought Galbraith might step under it but the lump of metal and rigid plastic crashed into the top of the windscreen and shattered across the inside of the car and across the drive like a small bomb. Leonard and Derin froze, then looked up. They ran into the building.

I turned to Aurora, whose hand was against her open mouth. I took it and pulled her to the door. I could hear feet thumping up the stairs. I was on the third floor so I had time.

"Lock the door, Aurora." I showed her the lock. "Lock it," I said, pulling the door closed behind me. I heard the latch snap in place as I ran down the hall to the top of the stairs where the fire extinguisher was, another requirement of office buildings regulation that I was suddenly very grateful for. I removed it from its wall fitting and charged down the stairs, releasing the safety seal as I went, the pain in my shoulder overcome by the rush of adrenalin. The narrow staircase and my elevation and momentum gave me an advantage as I met them coming up from the second floor. They were astonished to see me and even more astonished when I turned on the extinguisher, propelling foam into their faces. They raised their hands – Leonard was holding his Taser while Derin behind him waved his butterfly knife. I kept going, shoving the bottom of the extinguisher against Leonard's chest, forcing him back onto Derin. Derin collapsed beneath his colleague. I slipped on the foamy stairs as Leonard waved the Taser wildly, triggering it so that it crackled and sparked across its terminals. As my feet gave way I slid down the stairs trying to keep away from the flailing weapon, ending up on my knees straddling Leonard who was half-lying on Derin. I dropped the fire extinguisher, reached for his wrist with both hands and bent his arm backwards over his head until the Taser made contact with Derin's knife-holding arm. There was a horrible scream and the knife spun across the landing. Leonard released the trigger. His free hand wiped foam from his eyes then made a fist that connected with my lip. I didn't want to let go of his other wrist so I had to allow myself to be pummelled as I smashed his hand against the wall. Luckily he was hitting me with his left hand from a prone position so although the punches hurt they weren't immobilising. I worked my hand up to his little finger which I pulled away from the Taser, and kept pulling. Eventually it gave with a gratifying snap. He shouted and let go of the Taser. I grabbed it and rolled off them onto the landing, getting to my feet and running downstairs and outside.

I found Galbraith removing the bulk of the fax machine from the driver's seat of his pride and joy so he could leave. I picked up the briefcase where he'd put it down and that was when he noticed me. Despite the fact that I must have looked a sight he stared at me vacantly as I caught my breath.

"I'm keeping this," I said. "Until you get those psychopaths off my back." I could hear them in the hall. I went up to Galbraith and stood behind him, the Taser held up by his side. Derin and Leonard spilled out onto the drive, wild-eyed and covered in foam, Leonard holding his right hand to his chest, his little finger at an unnatural angle. They looked like they'd been part-digested and spat out by some monster who decided they didn't taste so good. The vision in my right eye was obscured. I wiped blood from it with my sleeve.

"Tell them to leave," I said to Galbraith. I briefly pulled the trigger on the Taser and the arc of crackling blue light appeared, reflecting off the dark walls of the building. Galbraith flinched but it had the effect of waking him from his reverie.

"Time to go, I think. Tell Badem it's over," said Galbraith in a monotone voice.

"This isn't over," Leonard said, addressing me with a big smile. Derin folded away his blade and followed Leonard round the other side of the Porsche and onto the street.

We turned with them and watched them go to the doctor's surgery two doors down and get into their car and drive off. I put the Taser in my pocket and felt my face.

"Right," I said to Galbraith. "We need to have a little chat, I think, don't you?"

28

GALBRAITH AND I SAT OPPOSITE EACH OTHER AT THE SMALL table in the communal kitchen. Aurora was asleep in Maggie's counselling room, curled up on the small couch where couples sat and tried to work out their issues. Now Galbraith – who'd only been convinced to stay after I'd threatened to call the police to the scene – and I had to work out our issues without the benefit of mediation. Bits of paper towel I'd stuck to the cut above my right eye had stemmed the bleeding. My cheek and lip were swollen and throbbing and my elbow, which had taken a knock on the stairs, was exchanging shooting pains with my shoulder. Galbraith, from a distance, looked like he'd stepped off his launch looking for cocktails. Up close, though, he had some golden stubble in admission of the lateness of the hour and the bottom of his eyelids were red with lack of sleep.

What with coaxing Aurora out of my office and getting her settled in Maggie's, he'd had time to compose himself and was smiling, ready for whatever I might throw at him.

"So, why don't you tell me what the hell's going on?" I asked.

"Nothing's going on. Badem's men must have taken

things into their own hands. When I speak to Badem I'm sure there will be consequences and a fulsome apology."

"Maybe even some compensation?" I said, but he missed the irony in my voice.

"I'm sure that can be arranged."

"How did they know we'd be here?"

"I've no idea."

"No idea, huh?"

He shrugged casually. I patted the attaché case which was on the floor by my side.

"So what's in here?"

"Medical notes, as I said."

"Badem's?"

"Yes," he said, running his thumb along the groove under his bottom lip. If we were playing poker I would have gone all in.

"Shall we have a look?" I pulled the case onto the table. It hadn't left my side since we'd come into the building and I'd bolted the front door behind us.

"You want to look at Badem's confidential medical records?"

"Indulge me, I've had a shit night so far."

"OK." He turned the case round so that the locks faced him and turned the dials, not bothering to hide the code which I memorised just for the hell of it. Releasing the brass locks, he opened the leather flaps and pulled out a grey folder thick with papers and showed it to me without opening it. When I reached out to take it he pulled it back and held it with both hands to his chest.

"No, I draw the line at you reading the notes. How would you like it if I went through one of your confidential files?" We locked eyes and I tipped the briefcase onto its side with the open mouth towards me, daring him to react. He froze, his forced smile trying to convince me that he didn't care that I was going through his stuff. Inside were some more giveaway pens, pads and medical brochures but what interested me was a large manila envelope with a string-tie closure. I pulled the envelope out and things shifted around inside it, settling on the bottom. I felt the contents. Round and small, like tiny marbles. Not heavy enough for marbles, though.

"What are these?" I asked.

"Be my guest," he said. I undid the string and opened it.

"Careful," he said. "Don't let them fall out."

I looked inside. Loose pearls of differing sizes along with some silk string. I reached in. They were cold to the touch and slightly gritty. Galbraith looked at me.

"My wife's pearls. They broke and I was going to get them fixed. It's one reason I wanted the case back so badly. I knew Aurora hadn't stolen them deliberately. They belonged to my mother you see, and her mother before her."

"She didn't seem so keen on them," I said. "Kristina I mean."

"She can be... caustic, sometimes. But they have sentimental value to me. They remind me of Mother." His eyes may have glistened at the mention of his mother. I put the envelope back and stood the case upright. He put the folder, which had no markings on its cover, back inside and closed it. All this fuss over some heirloom pearls.

"May I?" he asked with deliberate irony, gesturing at the case.

I nodded, suddenly feeling exhausted. I wasn't in much of a state to think this through. I wanted to ask whether he would talk to Badem about his men but I couldn't really trust what he said any more. Aurora had her passport and money and a ticket – that was all that mattered. Galbraith took the case and stood up. I dredged up a final question from my tired brain.

"What was that business about talking to Aurora alone? And let me have something real, Bill, not some spun version of the truth."

He turned to me, and I could see him calculating what to tell me. "OK, I'll be honest with you; I owe you that much given what's happened." He paused deliberately. I waited. "It's a little embarrassing," he said. I said nothing. "You understand that I'm trusting you with this information?" I just stared at him. He let out a long breath, then said, "I've been spending time with someone, a member of my surgical team. I had her back to the house when Kristina was away, which in retrospect was a stupid thing to do. Unfortunately Aurora saw us and ever since she left I've been a nervous wreck. I can't afford for it to come out, the tabloids would have a field day. Luckily it seems Aurora is clueless about the value of such information in the wrong hands. I just wanted to make sure she hadn't told anyone about it."

"And Badem?"

"I confided in Badem and he took things into his own hands. He insisted he would get her to the airport if I couldn't, to make sure she didn't speak to anyone before then.

I'm wishing now that I hadn't involved him." He sounded so reasonable when given the chance to pontificate.

"Is that why she left? Because she saw you with some woman?" I asked.

He shook his head. "I think she just wanted to go home." He moved to the door saying, "Send me your bill; I'll pay whatever you think reasonable." Then he was gone.

I wanted to go home and sleep but spent the next hour clearing the drive of debris. Luckily we weren't in a residential area so nobody had reported the sound of the fax crashing into the Porsche. Going back into the building I saw a plastic bag by the front door which contained some clothes and photos wrapped in a rubber band. I took it in, assuming by the photos that it belonged to Aurora – Galbraith must have left it. Then I cleaned up the stairs as best I could; the last thing I wanted was to give the other occupants an excuse to try to evict me and get in a nice trouble-free homeopath or chiropractor instead. Rummaging in the first-aid kit on the kitchen wall I found some butterfly closures to fix the cut above my eye. I then took some painkillers, more than the recommended dose, and checked in on Aurora.

She was curled up, face worry-free with sleep, clutching her precious passport and the envelope in her hands. It was chilly so I covered her with a rug draped over the back of her sofa. I let her sleep a little longer while deciding where to take her. A comfy-looking armchair opposite the sofa invited me to sit in it. I accepted, putting my feet up on the coffee table. I closed my eyes just for a minute as the painkillers kicked in.

* * *

I dreamt I was cycling my dad's heavy bike for dear life because I was being followed by two boys on racing bikes who were gaining on me. No matter how hard I cycled I couldn't get the damn thing to move; it was like cycling through treacle. Then I came to a stop and realised I couldn't reach the ground with my feet and just tipped over.

"George…"

"Mr George…"

I opened my eyes.

Maggie and Aurora peered down at me but I could only see them through my left eye. Light was coming through the window. I moved and everything hurt. Shit – I'd fallen asleep in Maggie's armchair. Thankfully Maggie looked more bemused than angry.

"What happened to you, George? Who is this woman?"

"Aurora," said Aurora, but I don't think that's what Maggie meant.

I sat up, feeling my face. "Sorry," I said.

"I've got clients coming in fifteen, you have to skedaddle. You can explain this later."

I stood up. My coccyx hurt from coming down the stairs. We all moved to the door.

"How did you get in?"

"There are keys to the rooms in the key safe in the kitchen. I'm sorry, your room is the first one that came to mind."

"You can explain this later, George."

"I'm not sure I can," I said. I hobbled away; I seemed to have also hurt my hip. I wasn't young enough for this sort of caper.

"Mr George, I got problem," Aurora said as we headed downstairs. I was keen to get home and sort myself out. Besides, I wanted to be out of the place before everyone else arrived to see me like this.

"I got problem, Mr George."

"You and me both, Aurora," I said, checking that I had my car keys and the mobile. My suit jacket pocket was ripped, which meant I had just one jacket left that wasn't. "Tell me in the car."

There was still some glass on the drive that I'd missed in the dark which I kicked into the grass border. We got in the Golf and I checked myself in the mirror. Not pretty. Aurora, who had a thumb inside her passport and the envelope of money in her hands, looked at me expectantly. That's right, she wanted to tell me something about her problems.

"What is it, Aurora?"

"Passport not good," she said.

"What do you mean, not good?" She opened the passport to where her thumb formed a bookmark and handed it to me. Squinting through my left eye I made out a colourful visa stuck to the page above which was a stamp partly obscured by Aurora's thumb: As A Domestic Worker In A Private Household for up to 180 Days.

The problem, which Aurora thoughtfully tapped on, was the Heathrow entry stamp on the visa – it was dated nearly a year ago.

29

I SAT IN THE CAR SOMEWHAT DEFLATED, THEN ANGRY AT Galbraith. Had he known about the expired visa? Maybe he hadn't, maybe he'd just taken the passport off Kristina and not even thought to check it. Then I was angry with Aurora. How had she not known about the visa? It must have been stamped when she came into the country, she must have had some idea of how long she could stay, even if she didn't have access to the passport. But she could have been told anything by her employers and had no choice but to believe them; maybe Kristina had told her the visa had been renewed.

I didn't really know where to take Aurora now. My plan had been to pop home, get changed, then drive her to Heathrow and wait around until she got her plane but that was now out of the question. As far as I could tell she was an illegal immigrant. What would happen if she tried to board a plane when she'd been in the country illegally for nearly six months? This was beyond me. I needed advice. In the meantime she needed somewhere to stay. Aurora nudged me and pointed through the window. Sandra, arriving for work.

Upstairs in the office, with Aurora in the bathroom, I

gave Sandra the highlights of the previous night and Aurora's current situation. She studied me, frowning thoughtfully as I sat in the chair feeling the swelling on my lip.

"I don't suppose you're going to call the police about these two psychos?"

"How can I? I'd have to tell them the whole sorry tale including about Aurora and who knows what they'd do with her. Don't worry, their time will come."

"I'll phone the charity that I spoke to; they'll at least be able to advise on her options. Meanwhile, what are you going to do with her?"

"I was thinking—"

"Forget it, I've got my sister-in-law coming to stay tonight for the weekend."

"Which sister-in-law?" Sandra didn't have a brother, and Jason and Ashley had different fathers.

"I only have one. I was married to Jason's father, not Ashley's."

"Of course. I thought you hated his guts?"

"I do, but I got on with his sister who agrees that he's an arsehole. He's got no interest in Jason but she comes once a year to catch up on what he's doing. The point is, George, I haven't got the room or the time to babysit runaway maids who are in the country illegally."

I raised my hands defeated but she hadn't finished.

"Can I point out that you have got room, since you're rattling about in a three-bedroomed house on your own most of the time? Surely your girlfriend won't mind Aurora being around, or is it going to cramp your style?"

"OK, OK. I'll take her back to mine," I said, standing with some difficulty.

"Go home and clean up," she said more gently. "Have some breakfast. I'll let you know what the charity says as soon as I've spoken to them."

I drove Aurora back to my place, explaining on the way what the situation was as best I could. When I killed the engine in my drive she gave me the cash from the envelope.

"You keep safe?" she asked, nodding.

I put Leonard's Taser in the drawer of the small telephone table in the hall where I found an old tobacco tin I used to stash my hash in before they genetically modified the stuff and it got too strong to smoke. Showing Aurora, I put her cash in the tin and put it back in the drawer. I took her into the living room, where she eyed my small TV. I gave her the remote and headed upstairs.

Linda had already left, of course. Whether it was last night, after I hadn't returned, or this morning, I didn't know. I showered, taking inventory of my various bruises and cuts. They were mainly cosmetic, apart from my elbow which as well as being bruised was painful when I picked anything up. I would have to get it looked at. I nearly wandered downstairs in my underwear before remembering Aurora was there, probably still recovering from the shock of not having a giant TV like Sandra's she could watch her beloved soaps on. I had at least upgraded from my old black-and-white cathode ray tube for something flat and in colour, albeit quite small according to current standards. Sandra had told me that the Galbraiths had given Aurora a large TV in her room – opium for the oppressed.

When I got into the living room she was hunched over it and jumped up when I came in. Force of habit, I assume.

"I make food?" she asked.

"No. I'll make food. If I can find anything." I pointed to the TV. "Do you ever watch Mr Galbraith on TV?" I asked.

"No," she said, switching it off.

"You can watch it if you want."

"Can I wash hair?" she asked, pulling at it.

"Of course." I led her to the bathroom and found some women's shampoo and a hairbrush that Olivia had left in a cabinet. I told her she could change in the spare room and went to look for a fresh towel. When I returned with it the shower was going so I opened the door to the spare room only to see Aurora naked, her back to me. I gently closed the door and put the towel in the bathroom.

In the kitchen I found a note on the table from Linda: *Woke to find you didn't come home last night! Hope everything is OK?*

I fired off a long text saying all was fine and that a case had dragged on and I'd slept at the office 'cause I hadn't wanted to wake her.

I cobbled together some cheese, olives and salad that Aurora didn't look too impressed with but as we ate our brunch she told me a little more about herself. She was the eldest of four girls and, although she was pleased to be going home, she was worried that they couldn't cope without the regular money she sent. I didn't remind her of the fact that, as things stood, it was possible she wouldn't be going anywhere.

"At least you have the money Mr Bill gave you," I said.

"Yes. Will pay for cancer, not for food."

"So what will you do?"

"Will find work."

"Doing what?"

"Domestic, of course. In Gulf."

She said this so matter-of-factly that I was taken aback. I'd assumed, naively, that this would be the end of her travails but I was wrong. Like hundreds of thousands of others she travelled abroad to support her family and that requirement hadn't changed. She looked unhappily around the kitchen then at me, her face set in a question that she couldn't quite verbalise.

"What is it, Aurora?"

"Mr George is married?" Mr George shook his head.

"Aurora clean the house," she declared. I remembered Sandra's battle over this matter. Judging by the almost clinical, pristine state of the Galbraiths' place, mine must have looked like a pigsty to Aurora. I did actually clean the place but it wasn't to her standards, that's for sure.

"Just the kitchen," I insisted, thinking it would at least give her something to do until I heard back from Sandra and we could figure out what options she had. Besides, if I had to listen to any more TV soap operas it might send me over the edge.

I found her some cleaning products and while she got started I checked in on the chess puzzle laid out on the dining-room table but my brain wasn't up to it. Anyway, it seemed a little odd to be sitting around playing chess by myself while

Aurora was cleaning. Instead I got to work darning my ripped jackets. Sewing was something that Kamal had insisted on teaching me after Olivia had left, claiming that men needed to become more self-sufficient in the domestic arena, calling our dependence on women a form of learned helplessness. If only he could see me now, having my kitchen cleaned by a Filipino domestic who'd escaped her abusive employers.

Aurora laughed at my efforts when I showed her the results of fixing the pocket on my jacket. I couldn't see why; it looked pretty good to me. The doorbell rang and she froze, the fear never far from the surface. I told her to wait in the kitchen and went to the front door. Linda stood there, her eyes widening when she saw my face.

"What the fuck, Georgie? What happened to you?" She pushed past me into the house. "I'm on my way to court to cover a trial. Thought I'd stop by and see how you were doing." She touched the swelling on my face. "Not very well, I see. What the hell happened?"

"It's a long story," I said.

"Well, I haven't got that long. Do you want me to kiss it better?" There was a noise from the kitchen. "Someone here?" she asked.

"Yes… a cleaner," I said. I'm not sure why I lied, except it was just easier than explaining everything. Anyway, it wasn't really a lie.

"About time you got someone in," she said, pulling me close. "Even if it puts the kibosh on some lunchtime nooky."

"I'm not in the best state for it anyway," I said. "Everything hurts."

"Poor baby," she said, mockingly. I walked her to the front door. "I've brought you the early edition of the *Argus*," she said, pulling it from her bag. "Yours truly is on the front page again." It was folded in half and I glanced at it to see a large picture of Jackie Rowling but was then obliged to indulge in some painful snogging with Linda before she departed.

"Will I see you tonight?" I asked, fearing, for a change, that she would say yes, in case Aurora would still be here.

"No, sorry. I was here last night, remember, and you fucked off?" she said good-naturedly. She gave me a final kiss and I closed the door after her. I turned the newspaper over to read the headline under the photo: JACKIE'S PARENTS REUNITED WITH DAUGHTER. I was aware of Aurora coming out of the kitchen.

She was standing at the kitchen door in a red apron, holding a stack of old newspapers. The apron was one of Olivia's – it had that bloody stupid maxim you see everywhere: Keep Calm and Carry On. Aurora didn't look very calm, nor did she look like she was going to carry on. White-faced, she just stared at me.

"Are you OK?" I asked.

She dropped the newspapers and rushed into the kitchen where I could hear her retching. I wanted to point out that there was a fully working toilet off the hall but it wasn't the time. I went in and held her freshly washed hair out of the way and ran the tap, washing bits of half-digested cheese and olives down the plughole. Then the front doorbell rang again.

30

I OPENED THE DOOR TO DENSLEY, WHICH WAS A BIT OF A surprise because he'd never been to my house before. He was also possibly the first black person to come onto my street in a social capacity, assuming that was the purpose of his visit.

"Come in. I hope the cheque hasn't bounced."

He smiled. "Nah, I'd have sent round the heavies for that," he said, stepping into the hall. He looked at my face and grimaced.

"I'd offer you a cuppa but the kitchen's out of commission at the moment," I said.

"Thanks, but I'm on my way home for lunch and the missus is on an evening shift which starts before I get back from work. We have lunch together, you see, otherwise I'd never see her."

I nodded, unsure of what to say, although I found myself slightly envious of his domestic arrangements.

"I stopped by this morning to tell you this but you'd left," he said. "You remember we had that break-in?"

I nodded. "Did your son manage to get anything on the CCTV footage?"

"Yes, he did. There were two blokes on it and – get this – all they did was go through the paperwork. That's all they did, and they wrote stuff down."

"That's weird," I said, although part of me was trying to work out why this would be of interest to me – was he wanting to hire me to find them?

"So Gary recognised one of the blokes," Densley was saying. "You remember Gary, the curly-haired guy who drove your car round when you were trying to shake those two men?"

He wasn't here to hire me at all. "Don't tell me. Gary recognised the guy who followed me on foot," I said.

"Yes. How did you know?"

"It's the only reason you'd be telling me this."

"I'm really sorry, George. I feel bad about it. That's why I came round in person."

"I'm the one who should feel bad, Densley. I shouldn't have got you involved in my business. At the time I didn't realise how desperate those guys were. I assume they were after my address."

"So am I too late?" he asked, pointing at my face.

"No, that's from a previous encounter."

"Well, if they do turn up and you need a hand, just give us a holler. I'm a bit old for the rough stuff myself, obviously, but I've got three guys who'd help out at the drop of a hat and lots of big spanners."

I smiled. "Thanks for the heads-up but let's hope it doesn't come to that; I'm getting too old for the rough stuff myself."

I picked up the phone after closing the door to Densley.

I was very careful about not giving out my address to people, especially clients, but I'd never had someone trying to track down where I live before. I didn't like it. I had to move Aurora out but needed to speak to Sandra first. I rang the office, hoping she was there. She was.

"Just about to call you, George… OK, so I spoke to the charity and they referred me to a lawyer, but I had trouble getting hold of her which is why I've taken so long getting back to you."

"And?"

"And the lawyer can't recommend that Aurora leave the country, given her current status, but when I pressed her she said she didn't think she'd be detained. After all, they'd want to deport her anyway and unless she wanted to go through a lengthy legal process to try to remain in the country then it's probably the best option."

I walked to the kitchen door to check on Aurora as Sandra was saying this; she was sitting at the table, head in hands. She didn't look up to trying to get through passport control in her current state.

"Thanks, Sandra." I checked my watch. "Her flight leaves in two and a half hours and it takes an hour and half to get there with no traffic so if we're going we'd better get a move on, providing that's what she wants to do."

"Oh, and the lawyer said that if she does leave and they see that she overstayed her visa then she's not going to be able to come back. She needs to know that."

I hung up and went to Aurora. "How are you feeling?"

As if realising she was sitting down, she stood up.

"Take it easy," I said. "You still look faint." I'd underestimated the toll her situation was taking on her. I sat her down again and filled a glass with water at the sink, which she'd cleaned out, bless her. She drank it in long gulps. I moved the neatly stacked newspapers she'd piled up ready for recycling from the other chair and sat down.

"What happened?" I asked.

She shrugged off my question and reached for the envelope in the back of her jeans pocket, unfolded it and took out the e-ticket and studied it wistfully, perhaps hoping that if she stared at the destination long enough she would be transported there. "Maybe try and go with old visa?" She looked at me, the desperation apparent on her face. "Please?" Well, at least she'd made the decision already.

"That was Sandra on the phone. She said they would probably let you leave." She nodded. "But if you do leave you'll probably never get another visa if you want to come back to the UK. Do you understand?"

"I never come back here again," she said with a fierce determination.

I blew some air from my cheeks and stood up. "OK then, we should go. For an international flight you usually need to be there a couple of hours beforehand," I said, as she took off the apron. "But since you have no luggage you might be OK."

I went upstairs and found a small case for her to put her few things in, just because I thought it might look better if she didn't turn up with a plastic bag.

She was anxious to leave, hovering at the front door. Had

she heard my conversation with Densley? "Thank you," she said. "For helping me."

"Thank me when you're on the plane."

I'd half expected to find Leonard and Derin waiting on the street when I reversed out of my drive but I couldn't see them. Perhaps they'd given up on me – after all, they'd broken into Densley's before last night. Perhaps that was wishful thinking on my part; I'm prone to wishful thinking.

I drove five miles per hour faster than the law allowed and on the M25 the incessantly flapping plastic in the back window blew out. Luckily it didn't cause a massive pile-up but flew high and off onto the hard shoulder. At least I could see in my rear-view mirror now, the downside being that the noise made it impossible to speak to Aurora, who was wringing her hands and moving her lips silently. Was she praying, or practising what she would say to border control? I'd told her to tell them a version of the truth about her daughter being ill and Galbraith helping her leave and just feigning innocence at the passport. I had Sandra on the phone for some of the way down, the hands-free earpiece in my ear, telling me which terminal I had to be at. I'd held the e-ticket on the steering wheel reading out the details so she could check Aurora in online to allow her to go straight to passport control. We were about twenty minutes away from the airport when Aurora shrieked.

"The money!"

Shit shit shit. The money, sitting uselessly in the tin in

the drawer in the hall of my house.

"Don't worry, I'll get the money to you," I said. "I can transfer it." I pulled up at the drop-off point outside the right terminal. There was simply no time to park in the car park and escort her, and now two heavily armed police officers sauntered over to have a look at the battered car, so any thought about leaving it unaccompanied in the drop-off zone was out of the question. This was breaking all my rules about being early.

"Do you know where to go?" I asked.

She nodded.

I wrote my phone number and email address on the printout.

"Call me if there's a problem, or if they detain you get them to call me. Email me when you arrive home with bank details of where to transfer the money, OK?"

I pulled out my wallet and gave her what little there was in it as walking-around cash. She sat there, clutching it, as if wanting to say something. I checked my watch and showed her it. Tears started to roll down her face.

"Aurora, what is it?"

She couldn't look at me. "I email you," she said. She got out of the car and ran into the building with the case. I sat there, hands on the wheel, engine running, when a black cab pulled in front of me. Out of it stepped Bill Galbraith with a suit carrier over his shoulder. Of course, his flight left soon after Aurora's. A casually dressed woman in her thirties followed him out, stowing a wallet in a messenger bag worn across her front. Then emerged a middle-aged man dressed half his age in jeans, T-shirt and leather jacket, pulling various aluminium cases from the back of the cab, the sort used to carry delicate equipment. I assumed they were his film crew. Galbraith didn't have his precious attaché case – so much for wanting to take it with him.

Without thinking I got out of the car. Galbraith, talking and laughing with the woman, her back to me, caught sight of me. He looked surprised but quickly recovered. I sat on the bonnet of my car, arms crossed, and waited, staring at him. His face had solidified into something unreadable and he told his companions he'd see them at the check-in desk. They trundled off without even noticing me.

He stepped forward, a question in his eyes.

"She's gone," I said. "If she hasn't been detained."

"Gone?"

"Yes, isn't that what you wanted?"

"Yes, yes of course, I just… What do you mean, hasn't been detained?"

"Her visa had expired," I said.

"Do you think it will be a problem?"

"I'm told not, and you'll be pleased to know she won't be allowed back into the country."

He nodded and walked into the terminal building.

I took a moment, enjoying the sun on my face, until some guy in a hi-vis jacket approached and told me in an officious tone that I had to leave once I'd dropped off my passengers. I saluted him and got in my car.

31

I KEPT CHECKING MY WATCH ON THE DRIVE BACK FROM Heathrow, hoping that Aurora's departure would pass with no phone calls. I had no way of knowing whether she'd got on the plane. Initially I worried that Galbraith would try to intercept her but my reasoning was that he'd be relieved that she'd left the country, unable to return. My anxiety eased once the departure time had passed and by the time I reached the outskirts of Cambridge I was all but humming a tune.

If Densley was the first black person to visit my street, then Badem's car was the first Bentley to be parked on it, that's for sure. Even the middle-class kids who lived here had congregated around it as they cycled home from school. I should have known that Galbraith would ring Badem after he'd seen me, but I wasn't sure why he would.

As I parked on my drive Iskender Badem got out of his car with some help from Derin. Leonard was nowhere to be seen. They came onto the drive and Derin joined me at the front door as Iskender waddled – there's no other word for it – towards us.

"Are you going to invite us in?" asked Badem, smiling. I opened the door. There was the Taser in the drawer in the telephone table but Derin was close behind me and I felt a sharp prodding in my back. A knife this time, not a Taser. A knife was much worse than a Taser. A Taser was temporary pain, a knife was permanent injury or worse: bleeding to death alone in your own house.

Derin and I went through to the living room. Badem disappeared into the kitchen and returned breathlessly dragging a chair on the floorboards which he placed facing the sofa. Derin put a firm hand on my shoulder and I was pushed onto it, the knife now at the side of my neck. He produced a cargo tie-down strap from somewhere and slipped it over my head and arms and the back of the chair, securing it until it was unbearably tight round my middle, pressing against my bladder.

By this time Badem, taking his time, had settled deep, very deep, into the old sofa. It complained noisily. He picked up yesterday's *Argus* from the coffee table and looked at the front page with Jackie's photo.

"Terrible business, this. I have a daughter the same age at a private school here in Cambridge. She's doing very well."

"You must be proud," I said.

Derin clouted me round my right ear so hard I nearly toppled over with the chair. He giggled and I imagined smashing his stupid face in.

Badem just sat there reading the newspaper as if nothing had happened.

"What do you want?" I asked, my ear ringing.

"Mr Galbraith wants to know how discreet you are going to be."

"About what?" I wasn't sure what Badem knew but I wasn't going to give him anything.

"I know Bill wanted the girl gone for his own reasons, but she is worth more here than back in the Philippines."

"To who?"

"To whom. To her family of course," he said.

"That's thoughtful of you. Doing what exactly?"

"Doing domestic service, my good man, much as she does now. What did you think?"

"It's in the nature of my job to think the worst. Plus you hear stories."

"I'm affronted, Mr Kocharyan, I really am. That you would think I would stoop to such sordidness. The fact is, since she's already in the country there are many people here who would like a live-in domestic without the hassle of bringing one in for just six months then having to get a new one." I wasn't sure where all this was headed but if it stopped me getting whacked round the head I thought it best to humour him.

"And they're happy to employ someone here illegally?"

He chuckled, seemingly at my lack of sophistication in these matters. He was right; I was being naive.

"OK, I get it," I said. "The fact that she would be here illegally could be used as leverage by a private employer. The fear of being detained by the authorities would mean she'd never want to leave the house."

"Quite so. The detention centres your government has

contracted out to private security companies are cruel places, especially for women."

Sometimes you get a flash of something – call it an insight – which is just your subconscious brain making connections without you knowing it and then knocking on the door of your conscious brain with it, saying: here you go, idiot.

"Did you provide the workers for Mrs Galbraith's business, the one that had to close down?" I asked Badem.

He smiled knowingly. "I also provide the girls for her current business." I found it hard to believe she would repeat her mistake.

"They're here illegally?"

"Legal, illegal, these are just labels assigned by whoever makes the laws within an arbitrarily drawn state border. They are simply artificial limitations to be worked round. Unfortunately a business is not like an individual employer. There's paperwork to submit and checks are done, so people have to appear legal. Of course that comes at a cost; in this case a small slice of pizza. The lovely Kristina gives me a slice of pizza for providing her with cheap workers, the workers give me a slice of pizza for providing them with the right piece of paper to be here. Everyone is happy."

"Especially you," I said, although I was dying to add something about him having too much pizza. Those women must be on a pittance if it was worth Kristina's while paying Badem rather than paying a decent wage. But perhaps the minimum wage was just another artificial limitation to get round.

"You could have made yourself a nice little finder's fee for the girl," he said. "Instead you insisted on playing the hero."

"Nobody offered me a finder's fee. How much is a Filipino woman worth these days to people-traffickers?"

"Ah, George, I sense you are being provocative. I do hope you're not going to invoke the Human Rights Act? The problem with globalised capitalism is that the movement of goods is encouraged, yet the movement of people is discouraged. I'm just facilitating the movement of people."

"Against their will."

He folded his hands over his stomach and contemplated me through narrowed eyes.

"I'm willing to bet that if you ask the girl whether she wants to stay here and work, and continue to send money home, she'd agree. Would that make you feel better about it, if it were her choice?" The trouble is he could be right. Having spoken to her about her need to support her family, Aurora might well have agreed to the arrangement, were it not for the desire to visit her daughter.

"Fascinating though this is, it's academic," I told him, "since she's now on a plane to Hong Kong. So why don't you tell me why the fuck you're here and then get out."

He glanced over my right shoulder and I received another mighty blow to the right ear from Derin. I struggled to stay in the chair, my ear ringing painfully. I had to turn my left ear towards Badem in order to hear what he said next.

"Next time I let him use the knife," he said. Derin waved the item in question in front of my eyes in case I'd forgotten about it.

"I really don't know what you want from me," I said, desperate to rub my ear.

"Of course you don't. You are one of life's miserable underdogs. It's in your genes. You Armenians either try to escape your past by overcompensating and becoming millionaires, or you wallow in victimhood. It's probably why you identify with the dispossessed and downtrodden." He belched lightly.

"Is this all because your buddy surgeon was seeing one of his staff? He told me about that himself. He was worried Aurora would tell someone but she didn't. Stupidly loyal to the end, you might say, or perhaps fearful."

"Men like Bill, who achieve things in life, have needs; they are a way of redressing the balance of achieving greatness. These are perceived as weaknesses by ordinary people so a man in his position has to be careful."

"So he does a bit of surgery and has to fuck around?"

He reddened dangerously and raised his voice. "You think being crude is the same as being clever, Kocharyan?" He glanced to my right again and Derin must already have had his hand raised because the blow came quickly. Being of hefty build he could put some weight behind it. Being slapped on the same side was getting tiresome, and the cargo strap was pressing on my bladder. I hadn't been to the toilet since taking Aurora to Heathrow, which was now over three hours ago.

"You are seeing some woman, I understand," Badem said, picking up the *Argus* again and showing it to me. "She works for this rag."

My blood ran cold. How the hell did he know about Linda? Had they been watching the house?

"Ah, you are suddenly silent, or is it that you can no longer hear me?" He chuckled at his own joke and his belly started to heave up and down. Derin showed his appreciation at his uncle's wit by joining him with giggles. I hoped Badem would go into one of his coughing fits and choke to death but he caught himself at the spluttering stage. He pointed to Linda's name under the headline. "If I as much as get a whiff of Bill's indiscretion in this sorry excuse for a newspaper, be it under her name or anyone else's, then Leonard and Derin will pay her a visit. Is that understood?" Derin patted my shoulder.

The doorbell rang and I hoped to God it wasn't Linda popping round unannounced. Badem seemed unfazed and gestured to Derin to go and answer. He smiled at me as we waited. I strained to hear who it was but there was no talking.

Derin came back in followed by Leonard, who looked pale and distracted. He ignored me and went over to Badem, leaning over to whisper in his ear for quite a long time, which the ringing in my ear made inaudible.

"How did that happen?" asked Badem, his unwieldy eyebrows coming together in a frown. More whispering followed. Badem nodded but didn't look happy.

Leonard turned to look at me, smiling. I didn't like it – it was the smile I imagine a spider has when something is struggling vainly to escape its web.

Badem tried to get up out of the sofa but it had moulded around his huge buttocks. Derin rushed over to help pull his uncle out. It wasn't a dignified exit for Badem and when he reached the door he stopped.

"Leonard, you nearly forgot," he said, holding out his hand.

"Sorry, Mr Badem." He reached inside his jacket and pulled out two identical-looking passports. The top one had PILIPINAS in gold lettering at the top. My heart sank.

Badem smiled at me, opened it and showed me the photo, but I already knew whose face I would see.

32

BADEM PUT AURORA'S PASSPORT IN HIS JACKET POCKET WITH its twin. They must have already known about Aurora's flight from Galbraith, and planned to be there. "Where is she?" I asked, feeling nauseous.

"She's safe, although it's not your concern, Mr Kocharyan. She's no longer your problem. You should be more worried about Linda. If you have any stupid ideas about going to the police, Leonard here has her address and he and Derin would love an excuse to pay her a visit."

Leonard pulled a piece of paper from his pocket and showed it to me. It was indeed Linda's address, a place where even I wasn't welcome. He grinned and I quickly tried standing up with the chair strapped to me but Derin pulled me back and put his hands on my shoulders, bearing down with his weight-lifting arms.

"Settle down," Badem said. "Now, I understand that Leonard and Derin have some brief business to conduct with you but I will wait in the car if you don't mind, as I'm squeamish. Don't be too long," he told Leonard, looking at his watch. "We have to pick Natasha up from her riding lesson."

"Right you are, Mr Badem," Leonard said to his retreating mass. He took a Taser from his pocket, a yellow one this time. I drew some consolation from the fact that his little finger was in a splint and taped to the finger next to it.

"Look," he said, with exaggerated cheeriness. "I've found another one." He waited expectantly until the front door opened and closed while I thought about spouting some cliché about how he didn't have to do this, but I guessed that he wouldn't be swayed. He pressed the Taser to my chest and smiled. "This is going to hurt."

Being Tasered is much like having severe muscle cramp, except you're having it in every muscle of your body simultaneously. Paralysed rigid and in appalling pain, time seemed to freeze and I was unable to speak except to make a noise like a tortured goat until he released the trigger and then what came from my mouth was repulsive in both tone and language and aimed at Leonard's grinning face. I may have spat at his smile. So of course he pulled the trigger again and I think he was telling the truth about having disabled the five-second safety because this time the pain lasted even longer and I felt as if I was disengaging from my body altogether. When he stopped this time I didn't curse, but so relieved was I that I whimpered like a cowed dog. On instruction from Leonard, Derin removed the strap and I bent double, my muscles stinging. I made my way to the sofa, supported by whatever I could lean on, hardly aware of Leonard or Derin. I vaguely heard them leave and sobbed to myself until I realised that my trousers were soaked. I staggered upstairs, tears coursing down my cheeks. I stripped off and forced myself under the shower, crouching as I didn't trust myself to stay upright.

I felt more human once dressed but flinched when the doorbell rang. The peephole revealed a fish-eye view of Kamal chaining his bicycle to my fence. I opened the door, checking the street behind him.

"Bloody hell, George, what happened? You look as bad as your car. Were you in an accident?" Without waiting for an answer he pushed past me into the hall. I closed the door, grateful he was here. He was dressed in a corduroy jacket over a proper shirt.

"Do you want a drink?" I asked. "I want a drink." I went to the kitchen and grabbed a cold beer from the fridge. I took two ibuprofen from a pack on the table.

"It's not quite five o'clock," Kamal said, sitting at the table and watching me, disapproving, as I swallowed the pills and glugged from the neck of the bottle. The beer, which was nothing special, felt so good, so satisfyingly deserved, that it was difficult to stop drinking until the bottle was empty. I sat down opposite Kamal who was watching me all the while.

"Are you OK?" he asked, frowning with concern.

"I'll be fine."

"You going to tell me what's going on?"

"I've fucked up big time," I said. "I've taken someone out of the frying pan and thrown them into the fire."

"Maybe I will have that beer." He got up and took one from the fridge. "Tell me what you can."

So I told him the whole sorry story without giving too much away although as he already knew about my interest in

Galbraith, he soon put two and two together. He stroked his ridiculous moustache.

"Let me get this straight. The Filipino girl I helped you find was working for Galbraith and disappeared with his briefcase because she wanted her passport and you negotiated an exchange and took her to the airport and she's now in the possession of Galbraith's patient who was also looking for her because Galbraith had told him his medical notes were in the briefcase?"

"Something like that." I'd left out the pearls because they were an irrelevant side issue.

"And you can't go to the police because...?"

"She's in the country illegally. If she gets into the hands of the authorities they might stick her in a detention centre for weeks, if not months, before deporting her. That's if they can even be bothered to look for her. It's conceivable that she might have been convinced to go with them of her own free will. She might have been offered more money to work here illegally for someone else." I didn't tell him of the threat made to Linda. I had thought about going to Stubbing unofficially but, knowing her, she would put duty before anything. And I couldn't see Linda being happy to move again or be placed under protection from some thugs.

"Maybe you should have gone to the police before you took her to the airport," he said.

"Maybe. Hindsight is a wonderful thing." I opened another beer and began to feel a little more human and less like a stunned heifer.

"So what happens now?"

"I don't know. I'll have another drink and think about it." But something he'd said was nagging at me. He was asking something about poker but I was only half listening. I was picturing Badem's notes in the briefcase.

"I've got a question," I said.

"You haven't answered my question about whether you're coming to poker tonight?"

"Jesus, is it Friday already? I think I'll give it a miss, for obvious reasons."

"Thought so. What's your question?"

"Patients' medical notes. There'd be like a sticker or something that identifies the patient?"

"Of course. Patient name, date of birth, hospital number. I transport notes all the time from Medical Records to clinics or the wards, and back again."

"Really? So could you check to see if someone's notes were in the hospital?"

"I'm not getting hold of anyone's medical records, George," he said, a warning in his voice.

"I'm not asking you to. I just want to know if someone's notes are in the hospital or not."

"It's difficult to tell whether they've left the hospital, unless they've gone to another hospital. I think the system tells you whose clinic or which ward they were checked out to, but consultants are notorious for keeping notes in the boot of their car… Ah, I think I see where you're going with this."

"Good, 'cause I'm not sure myself where I'm going with this. So all you can tell for certain is whether a particular set of notes has been checked out of Medical Records?"

"That's right."

"So if I gave you a name, you could check it? All I want to know is if the notes are there or not, and if they are, when they were last checked back in."

"You think Galbraith lied to this guy about his notes?"

"I don't know. I just know that I saw what I was told were the notes but they were in a bog-standard grey folder with nothing on the outside."

"The notes are usually blue, heavy-duty cardboard; they get handled a lot. There's usually a mess of papers inside, pharmacy slips, test results, you name it." That didn't sound like what I'd seen in Galbraith's case. I wasn't sure it was worth pursuing but it was something Galbraith didn't want me to see, and that sort of thing always piques my interest. How it would help Aurora I'd no clue, but you never know what might turn out to be useful.

"Can you check it out?" I asked.

He ummed and aahed but eventually agreed to do so when he was on duty the next day. I wrote down Iskender Badem's name.

"I better get going," he said, taking the slip of paper and standing up.

"Why did you stop round, anyway?" I asked. "I'm not on your way home."

"Yeah, I was, erm, I'm actually on my way to visit someone nearby and wanted to tell you about Chris, my lodger." I filed the shy reference to visiting someone nearby – a conversation for another time. "You know how yesterday he was going on about his director who was sacked?"

"Yes?"

"Apparently all the computers in the department were taken away by Human Resources this morning. Something about IT needing to audit them because the director had access."

I was struggling to muster up a reason to care about any of this right now. I just wanted to go upstairs and have a bath with a drink in hand, even though I'd just showered. I got up.

Kamal sensed my ambivalence. "I'll cut to the chase. Chris spoke to someone he's friendly with in IT who told him that the director's computer had nothing on it when they had a look, but that the porn was on a USB stick plugged into his computer."

I nodded, walking Kamal to the front door. "So someone could have just stuck it in his machine and made an anonymous call."

"Exactly. I mean, maybe Chris is right, maybe this was all to pull the rug out from under the report."

"It's a bit extreme," I said. "I mean what could it possibly say that would justify ruining someone's career, not to mention their life, like that?"

"Something that ruined your own career?" he said.

As I watched him unchain his bike I wondered whether being Tasered scrambled your brain for the better or worse.

"Listen, ask Chris whether Galbraith would have received a copy of the audit report as a matter of courtesy. And get back to me on those notes."

"Does this mean I'm on the payroll?"

"I'm giving you free lessons in the vagaries of human nature. What more do you bloody want?"

33

I WAS WOKEN FROM A LONG SLEEP BY SOMEONE LEANING ON the doorbell, followed by knocking, then testing the bell again. I pulled a robe on and staggered downstairs, every bit of me annoyed.

Linda stood there, dangling a paper bag of something.

"Croissants," she declared, then peered at me. "You look worse today than you did yesterday." She swept past me into the kitchen and I could hear her fill the kettle as I checked my face in the hall mirror. Things were turning a nice mix of purple and blue.

I went into the kitchen and sat down. I had tinnitus in my right ear – a faint but constant buzzing.

"Coffee?" she asked.

I grunted as she put the wrong amount of coffee into the cafetière. I'd tried numerous times to explain that two level scoops was just right and that she should wait thirty seconds after the kettle had boiled before pouring on the water. This morning, however, I let it ride. "You going to tell me what the face is all about?" she asked, putting the croissants on a plate.

"It's a case I've been working on."

"Well duh, I didn't think you'd taken up a career in boxing," she said, bringing the coffee and sitting opposite, smiling. She reached out and stroked my eye and swollen lip. "Poor baby," she said. "Does it hurt?"

"Only when I laugh."

"Ha ha. So who did this to you?"

"Bullies."

"Again, duh. But who were they, what did they want?" she asked, ripping a croissant in two.

"Bullies don't want anything, they just need someone to torment."

She poured the coffee. "I get it; you don't want to talk about it."

"Sorry," I said. "It's just that if I tell you about it you're so clever you'll easily put two and two together and realise who my client is. Next thing you know it'll be in the *Argus*."

"Mmmm. So it's someone well known enough to write about. That's just piqued my interest even more." I sipped the weak coffee and decided it might be better soaked up in croissant.

"However, I have enough on my plate at the moment. The police here may have matched the dead girl with a Polish teenager reported missing by her parents. She left Poland several months ago and they hadn't heard from her since. They've arrived here today and I plan to interview them."

"How did the Poles get wind of it?"

"The police here sent photos of the dead girl to Europol, since they couldn't link her to any reported missing people in the UK. They think it's the same girl but the parents are arriving to identify the body."

"And you've got an interview with them?"

"Not yet, but I will," she said, winking. "I think they might go up to Byron's Pool to see the tributes there. Assuming it is their daughter of course. If she is then Stubbing will want to make a photo public – one from when she was alive, obviously – in the hope people will recognise her."

"You want to take them to the place their daughter was murdered?"

She shrugged. "She wasn't murdered there, she was found there. If it was me I'd want to see it. Anyway, I thought you might want to meet up afterwards; we could have lunch in Grantchester."

Visiting the site where a dead girl had been found seemed prurient to me but at least I'd be able to keep an eye on Linda, and make sure Leonard and Derin weren't keeping tabs on her.

"I'd nothing else planned except sitting around feeling sorry for myself," I said, which was true.

"Ahhh... poor Georgie." Her hand went to my face again. Her touch was cool and gentle.

"I seem to remember you offered to kiss it better yesterday," I said.

"I did, but you told me you weren't up to it. Plus you had that cleaner here, remember?" She took her hand from my face and smiled crookedly to let me know that she didn't quite believe me about the cleaner.

I gestured around the kitchen. "Have you ever seen the sink sparkle so?"

"It is very clean," she acknowledged grudgingly. I took her hands and made a show of looking into her eyes.

"Don't we owe it to ourselves, Linda, to at least try and find out whether I'm up to it or not?" She pulled her hands from mine and stood up.

"I think we already know the answer to that, don't we?" She sashayed to the door, then looked at me over her shoulder. "Well? I'm not bloody carrying you upstairs."

Afterwards, I downed painkillers in the kitchen as Linda made a lot of noise in the shower. There was a message left on the mobile from Kristina Galbraith, greeting-free as per.

"I wonder if we could meet some time today. I'd like to follow up on our conversation. Can you come to the house this evening at six-thirty?" She didn't say what she wanted. A day ago I would have told her to throw herself in the sea but she could be a useful conduit to finding what had happened to Aurora. I rang her back and left a message confirming that I would come to the house.

We drove up to Grantchester in Linda's car (with me surreptitiously checking that nobody was following), where we had lunch at a pub crowded with tourists looking for the ghost of Rupert Brooke. I wanted to tell them he was buried just miles from where Olivia was restoring a farmhouse with her lover but they might have regarded me with pity, and there's nothing worse than that.

We walked off our lunch by going down to Byron's Pool. It was busy which was good for Linda, who wanted to capture some vox-pop about what it was like to visit a walking spot where a body had been found, or some such ghoulish nonsense. I left her to it. At the base of the post of the height restriction barrier – where presumably the car park had been cordoned off by police – was an unhappy collection of faded and fresh flowers with a now sodden teddy bear thrown in. Lots of handwritten messages from the general public had been stuck in the flowers and taped to the post, many of them illegible due to overnight rain. Those that had survived because they'd been put in plastic bags looked rather sad. Leonard and Derin were nowhere to be seen and the whole setting was making me depressed. As I walked back towards the road Stubbing drove up in an unmarked car, parking before the barrier. She opened the back door and a middle-aged couple got out – they must have identified the body as their daughter's. Looking tired and shell-shocked Stubbing led them to the barrier where she stood back as they looked at the offerings left for an unknown woman. The mother, petite and lank-haired, clung to a pot-bellied man with a smooth shiny head who made no attempt to stem his tears. Linda was hovering, trying to catch Stubbing's eye. Stubbing nodded and gestured to her.

I couldn't watch. I walked back to the pub and sat in the garden with a fresh pint, contemplating what it was that motivated people to leave messages and flowers for complete strangers. Was it a form of collective mourning? I reached no conclusions worth sharing but became aware that I was sitting alone at a table in an otherwise busy garden being suspiciously side-eyed. I remembered that I looked like I'd been in a fight, which I suppose I had, albeit one-sided.

I was at a loss as to what to do about Aurora, if I could do anything, and had no reason to think she was in physical danger. I felt angry with her at letting herself be convinced to leave with Leonard at the airport. All she'd had to do was go through passport control; I couldn't imagine he'd risk forcing her anywhere in a crowded airport with armed police everywhere. However it happened, things did not sit easy with me, and I felt some responsibility for her predicament. But maybe there was a way back in via Kristina that didn't involve antagonising Badem and putting Linda at risk.

The pub had emptied when she returned, a glow in her eyes and a large envelope in her hands. She was itching to be off.

"Did you speak to them?"

"Yes of course." She waved the envelope. "They've brought a picture of their daughter with them. Her name's Bogdana." In the car back to Cambridge I asked her what she'd learnt.

"You'll have to read it on Monday like everyone else. You don't tell me what you're working on."

"Fine. What were they like, her parents?"

"Sweet couple, unsophisticated in a way. He's a carpenter, she works in a school as an administrator. I'm going to talk to them properly tomorrow with an interpreter."

"They're happy to be interviewed?"

"Of course; they want to know what happened to their daughter and getting her story out there is going to help."

She dropped me off at the end of my road. The previous

day's events, the morning's sex, the lunchtime beer, the depressing sight at Byron's Pool – it had all taken its toll. When I got in I crawled onto the unmade bed that still smelled of Linda and submitted to the Sandman.

34

GALBRAITH'S PORSCHE WASN'T IN THEIR DRIVE, NO DOUBT
undergoing some satisfyingly expensive repairs somewhere. I
pulled up behind the Range Rover, my back window freshly
covered with my own efforts to keep probable rain out. As I
waited for Kristina to answer the door, my phone declared a
text from Kamal: *Notes of IB currently in medical records, last
checked out for follow-up clinic 2 weeks ago. Kx.* So Galbraith
had lied: those weren't Badem's notes in his briefcase. I was
increasingly curious about what was. Then I got a second text
from him which made me ninety per cent sure: *WG would
have received copy of audit.*

She opened the door, flushed and in her purple running
gear. She looked at my battered face with interest but no
comment, and let me in.

"You're early. Wait upstairs; I'll be five minutes."

With some effort I climbed the stairs to the open-plan
living space to find a view of the low sun struggling through
some dark clouds over the distant fields. A low growl came
from the sofa. Misha was curled there, his head following me
around the room. I decided ignoring the mutt would teach

him some manners. I examined the sound system. Only a man would spend so much on music technology. The speaker cable alone probably cost more than my hi-fi system, such as it was. There were hundreds of records, most of them classical and jazz. To the left of this setup was an archway into another room. I stepped through it to have a look. It was a large space, with windows onto three aspects. In the middle was a glass desk on a Turkish rug. The desk was empty apart from a closed MacBook Air sitting neatly in front of an expensive-looking ergonomic chair with lots of levers, the sort that you had to keep the manual handy to operate. Medical books lined the wall around the window behind the desk. There, under the window that faced the front of the house, sat Galbraith's attaché case.

"That's Bill's study," Kristina said behind me.

She wore the kind of black dress that women in films ask gooey-eyed men to help zip up at the back. My limited expertise in that area wasn't required, however, and she put some heels down next to the sofa and walked on stockinged feet over to the kitchen area where she poured a little red wine into two ridiculously large glasses and came back to sit on the white leather sofa. She leant over and put a glass on the table near me. I chose a white leather cube to perch on. Misha stood on his hind legs and I was treated to a thankfully brief smooching show. He then lay back down next to her and watched me warily, smacking his lips in satisfaction.

"Were you hit by a car?" she asked.

"I fell down the stairs at work."

"I wondered, because my husband said he hit something

with his car, a small deer or something. We have them round here." She smiled, and I realised she was making a joke so I showed her a grin.

"That wasn't me, no," I said.

"He's having to have the seats reupholstered." She lifted her glass in a toast. "I wanted to thank you for returning his briefcase."

"And you got your pearls back," I said, thinking she could have done this on the phone. But I picked up the glass.

She shrugged. "I haven't seen them yet. Apparently Aurora broke them, so he's getting them restrung."

I didn't tell her that the pearls had already been broken – you don't play your hand without some money on the table. It was worth finding out what she knew and didn't know.

"So I put her on a plane to Manila," I said. Her eyes widened in surprise, but I couldn't tell whether she knew Aurora hadn't boarded the plane.

"Really? That's good." Her hand went unconsciously to Misha, who squirmed in pleasure under the ministrations of her fingers.

"Yes, she's probably with her daughter as we speak." She nodded and I was unable to resist continuing the charade.

"It was good of you to hand over the passport," I said, as if it were an act of extraordinary magnanimity. Of course, her husband may have just taken it from her but I let her soak up the compliment. She shrugged like it was nothing and put the lipstick-stained glass down on the table, sitting forward, her knees together.

"So did she tell you anything before she left?"

"About what?" I asked. This was why I was here. "You asked me this before. What is it you're so worried she's told me about?" I tried to cross my legs but it's difficult on a stool with no back so I gave up. She stared at me with open hostility. I felt self-conscious and touched my face. The swelling on my lip had certainly gone down. She was about to speak when a phone rang somewhere. Putting the glass down again she got up and went to the source in the kitchen area. She picked up a mobile from the counter and took it into a room, closing the door behind her.

Without giving it much thought I got up, went into Galbraith's study and moved quickly to the case. Would I remember the code? My hands sweaty, listening for Kristina, I tried the combination. The first attempt I got it wrong. Less haste, more speed, George, my father used to say. I managed it on the second go and got the flaps open. Inside was as before, the grey folder and the envelope with the pearls. I took out the folder and flicked through it: charts, text, tables of figures, all fastened together. I heard a noise and nearly jumped out of my skin when I saw Misha standing in the doorway, little head cocked. Ignoring him I tried to open the window overlooking the drive but had trouble figuring out how to open the bugger, because being an architect-designed house it couldn't be a normal window. A door opened somewhere as I finally got it open and I pitched the folder into a bush next to her Range Rover, left the window open because I didn't have time to close it, closed the flaps and locks on the case without having time to spin the dials, then wandered out casually, bending to stroke Misha who snarled at me. Kristina was picking up her wine from the table.

"Sorry, I was looking for the bathroom," I said, feeling sweaty, my heart beating hard, although the worst-case scenario would have been Kristina throwing me out. She pointed to a door off the kitchen area. I went in and wet my face circumspectly in the marbled washroom, then dabbed it dry with a soft towel that smelled of lavender.

Kristina was on the sofa putting on the heels when I emerged. I sat in an armchair this time, at ninety degrees to her.

"Where were we?" she asked.

"You were worried about what Aurora might have told me."

She finished buckling the thin straps at her ankles and looked at me, ready with something to say.

"It's just that I think Bill has been seeing someone from work, and Aurora may have seen her." She gestured at the room. "Here."

"You believe he's involved with someone else?"

"Was," she said, without hesitation. "It ran its course as these things do. But I'm less worried about the fact that it happened than the effect on his career should it come out. You understand?"

I did understand. She didn't care about him sleeping around – how could she if she was indulging herself? What did concern her was a loss of his status, which would affect her.

She stood up and smoothed down her dress, saying, "Well?" For a crazy second I thought she was asking me how she looked but I bit my tongue before realising that she was asking whether Aurora had said anything.

"She didn't say anything to me," I said. "And I don't think she spoke to anyone else about it. Is this why you asked me here?" It had started to rain, and I was worried about the folder outside in the bush and wanted to retrieve it before she went out. She moved to the stairs and smiled at me, which was disconcerting given its rarity. She also stuck out her hand.

"I assume we can count on your discretion?" she said, looking into my eyes. She held onto my hand a few seconds too long.

"An unnecessary question," I said.

We stood at the top of the stairs until I understood that I was to make my own way down. I had one last curveball to throw at her.

"How well do you know Iskender Badem?" I asked, daring to look again into the dark wells of her eyes.

She frowned, asking, "How do you know him?"

"He's a patient of your husband's, a friend even. His medical notes were in the briefcase, so he had, shall we say, an interest in retrieving it."

She appeared taken aback by this but shook it off.

"He's been to dinner once or twice but otherwise… Why do you ask?"

"Just curious."

She nodded and smiled politely as I went down the stairs. I looked up when I reached the bottom. She stood, arms crossed, staring down at me, unsmiling. I let myself out into the drizzle, moving quickly to the bush in case she went to the window. The folder was damp so I tucked it into my jacket and got into my car which I reversed into the turning area before driving out.

I drove into the pub car park down the road and parked facing the exit, so I could see when she left, providing she headed into Cambridge. After ten minutes of listening to the rain drumming on the plastic over the back window and switching on the wipers intermittently she still hadn't emerged, so I had a proper look at the report I'd stolen. A lot of statistical tables and charts comparing readmission rates, complications, deaths by procedure – nothing I could make sense of. I started the engine. A taxi coming from the direction of Cambridge slowed as the driver peered through the rain for an address. Her good-looking special friend from the afternoon-delight hotel was in the back, pointing down towards the Galbraiths'. Of course, she wouldn't drive in heels – he must be picking her up. I pulled out enough so that I could see down the road. The taxi stopped and he got out, clutching a bunch of flowers. The taxi left and he disappeared from view. I waited for another ten minutes, then decided they were having a cosy night in.

I nearly left for home but on a whim I parked the car properly then retrieved the digital camera that I keep in the glove compartment. It wasn't heavy duty – I keep that stuff in the office – but it came in handy at opportune moments like this. I mean, what private investigator doesn't enjoy standing in the rain taking photos of cavorting lovers?

35

WHEN I STOPPED BY KAMAL'S AFTER STANDING IN THE RAIN outside Kristina's taking photos, I learnt that his lodger Chris was out with friends, since it was the normal thing to do on a Saturday night. So I left the folder from Galbraith's case with Kamal for him to give to Chris to decipher, with a message for him to call me in the morning. I also asked Kamal to get me the name of Galbraith's senior registrar, the one who did all the work and was rumoured to be self-medicating. I thought I might as well make a pretence at working for Mrs G; maybe Galbraith had told me the truth when he'd said that Aurora had seen him bring someone home from work. It would make sense that he was leading someone on romantically that he was leaning on professionally. He was certainly right about the effect an affair would have on his TV career, especially if he was sleeping with someone junior to him. I now wished that I'd pressed Aurora about it, but the last few days had been nuts and I seemed to have been reacting to events rather than trying to steer them – ever the story of my working life.

Kamal and I had a couple of kebabs at a lively and unpretentious place on Mill Road and he told me about the woman he'd been on his way to visit when he'd stopped by yesterday – a radiologist at the hospital who'd been badgering him to go round for dinner.

When I got home I set out a fresh chess game with the heavy pieces. My father had an old book of Armenian Grandmaster games and I planned to run through a Petrosian game from his successful 1963 World Championship challenge against Botvinnik. I also fired up my old computer, since I hadn't checked my emails for days – not that anyone sent me emails. Olivia used to send me updates on their Greek restoration plans and for a while I had even followed her on Facebook until I realised everyone on Facebook was having a wonderful life and had wonderful children and wonderful partners and I didn't. So I quit and immediately felt better.

I poured myself a whisky, found some Bach on the radio, and played through the Petrosian-Botvinnik opening until the doorbell disturbed my peace. I took my drink and put it on the telephone table in the hall where I opened the drawer slightly to make sure the Taser was handy, then switched on the outside light and looked through the peephole. Stubbing. Sighing, I opened the door. She was in her cheap work suit, her hands in her jacket pockets.

"What's the rumpus?" I asked her.

She nodded at the hall. "May I?"

"If you must." I led her through to the living room, picking up my drink and closing the table drawer with my hip as I passed so she wouldn't see the Taser; I doubted she would turn a blind eye to my having it in my possession.

"Would you like a drink or are you on duty?"

"I am on duty, as it happens." She sat in the depression left in the sofa by Badem. Her face was pale and she had grey rings forming under her eyes.

"You don't mind if I imbibe?" I said.

"Have you been in an accident?"

I pointed to my face. "You mean this?"

"That and your car."

"Occupational hazard." I sat in the armchair.

"If you need to report an assault or accident I can point you in the right direction," she said, distractedly.

"Is this a continuation of our chat the other day?" Which reminded me. "Did you run the licence plate I gave you?" I asked.

"No I didn't, I've got more important things on at the moment." She took out a black notebook from her jacket pocket and flicked through it.

"Do you know an Aurora de la Cruz?"

I tried to hide my alarm as she studied me with her professional face on, features expertly inexpressive, a face honed from doing hundreds of interviews.

"Yes, I do," I said.

"When did you last see her?"

There was little point in lying to her. "Yesterday afternoon, around two. I dropped her outside Terminal Three at Heathrow Airport."

"Heathrow. And she was headed where?"

"Manila, via Hong Kong. Why, what's happened?" She took out a smartphone and flicked through some stuff and then seemed to pinch the screen and peer at it.

"Can you prove that you took her to the airport?" she asked. "A parking ticket, that sort of thing."

"You'll find I'm on CCTV of the drop-off area outside Terminal Three. I didn't have time to park."

"And you haven't heard from her since you dropped her off?"

"No."

She wrote something down. "I'm assuming she's the same woman you told me you were going to meet outside the church in Cherry Hinton, the one whose briefcase you said was being stolen by two men?"

"Why do you assume that?"

"Because the person who reported the fracas outside the church was a Filipino and described the woman as Filipino. So unless you are having dealings with lots of Filipino women then I am assuming she is one and the same person." She said this all very matter-of-factly and I nodded.

"You told me she was your client, right?" she asked, cocking her head slightly. What with the events of the past few days and my brain being fried I was having trouble remembering what lie I'd told Stubbing.

"Has something happened to her?" I asked.

She blew air from her cheeks. "Someone reported a body by the side of the A14 just outside Cambridge. Looks like a hit and run."

"Jesus..." Fuck, fuck, fuck. I put my drink down as Stubbing spoke.

"I'm trying to get footage from the traffic cameras that hopefully cover the spot, but it's Saturday night and apparently people don't work Saturday nights."

I stared at her as she spoke.

"All she had on her was a printout of a ticket, with your email address and phone number on it. It checks out with what you told me about the flight, although obviously she didn't catch it."

"You've checked, have you?" I asked, stupidly, in the vain hope that she was in Manila and that everything I'd heard or seen to the contrary was just a bad dream I'd had.

"Oh, thanks for reminding me, Kocky, I'll get right on it. Of course I bloody checked. I haven't had a chance to get her status from Visas and Immigration but I imagine they're another five-day-a-week work-shy outfit. Unless it's terrorism-related of course, then everything is immediately available."

I nodded because I didn't know what else to do in response to her little rant.

"So what were you doing for her?" she asked.

"Getting her to the airport," I said.

Given that Aurora was dead I didn't really have much choice in divulging information to Stubbing. However, I wasn't going to give it up too easily. Aurora linked to Galbraith who linked to Badem who'd just threatened Linda.

"How did you identify the body if all she had on her was the printout?" I asked.

"We haven't. That's why I'm here. I was hoping you could, somehow."

"What do you mean, somehow?"

She paused, glanced at my drink and said, "Whatever hit her was big and heavy and it looks like she was dragged beneath it for a distance. She may even have been hit by more than one vehicle; it's been known to happen. What I'm saying is that there's not a lot to actually identify."

I felt queasy. I took a sip of my drink but it tasted like cleaning fluid.

"She had black hair," I said.

"Yes, that would fit, and the skin colour would make sense. But it's hardly an ID." Stubbing tucked a stray strand from her scraped-back hair behind her ear and I remembered something.

"She was here for a couple of hours before her flight. She borrowed a hairbrush that belonged to… that was left here."

She shrugged. "I can take some hairs but hair isn't ideal for DNA testing. It all depends on whether the roots are intact."

"Shall I get it?" I asked.

"Hang on, before we do that. There is an identifying mark on the body which you may have seen."

"OK?"

"A tattoo, on the lower back," Stubbing said, touching her own lower back to demonstrate. "What's called a tramp stamp."

"For Christ's sake, Stubbing."

She looked at me questioningly and brandished her phone. "I have a photo of it."

"Shut up," I said, forcefully. I stood up, livid. Then I remembered something: I had briefly seen Aurora naked from behind, when I'd taken her the towel.

"Why are you smiling?" she asked.

I was so relieved I didn't even care what Stubbing would

think. "She didn't have a tattoo," I said.

"Are you sure? You didn't just see her bending over with her knickers showing?"

"Yes, definitely. I've seen her fully naked from behind." There, put that in your smutty pipe and puff on it, Stubbing.

Smirking briefly, she wrote something in her little book. I sat down again and took a sip of whisky. It tasted like whisky this time.

"So," she said. "I still have a dead unidentified woman on my hands. Which brings us to the question of how this woman had Aurora de la Cruz's ticket on her person."

"I really don't have a clue," I said truthfully.

"Why didn't she catch the flight?"

My relief at learning Aurora wasn't dead was short-lived. I could tell Stubbing everything and someone might even be able to track Aurora down, although it wouldn't be a high priority. But if found she would then become part of the system's machinery in dealing with illegals. Plus there was Badem's threat to factor in. Luckily I was spared the need to answer by the doorbell ringing.

"That'll be for me," Stubbing said, rising. "I came straight from the RTA in a patrol car." She went to the front door and I followed. A young policewoman in uniform, cap in hand, stood under the porch light. Stubbing stepped out and they had a whispered conversation. Stubbing turned to me.

"We'll speak again tomorrow. Make sure you're available."

"If I'm not in, it'll only be because I've gone to church," I said, but her attention was already on other things.

36

OBVIOUSLY I WAS JUST AS CURIOUS AS STUBBING AS TO HOW
Aurora's ticket had ended up on the dead woman. Had she
been trying to escape from a car? I recalled Leonard giving
Badem two passports after coming from the airport. Where
had he taken Aurora? After all, he hadn't been that long
behind me. He might even have made it back to Cambridge
before me since I'd been driving without any urgency to cut
down the noise and in-car turbulence created by the lack of
a rear window. So he could have taken her somewhere before
bringing the passports to Badem, somewhere off the A14.

All this I mulled over while washing down a Sunday
breakfast of bacon and egg with coffee. Afterwards, in the
dining room, I uploaded the photos I'd taken last night of
Kristina and her lover. The compact camera had a limited
zoom lens but since it had been raining and people shouldn't
live in glass houses, I'd managed to capture a few choice
pictures. They'd closed the blinds when things got seriously
carnal but you got the very definite impression from the
pictures that they weren't planning a game of Scrabble.

I made fresh coffee and wandered outside with it to check

E. G. RODFORD

on the growth of my brambles. My neighbour was currently
hacking at them where they were growing into his pristine
garden and throwing the cuttings back over the fence. I was
about to cough loudly so he knew I could see him when the
landline rang inside.

"Hello?"

"George, it's Kamal. Chris has had a read of that report
and wants to talk to you."

"I can't leave the house," I said. "Why don't you come
over for coffee?"

"I can't," he said. "But I'll send Chris over."

I got dressed, stripped the bed and put the bedding in
the washing machine. I then tidied up the kitchen and, when
the bell went, let Chris in, who'd arrived on bicycle. I made
coffee and we sat at the kitchen table. Chris was clutching the
report and champing at the bit.

"I read this last night when I was drunk and then again
this morning just to make sure I'd read it correctly."

"You didn't share any of it, did you? On Twitter or
Facebook?" I asked.

"Just because I'm young it doesn't mean I'm stupid.
Although I do think it should be made public," he said.

"Hang on there, Caped Crusader. Let's hear what it is
first, then I'll decide what to do with it."

Chris looked at me with ill-disguised scorn. He composed
himself and began.

"What you have here is an audit report of all the
operations done by Mr Galbraith and his team over the last
two years. This period includes pre and post his TV series,

so it gives a nice comparison of the time before and after. The report looks at complications, readmission rates, deaths, etcetera, and compares them to the national average right down to procedure level. What the director did was to get people to go through the physical notes, not just rely on the codes entered into the system which is done afterwards. It's a huge amount of work."

"OK, you've lost me a little. What does the comparison with national rates show?"

"Nothing. Overall, performance falls within acceptable parameters. You could even argue that, since this is Addenbrooke's we're talking about, it might attract more complex cases than other hospitals so in that sense the odds are stacked against it."

"So where's the news?"

"The news is the analyses within the consultant firm. Remember how I said that there are several surgeons operating under a consultant's name?" I nodded. "Well, the analysis compares them all, and breaks down procedures according to who did them, and then compares that to the national average. So it's looking at things at a micro level rather than a macro level."

"OK, so what does that show?"

"That shows that Galbraith has the worst outcomes of all the surgeons in his team. He's mediocre at best, but on some complex procedures he's well below national average with higher death rates and readmissions."

"But—"

He put up a hand to silence me. "Also, the number of

procedures he's been doing has almost halved since he started appearing on TV. His senior registrar has taken up the slack, and as a result her complication rate is on the rise. So overall things are declining, but looking at his firm as a whole it's still performing OK."

He sipped his coffee and looked at the folder in front of him. I thought about what he'd said. I could understand now why Galbraith wanted the case back so badly.

"How many copies, physical copies, of this would there be?"

He shrugged. "The meeting planned for tomorrow was with the chief exec and clinical director, and Mr Galbraith would have had one. Where did you get this?"

"I borrowed it," I said, sliding it towards myself across the table.

"Borrowed it from whom?"

"Never you mind."

"What will you do with it?"

"Nothing. I'm sure the chief executive is going to deal with it in his own way."

"Her own way."

"Her own way. You say she's got a copy and presumably she understands the significance of it?"

"I guess. But now that the person driving it has been taken out, it will just fall by the wayside. And Galbraith is a high-profile figure for the hospital. He's wheeled out to meet the bigwigs from pharmaceutical companies who are building on campus."

"Look, I'm sure she'll do the right thing. She has a duty of care to patients, or something like that."

He looked crestfallen, perhaps thinking he could storm the citadels of the hospital with the report and avenge his wronged director. He sat up as if struck by lightning.

"Is that Galbraith's copy?" he asked. Before I could answer he said, "Wait a minute, it can only be his. Is it him you're working for?" He stood up, scraping the chair legs against the tiles.

I laughed at the absurdity of this suggestion, but it obviously wasn't the reaction he was looking for. He stormed out of the kitchen and slammed the front door, making the wine glasses on the shelf tinkle.

I could have gone after him, but to be honest, the whole thing wasn't exactly top of my agenda; it's not like I was being paid to look into it. I should really have been more concerned that as soon as Galbraith returned from the US he would realise that the report was gone, and it wouldn't take him long to work out that I was the only possible culprit. Which in turn would lead to another bloody call to Badem, which never resulted in anything life-affirming. Instead, here I was waiting for Stubbing to get back to me and deciding what I could say to her without dragging Linda into the mix.

Around four the phone rang but it was just Kamal again.

"What did you say to Chris? He seems pissed off."

"He thinks I'm working for Galbraith."

"Well, aren't you?"

"Not in the way he thinks. Is this why you rang?"

"No, it's about Galbraith's registrar. Remember telling me that it pays to pretend to be a smoker to get information because now smokers from all strata of an organisation are forced to mingle in designated smoking areas? Anyway, I went to the smokers' lounge, and you should pay me because it's disgusting in there and I breathed in a lot of carcinogenic smoke."

"I promise to visit you in hospital if you get lung cancer," I said.

"Hmm. Anyway, I talked to a medical secretary who works in surgery. She said that she knows for a fact that Galbraith's registrar lodged a formal complaint against him with HR."

"What sort of complaint?"

"Bullying, apparently, which covers a multitude of sins," he said. "Make no mistake, she hates his guts and makes no bones about it, it seems." None of this was exactly a recipe for romance, I decided, after I'd thanked him and hung up.

I went to the dining room and studied the chess board, playing a few more moves of the Petrosian-Botvinnik game from the chess book open by the board. I was distracted by the photos of Kristina and her lover that were still up on the computer screen at the other end of the table.

There's a misconception that chess grandmasters calculate many more moves ahead than average players. But they don't; in fact they might consider fewer moves than a lesser player because of their experience. They instinctively know that certain variations are simply not worth taking into account and can be dismissed, whereas others deserve more analysis. Weaker players have to spend time looking at every option because they haven't got that experience.

I couldn't honestly pretend that I'd taken those photos with a specific purpose in mind, but experience told me that it was a better move than not taking them. I'm not saying that I'm a grandmaster of investigative work or anything but it slowly dawned on me how I could use the photos for a positive purpose, namely to help Aurora.

37

"WHAT DO YOU WANT?" WAS KRISTINA'S RESPONSE THROUGH
the intercom on the gate when I turned up at The Willows
unannounced.

"I need to talk to you," I said.

"About what?"

"About Aurora."

There was a moment's silence before the gate started
to open.

Her eyes didn't light up nor did she break into a big grin
when she opened the door – quite the opposite. She was
makeup-free and barefoot in jeans and T-shirt and her hair
was up in an untidy bun. I cleverly deduced that the company
she'd had last night had left and she wasn't expecting anyone
else, least of all me. Little Misha wasn't pleased to see me
either, and ran around her feet yapping, perhaps having an
animal sense of why I was here. A quick kick might have
taught it some manners but one of my basic rules is not to
kick children or animals, however annoying they might be.

She glanced at the envelope in my hand and tried to read
my face.

"There's something I need to ask you," I said. Displeasure marked her face as I followed her up the stairs. The place was beginning to feel like home. Jazz fusion came from a record spinning on the turntable and the flowers I'd seen arriving yesterday were in a white vase on the kitchen counter. She turned the music down and pointed to an armchair. She sat on the sofa, legs tucked under her, and picked up a glass of something hot with mint leaves in it. Misha joined her and watched me, a protective look in his beady eyes, seemingly unaware that I was thirty times his size and could easily squash him. I put that from my mind and tried to concentrate on Kristina – this wasn't a conversation I was looking forward to.

"Remember I mentioned Aurora yesterday?" I asked, just to ease us into it.

"Yes, what of her?"

"She didn't actually leave the country after all." I studied her reaction but she just looked confused.

"So why did you tell me she had?"

"I wasn't sure what you knew or didn't know about her whereabouts."

"What?"

"I asked you about Iskender Badem yesterday and you said you didn't know him that well, which is not what he's led me to believe."

She clearly didn't like that but said nothing so I carried on.

"She was prevented from leaving the UK by one of his men."

"So she's still in the country?"

"Badem probably has her stashed somewhere along with other illegals he provides to unscrupulous employers." I let that sink in a second then said, "I'm particularly interested in your business relationship with him."

She smiled unpleasantly. "On whose behalf are you here?"

"Aurora's," I said without thinking. She laughed and it was as belittling and dismissive as the smile. Misha looked up at her in alarm.

"You are a funny man. Is she paying you?"

"Do you want to know why I'm here or not?"

"I'm dying to know. Please tell me."

"Badem has Aurora here. He also has her passport. I would like her and her passport back."

"OK. And you're telling me this because…?"

"Because I need you to get her and her passport for me. As soon as possible. Now in fact."

She looked suitably astonished, then, slowly putting her tea down she untucked her legs and made a steeple of her fingers, perhaps in the hope that it gave her composure.

"What makes you think I have a business relationship with Iskender?"

"Because he was quite open about your staffing arrangements." A flicker in the eyes told me I'd hit home. Her fingers parted and she reached for Misha, looking down at the mutt as he rolled over and she scratched his tummy. I idly wondered who was cleaning up his little shits since Aurora had left.

"All my employees are here legally," she said. Which was

interesting, because I hadn't said they weren't.

"Maybe they look legal. But what if Immigration were persuaded to conduct a proper scrutiny of your employees' documents? Would you survive a second charge of employing people illegally?"

"I can get rid of those women with a phone call," she said, snapping her fingers. At least she wasn't denying anything.

"I'm not sure how Badem would like you cutting off his income stream like that. He doesn't strike me as an understanding type of fellow."

She studied me to see how serious I was. I guess I must have looked pretty serious.

"Even if I agreed to talk to him what makes you think he'll hand her over? He'll probably just laugh at me and deal with you himself. Do you understand what I mean?"

I pointed at my bruised face. "I understand perfectly – it's his modus operandi. If that is what he says, and it's likely it will be, you'll have to convince him that it's in his interest."

"Just like that."

"Look, he won't want the authorities looking into him as a possible people-trafficker. Explain to him that he's giving up one woman in order to keep many."

"Wow. She means this much to you, Aurora?" She forced a laugh. "Are you going to keep her for yourself?"

"Do you really care what happens to her?"

She shrugged. "I need time to think about it."

"There isn't time to think about it. He might move her, if he hasn't already."

"Go and see him yourself then," she said, dismissing me

with an impatient wave. "Why should I do it for you?"

I pointed to my face again. "He won't do this to you."

She shook her head. "I can't do it," she said, adamant.

I had hoped it wouldn't come to this.

I opened the envelope and took out the printout with the four photos of her and her silver-fox lover embraced. There was a particularly good one of her dress pulled up and his hands cupping her lacy-knickered buttocks. I held it up so she could see it. She leaned forward to have a look. Her face drained of blood then set like concrete and she muttered something in Russian.

"Do you know who that is?" she whispered, pointing at the sheet.

"Someone who wouldn't want this made public any more than you would, I'm guessing." She got up and walked about the room, thinking, watched by me and Misha. I gave her a bit of time, listening to the music before saying, "You can even tell him that he can come after me once I have put Aurora on a plane. That might satisfy his warped sense of honour. But this…" I wiggled the sheet, "…this is your motivation to be really convincing. I'm guessing this revelation would be embarrassing to you and the other party, not to mention damaging to your husband's career if it were sent to a tabloid."

She stopped pacing and leant against the kitchen counter. She couldn't look at me but gave a curt nod, which I took as acquiescence that she would do it.

"Call him now," I said.

"He'll want to meet; he doesn't talk business on the phone."

"Fine, I want to hear you call him and arrange to meet."

She looked at me with disgust, got a small glass from a cupboard and filled it from the tap. She picked up her phone and sipped the water before dialling.

"It's me," she said. "I need to speak to you. I have that Armenian detective with me." She looked at me, expressionless, as she listened. "It's about the woman who worked at the house," she said. Then, "No, as soon as possible. I'll explain when we meet – without the detective." She hung up.

I stood up. "Good. Call me after you've met."

Her face darkened and her eyes went an odd shade of black. "What a seedy little Armenian you are."

I held up the photos. "Do you want to keep this copy, as motivation?"

In one movement she reached for the vase of flowers and hurled it at me. It went high, spewing flowers and water, but I ducked instinctively. Hitting the turntable behind me it fragmented, bringing the music to a crashing end and sending the turntable to the floor in pieces. Misha shot from the sofa and disappeared into the study. Yellow petals strewn on the floor were a colourful contrast to the clinical decor.

"I'll take that as a no," I said, putting the sheet back in the envelope. I made it to the stairs without anything hitting the back of my head.

I waited in my car down the road, pointing towards Cambridge. I waited with an unpleasant whiff of self-disgust in the car. I had no desire to ruin Kristina's marriage, whatever I might think of her. Despite my job, I happen to believe that what people get up to as consenting adults is their own business. I justified my actions by thinking of her association with Badem, and of Aurora's plight. I felt a certain responsibility for what had happened to her, and needed to rectify it, even if it did mean putting up with my own bad smell.

About fifteen minutes later her Range Rover emerged from The Willows and headed in the opposite direction, away from Cambridge. I did a quick U-turn and followed.

38

PARKED IN THE TYRE INFLATION AREA OUTSIDE A SERVICE
station with an American-style diner attached, I watched
Derin in the distance leaning against the back of Badem's
Bentley, which was parked outside the diner. He was digging
inside his nostril with his little finger. Large clouds of blue
smoke emanated from a gap in the rear window – I could almost
smell the cigar. Kristina had parked nearby and was inside the
Bentley. A cigar was tossed out before the window slid closed.
I would have given anything to overhear the conversation and
had Derin not been outside might have risked approaching
the back of the car, although a sound-proofed Bentley doesn't
yield its occupants' secrets easily. About five minutes later
Kristina got out and spoke to Derin, who went to the open
door and stuck his head inside. Kristina dialled a number and
put the phone to her ear. My phone rang.

"I've spoken to Badem," she said, her Russian drawl
more pronounced than usual. "He will bring Aurora to you
this evening."

"So you managed to convince him?"

"Of course."

"You told him about your problem?"

"No, of course not," she said, then her voice softened. "So will you destroy the photos now?"

"When I have Aurora. Where and when will he deliver her?"

"To your house. Later. He has to pick her up."

"We'll talk soon," I said, hanging up – let her sweat for a while.

I watched her hang up, go back and say something to Badem whilst wagging her finger, then get in her car and drive off.

I stuck with Badem, for the simple reason that I didn't believe anything she might have said to Badem or to me. She might have told him that I was being a nuisance and asked him to deal with me. I needed to anticipate the worst. The Bentley, however, didn't move. Instead, Badem was helped out and made his way into the aluminium-clad diner. He squeezed into a booth and a waitress in a red apron and cap took his order. Derin remained with the Bentley, lighting up a cigarette as he checked his phone, possibly for Facebook likes. As I watched Badem scoff a burger he didn't need, Leonard turned up in the Ford Focus. Derin waved to him and he pulled up alongside. Leonard got out and handed Derin something he pulled from his jacket. From my vantage point near the petrol station I couldn't see what it was apart from something he could hold in his hand. I was on view to people filling up with petrol but I got out the small pair of binos I keep in the glove compartment and had a quick look – it was a passport. Maybe he was going to do as I'd asked.

Badem came out and had a conflab with Leonard and Derin. There seemed to be some sort of discussion as to what they were wearing. Derin was in trackies and weightlifting tank-top to show off his chest and arms. Leonard was in a jacket and jeans. Derin sulkily gave Leonard back the passport. Badem got into the back of his Bentley again and Derin into the driving seat. Leonard settled into the Ford Focus and I decided that he was the one to follow.

I tailed Leonard north of Cambridge, crossing the A14 into Fenland territory where the horizon stretches three hundred and sixty degrees and produces the type of melancholic washed-out landscape favoured by artists yearning for actual scenery. He was a cautious driver, and the advantage of the flat terrain was that I could keep my distance since his car was easy to spot. The roads got narrower and the houses more infrequent and eventually he turned onto a potholed muddy track that led to a farmhouse. I parked just beyond the entrance on a grassy verge behind a hedge, finding the small pair of binos in the glove compartment – there was no problem using them out here. I had to get out for a better vantage point. The farmhouse was dilapidated, the rendering falling from the walls and the windows obscured by ivy. Run-down wooden outbuildings completed the picture. Leonard removed some bags of shopping from the back of the car, then let himself into the house with a key. There were no other vehicles visible and I was torn between getting closer or waiting. The decision was made for me as Leonard emerged from the house with an anxious-looking Aurora in tow. He closed and locked the front door behind him while she waited, then ushered her into the back of the Focus.

I was obviously relieved to see Aurora, but her appearance made obvious my lack of a plan beyond locating her. For all I knew Leonard was going to deliver her to my house along with her passport, but I had doubts. What I did have on my side was the element of surprise – I could block his exit now and try to overpower him, although I felt a little vulnerable, especially in my already battered state. Plus he was likely to have a Taser on him. The Ford was making its careful way down the uneven track towards the main road. I got in my car and prayed he'd be heading back in the direction he'd come from. I quickly drove on and reversed into the entrance to a field further down the road. I ducked down as he pulled up to the road. He drove away from me, the way he'd come.

To my surprise Leonard drove into Cambridge, even heading towards my part of town north of the river and then approaching my road. Maybe they were actually bringing Aurora to me. But he passed it and parked on a broad tree-lined road four blocks down. The houses here were large semi-detached affairs with an art deco feel set well back from the road. It was near the river, just a five-minute walk from the centre of town and a prime location for families. Rich families. Leonard and Aurora got out of the Focus and he led her up a drive, his hand on her upper arm. From my position nearby I could make them out as he rang the bell. He tried to adjust her hair but she batted his hand away. Before he could admonish her the door opened and he smiled and they both went inside.

Five minutes later he came out of the house, and, from

behind a tree, I watched him get in his car and drive off. I went to the Golf and flicked through a business card holder I kept there. I collected any business cards I came across – they could be as convincing as a driving licence for a brief enough period, given the right patter. I found one from someone at the Department for Work and Pensions; I'd done occasional work for them investigating claimants. It would have to do. I went up to the house Leonard had come out of and pressed the doorbell. A pale-skinned auburn-haired woman in a dressing-gown and slippers with the misleadingly older face of a long-term drinker opened the door, releasing the sound of shouting children. Suitcases and cardboard boxes lined the hall. They were either leaving or had just arrived – I suspected the latter; it would be Badem's way of getting her out of the way and making some money at the same time. The woman held Aurora's passport in her hand.

"Yes?"

I flashed the business card. "I'm from the Department for Work and Pensions," I said, mustering some officiousness. "We're investigating reports of illegal workers in this area."

Her face reddened as I looked meaningfully at the passport.

"I'm looking for one Aurora de la Cruz," I said, reaching out. "Is that her passport?" She recovered her composure, pulling it to her chest.

"Do you have some identification?"

"We can involve the police if you prefer?" I took out my mobile. "I know she's here. If you check her passport you'll see her visa ran out some time ago."

A child, a preteen girl, emerged from a doorway behind her. She was clutching Aurora's hand, pulling her into the hallway. Aurora looked appropriately staggered to see me.

"Mummy, is she coming to Scotland with us?" the girl said in a wheedling voice.

I reached out and grabbed the passport where it was exposed and we had a slight tug of war. I gestured to Aurora to come forward. She untwined her hand from the girl's grasp and stepped towards me uncertainly. As she reached the door the woman put her free hand out to stop her progress. Aurora tried to push past but the woman grabbed her arm. I teased the passport free while she was distracted. She reached out for it, letting go of Aurora.

"I paid good money for her," the woman said.

"That in itself is an admission," I said, as Aurora emerged from the house and stood slightly behind me. "You may want to consult a lawyer proficient in human-trafficking law before saying anything else."

"We didn't know—"

"Ignorance is not an excuse in the eyes of the law. Someone will be round to take a statement," I said. I made a contrite face to the woman and leant forward conspiratorially, getting a whiff of stale gin. "Look, I shouldn't really be telling you this but it's probably best not to contact the people you got her from; you'll only implicate yourself further." We walked off and once we were out of sight I gave a bewildered-looking Aurora her passport.

39

AURORA HAD NOTHING WITH HER, NO CASE, NOTHING, NOT even the little money I'd given her at the airport. The dressing from her earlier brush with Derin's knife had come off and the small wound had bled afresh and rescabbed. We drove to Sandra's house. I wasn't about to go home if that's where Kristina told me to wait.

"Are you going to tell me what happened?" I asked Aurora as I checked the rear-view mirror for potential followers.

She stared at her fingers. In the confines of the car I could detect the sweet odour of stale sweat.

"You still have the money?" she asked.

"Of course. It's where I showed you. I'll get it later."

She nodded. "I should maybe go to embassy."

"Slow down, Aurora. It's Sunday night, it won't be open. Let's think about what to do after you've had something to eat."

"Yes, and shower would be nice." She grimaced.

Sandra looked surprised when she opened the door slightly on the chain. She released it, opening up.

"What's up, George? It's Sunday night and my ex-sister-in-law's just left. She's not the most relaxing of people to have around."

"Sorry, I'd forgotten she was in town. The thing is, Aurora didn't leave the country as planned."

"What do you mean? You drove her to the airport on Friday. Did she miss the flight?"

"It's a long story."

"Give me the bloody highlights."

"OK. She was intercepted at the airport after I dropped her off and when I got back home I was slapped around and Tasered. The people who did it, likely as not people-traffickers, picked her up at the airport. Yesterday I was told she'd been found squashed on the A14 but they'd actually stashed her somewhere in the Fens and now she's in my car in filthy clothes minus the suitcase I gave her. I don't know what she's been through between the airport and here because she's too upset to be able to talk to me and needs a shower. Plus I have no change of clothes to give her."

She looked over my shoulder at the car. "Bloody hell. Why didn't you just say she was here?"

"Before you ask, I can't take her home: they know where I live and might find out that I have her."

She sighed. "Has she eaten?"

Aurora sat wet-haired in a large bathrobe at the kitchen table. The sleeves were rolled up and she sipped gingerly at a hot cup of tea.

"I've ordered some pizza," Sandra said.

Aurora nodded and smiled at her. "Thank you for having me." Sandra patted her arm.

"Do you want to tell me what happened at the airport?" I asked gently.

Putting the cup down, she tucked her damp hair behind her ears.

"A man stopped me before the passport control. Ask for passport."

"The man with the beard, who picked you up tonight? From Cherry Hinton?"

"No, he was there later, with car. I never seen this man before. He took passport from my hands and looked at it. Then he said to go with him."

"And you went?"

"I thought he was official man," she said, sounding distressed at her own gullibility.

"Yes, of course," I said. "Listen, most people would have done the same. So where was the bearded man?"

"He was waiting next to car. Official man give him passport and beard man give him envelope and he go. Then beard man tell me we going to Cambridge."

"And you got in the car?"

"What can I do?" she said. She was trembling either with anger or frustration. "He had passport!"

"Aurora, I'm not judging you, I just want to know what happened."

"That's what happened. There was other woman in car, from my country."

"She died?"

"You know?" I nodded and she covered her face with her hands.

"That's enough, George," Sandra said, making eyes at me.

There was a knock at the front door and on Sandra's prompting I went to pay for the pizza which I took into the kitchen.

In contrast to my interrogation, Sandra fussed over Aurora and served her a slice of pizza which she wolfed.

"I think it's probably best, Aurora, if you stay with Sandra tonight because I'm not sure if they know that you're not at your new employer's and they know my address." I looked at Sandra. "Is that OK?" I asked, smiling, knowing I was putting her on the spot.

"It's fine, George."

"I'll bring your money tomorrow first thing," I told Aurora. "We'll use some of it to buy a ticket and then I'll take you to the airport. And this time we'll allow plenty of time."

"Wouldn't it be better to book a flight online now?" asked Sandra. "We can use the office credit card."

"Yes, excellent idea," I said.

"I pay you," Aurora said.

"Better still, we'll charge it to Galbraith," I said, smiling to myself. Why hadn't I thought of that before?

"Thank you, Mr George."

"Could you please just call me George, Aurora? Not Mr George."

"OK… George." She managed a smile.

We browsed the Web but the earliest flight we could book

was for a ten-thirty a.m. from Heathrow for the Tuesday, the day after tomorrow. We bought a ticket anyway.

"Now, when you've finished eating shall we try and find some clothes for you?" Sandra asked Aurora. "Nothing of mine is going to fit so you'll have to wear Jason's. We'll raid his wardrobe since he isn't here."

I stood up to make a move. "I'll see you out," Sandra said. In the hallway I turned to her.

"You'll try and speak to her, right?" I asked, softly. "See what happened after she left the airport."

"Sure, but I'm not going to force it. By the way, I was going to tell you tomorrow but since you're here…"

"What is it?"

"Remember the Toyota lease car you asked me to chase up? Yesterday I finally got hold of some young lad at the leasing company; he's new there and I managed to get the name of the organisation the Toyota is leased to out of him."

"Do I have to waterboard it out of you or what?" I asked.

She smirked. "Cambridgeshire Police."

"Say that again."

"The name on the lease is Cambridgeshire Constabulary, not an individual."

Darkness had fallen by the time I drove home, mulling over what Sandra had just told me. Trying to process this information on top of everything else was hard work – my brain was like a sponge to which people kept adding water that it couldn't hope to retain. Kristina Galbraith was seeing a bloody policeman? Of course he could be an administrator or a manager – Cambridgeshire Constabulary covered a large geographical area and number of people, and management metastasized in every profession – but it would have to be someone senior, that's for sure. His age, the confident way he held himself, the snazzy suit. Yes, he'd been slumming it in a corporate lease car, probably to be inconspicuous, but Kristina wasn't the type to fuck around with a nobody. I wasn't sure of the significance of this information at the moment, except that it explained Kristina's reaction to the photos when I'd showed them to her. I filed it under "interesting" as I parked one street down from mine. I made a sweep of the cars near my house but couldn't see anything suspicious. The house was dark and unwelcoming and as soon as I was inside I rang Linda, to see if she wanted to come over and fool around.

"I'm off to London in the morning," she said.

"Work?"

"Actually I have an interview."

"Really? Where? You kept that quiet," I said, sounding more aggrieved than I wanted to. She was the first to break the small silence that followed, and ignored my questions.

"How about I come by tomorrow, when I get back? I'll pick up some food on the way from the station. Will you be there?"

"Yes, but I don't know what time," I said, then without thinking about it, "I'll leave you a front-door key under the rubbish bin behind the side gate."

"Sounds good, Georgie. Oh, and make sure you look out for my story tomorrow morning, it should be another front pager above the fold."

As soon as I hung up the phone rang. It was Stubbing, sounding tired.

"George, I'd like you to come and see me first thing tomorrow."

"What for?"

"You'll find out. I'll see you at nine sharp."

"Should I bring croissants?" I asked, but she'd already hung up.

40

I DIDN'T SLEEP WELL, WAKING UP AT THE SLIGHTEST NOISE and getting out of bed to look through the window onto the street. There was little point worrying about what Stubbing might want but I tried to get back to sleep.

I eventually drifted off about four until I woke, if not quite from a nightmare, then from an unpleasant dream, one bad enough to disturb my sleep. I was on my father's bicycle again but this time cycling in a tunnel where the roof was getting lower and lower until eventually I was bent double over the handlebars and my back scraped the brickwork. I was ringing the bicycle bell when I woke but realised it was the landline. The clock read six-thirty. Once I'd managed to get out of bed it stopped ringing. I pelted my aching body with hot water, greeting my various bruises like the old friends they'd become. The phone rang again as I stepped out of the shower. Still wet and wrapped in a towel I checked the mobile. A message from Sandra asked me to ring her as soon as.

"Aurora's told me about what happened in the car after she was picked up at the airport, although you'll probably want to hear it for yourself."

"Give me a synopsis," I said. "We got up to how she was bamboozled into getting in the car with Leonard at the airport."

"That's right. Let's see... So she's with another Filipino woman in the car from Heathrow. They're talking, exchanging their stories all the way back to Cambridge, in whatever language they speak, I guess, and this drives him nuts, apparently, the driver, 'cause he can't understand what they're saying. He keeps shouting at them to shut up. The other woman tells Aurora that she plans to make a run for it. So Aurora gives her the piece of paper, the e-ticket or whatever, with your number on it, so she can call you. By this time the driver's livid and stops the car in a lay-by or something. Her companion puts the piece of paper in her pocket so he doesn't see it when he turns round and starts hurling abuse at them, actually spitting on them. So out of nowhere this woman punches him in the nose. At that point he gets a zapper, like the one you showed me, from the glove box, and just zaps her. Aurora is terrified at this point, obviously, but he starts the car and as they're moving off the woman just gets out.

"The thing is, her door is roadside and it's raining and she just runs when she gets out and almost immediately, bam, she's hit by a bloody lorry and carried down the road. The lorry just keeps going, like the driver didn't notice, and maybe he didn't, who knows. It's raining and busy. The driver just takes off, and about fifteen minutes later reaches some house in the country. She said there were about twenty other women there, a mix of nationalities which she's a bit hazy on. Anyway, they weren't locked in their rooms or anything, just sitting around, cooking and chatting. She spoke to one of them who said that people leave and new people arrive, and that nobody is there longer than a week. None of them had their passports so I'm guessing that either they're arriving here illegally and are waiting to be found work, or they're being trafficked into the country. Either way the place is some sort of halfway house."

"Yes, I know the place," I said. "I followed one of Badem's men there yesterday evening. That's where he picked Aurora up from."

"So those other women are still there?"

"He took some bags of shopping into the house, so I guess so."

"So shouldn't we tell someone about it?"

"Yes, but I'd like to do it without getting Aurora involved, otherwise she'll be sucked into the system. Listen, while it's still fresh, make some notes of what she said about the incident on the A14, and whatever she told you about where she was taken. I think it would be useful to get a statement from her."

"But not go to the police?"

"I'd like to give the police something to work with so this guy is dealt with, but without risking Aurora. I know who he is but it would be good to somehow tie him to the woman's death. I'll ring Rhianna about it this morning." Rhianna was the solicitor I occasionally consulted when negotiating legal minefields.

"What's the matter?"

"What?" I asked.

"Not you, George. Hang on a second will you…" Her voice grew faint as she spoke to someone else. I mused. A statement from Aurora on the death of the woman on the A14 would be something concrete I could give Stubbing, along with the location of the other women in the Fenland farmhouse. For all I knew the farmhouse was legit, but given it was linked to Badem, that seemed unlikely. At the very least it would get Leonard investigated. As long as Badem didn't know that I knew about the house, he would be unlikely to move them out of there, so twenty-four hours wouldn't make a huge difference.

"George?"

"What is it?" I asked.

"You should get over here now."

"What's going on?"

"Aurora's in a state. Seems to be having a panic attack or something."

"Not again. What happened?"

"I don't know, George, just get over here."

"OK, but I have to be at Parkside police station at nine."

I quickly took Aurora's cash from the tin in the hall and put it in an envelope then picked up the clinical audit report filched from Galbraith's case which I wanted to scan at the office. As I left the house I put the spare key as promised under the wheelie bin for Linda. Perhaps it marked a new transition in our relationship, or perhaps it was just too little too late on my behalf when suddenly faced with the prospect of Linda moving to London.

After remembering where I'd parked the car last night I took a circuitous route to Sandra's in case I was followed, but I was still surprised that Badem or his goons hadn't turned up. Was he hoping I'd just move on when Aurora hadn't turned up yesterday evening?

Sandra opened the door, and I was reassured to see her looking annoyed rather than upset.

"What's the rumpus?" I asked.

"I don't know, she insists on talking to you," Sandra said, sounding peeved. "The newspaper dropped through the letterbox and she freaked out." She handed me the offending copy of the *Argus*.

On the front, above the centrefold as Linda had said, was a picture of a new smiling blond girl, under the full width headline EXCLUSIVE: DEAD GIRL FOUND AT BYRON'S POOL IDENTIFIED emblazoned above it. The subheading read: BOGDANA SUMIŃSKI IDENTIFIED BY PARENTS. PEOPLE-TRAFFICKING LINK SUSPECTED. I flipped it over to see another story – PARENTS VISIT SITE WHERE DAUGHTER'S BODY FOUND – with a photo of the makeshift shrine in front of the height barrier.

"Where's Aurora?"

"In the living room."

She was on the sofa in jeans rolled up at the ankles and an oversized T-shirt with the name of a band I didn't recognise printed on it. The clothes made her look like she'd shrunk. She was staring at an untouched cup of tea, her eyes wide and face pale. I sat down next to her but she couldn't, or wouldn't, look me in the eye. I put the newspaper on the table and she flinched.

I gave her the envelope with her money in it. She nodded and placed it on the newspaper.

"Sandra told me about what happened to you in the car," I said to her. "Must have been traumatic."

"Traumatic?"

"Upsetting. Sad."

"Yes, but for other woman was worse," she said. She was staring at the envelope.

"Of course. But you saw it."

She turned to me. "Will anything happen to him, the man with the beard?"

"Yes. And I will tell the police about the place he took you. As soon as you get on the plane tomorrow."

She nodded but said nothing, then sighed. It was a tremulous sigh, full of feeling.

"What is it, Aurora?" I pressed.

She took a breath and raised her head. "I have to tell you something," she said, and it was the first time she'd spoken to me in this way, like someone much older. "Something I didn't tell you before because I didn't know…"

"OK." I imagined it must be something that had happened at the farmhouse Leonard had taken her to, something she couldn't tell us before. She removed the envelope so that Bogdana's picture was visible. She pointed at it.

"I seen this girl. Walking, smiling, speaking."

"Are you talking about Bogdana?"

"Bogdana, yes. Yes, I saw her at the house." She reached out to touch the photo gently.

"You mean the house you were taken to yesterday by the bearded man?" I asked her.

She looked at me, frowning. "No, the house of Mr and Mrs Galbraith."

41

FROM WHAT I COULD GATHER FROM AURORA IN THE FEW
minutes I had before rushing off to see Stubbing, Bogdana
had occasionally been to the house to help Aurora out when
there was a dinner party, sometimes sleeping on Aurora's
floor until Mrs Galbraith took her back to wherever she'd
come from in the morning. She'd been there the Tuesday
night, as the Galbraiths had hosted people for dinner, and,
as on previous occasions, had remained behind to help clear
up. That night, the night before Aurora left with the briefcase
and Bogdana's body was found at Byron's Pool, Kristina had
left to drop a guest at the station and Mr Galbraith had told
Aurora to go to her room, and had locked the door from the
outside. That's the last she'd seen of Bogdana. She wasn't let
out of her room until the following morning.

"Was that normal, to be locked in your room?" I asked.

"Sometimes," she said, shrugging. "Sometimes they
want private time."

"So Bogdana didn't sleep in your room that night?"

"No, no."

"Maybe Bogdana left with Mrs Galbraith? If she was

going to the station?" I glanced at her and she shrugged.

"No. But Mrs Kristina come back very late. Three in morning."

"How do you know?"

"I hear car. Her car sound different to his car. Then she leave again five in morning."

"Is that normal?"

"No, sometimes she leave at night but not come back."

"Did anyone else see Bogdana that night? Any of the guests?"

"She mostly work in kitchen. But people like that not see people like us. You understand?"

Yes, I understood. People like her, people making and serving the food, cleaning up afterwards, remained invisible to people who attended that sort of dinner.

I now understood why Bill was so keen to see Aurora leave the country and why Kristina was so worried about what Aurora might have told me. Of course Aurora hadn't realised the significance of what she'd seen until this morning. If it was significant – for all I knew Bogdana had gone home that night. At the very least The Willows was one of the last places she'd been seen alive. The Galbraiths would see Bogdana's photo in the paper at some point today, as would Badem. My hope was that they'd assume Aurora had already left with her new family.

"Will I have to talk to police?" she asked.

"I don't know. I have to get advice."

"My daughter is sick," Aurora said.

"Yes I know," I said. "Leukaemia?"

"Yes. But she is very sick. Not recover. You understand?"

Her eyes welled and I put my hand on hers.

"You need to get home to see her," I said. She nodded, unable to speak.

As I left I asked Sandra to keep Aurora at her house until I sorted out a meeting with Rhianna.

"What's going on, George?"

"In a sentence: Aurora saw the girl found at Byron's Pool at the Galbraiths."

At Parkside police station, after announcing myself and waiting for Stubbing to summon me, I sat and read Linda's story on Bogdana. According to her parents the seventeen-year-old had befriended a woman in Poland who convinced her that if she parted with some money she could find work in the UK as an au pair. Her parents refused to give her the cash and she left without their blessing, saying she would work off the debt. They alerted the Polish authorities. The rest was what Linda had told me on Saturday, but more dramatically put. What Linda didn't know was that somewhere along the line between leaving home and being found dead at Byron's Pool, she'd ended up at the Galbraiths' house.

As I looked up from the paper who should walk into the police station but Kristina Galbraith's handsome boyfriend. He carried a brown briefcase in one hand and a cardboard takeaway cup in the other. He smiled charmingly at the woman behind the glass and she reciprocated, buzzing him through the steel door which he opened by pushing on it with his backside, facing me as he went through – but showed no sign of recognition. I considered asking the woman behind the glass who he was but the door opened and Stubbing appeared.

"Let's go on to Parker's," she said, striding purposefully out of the building ahead of me.

"Have you had any luck with the hit and run?" I asked when I caught up with her. It was a sun-soaked morning as we crossed the road.

"You're not my boss, Kocky."

"Did you manage to get any traffic camera footage from the A14?"

"Annoyingly persistent for this time of the morning, aren't we? Yes, but since it was raining at the time and it's at a distance I didn't get a licence plate or even the car model. But that's not why I asked you here," she said, as we found a bench under the line of lime trees that edged the green. She unbuttoned her jacket and we sat down. "Last night we stopped the Ford Focus you mentioned, and picked up one Leonard Diski."

It took me a few seconds to realise that she was referring to our conversation about the Cherry Hinton episode when I'd given her the licence plate number. I hadn't thought she'd follow through on it.

"You guys are on the ball," I said.

"The plate was in the system, the traffic cops did the rest. I've got a nice photo of him and another man crossing the railway tracks in the Focus after the barrier started to come down. To be fair, it was his companion who was driving, but it does corroborate your story about the altercation outside the church."

"Glad to hear it," I said.

"I've got questions, before you get too smug."

I waited expectantly, watching a couple of older joggers trudge round the perimeter.

"He says they were there to retrieve a briefcase from this Aurora de la Cruz. That she'd stolen it from local hero Bill Galbraith."

"Stolen is a pejorative word," I said.

She snorted. "It's also a fairly black-and-white term, with little room for ambiguity."

"Aurora thought her passport was in it. Her employers were keeping it from her."

"So she hired you to get her passport back and they were hired by Bill Galbraith to get the briefcase back?"

"I don't know that they were hired. They somehow inserted themselves into the situation."

She shook her head. "I'll be inserting something into you if you don't start talking."

I sighed, working out how I could neutralise Leonard and Derin without Badem knowing it was me. "Maybe Bill Galbraith did hire them, maybe he needed someone else who was less, shall we say, squeamish, about picking the briefcase up. I was on my way to meet her outside the church so we could have a face-to-face with Galbraith to exchange the briefcase for her passport when those goons turned up. Afterwards Galbraith apologised. He said wires had been crossed and things had gotten out of hand."

She turned to stare at me. "How does someone like Galbraith even know people like that?"

I shrugged. "Through a patient? He told me there were some patients' notes in the briefcase."

"And were there?"

I shrugged again.

She kept her gaze on me and it was becoming uncomfortable. I'd wanted to wait until tomorrow but she was forcing my hand, or rather I'd forced my own hand since I was the one who'd pointed her in the direction of Leonard and Derin. But of course that was before Badem had issued threats against Linda if I involved the police.

"Don't you have more important things to worry about? Like a murder case?" I said.

"Unlike you I have to worry about more than one thing at a time. Come on, stop stalling and spill whatever beans are giving you wind."

"You couldn't identify the car the woman jumped out of on the A14, right?"

"I just told you that."

"What if I told you that it was the Ford Focus, with this Leonard Diski driving."

"I'd ask you to fucking elaborate."

"Did you find a Taser on him, or in the car?"

She just looked at me and I have to say she'd be good at the poker table. She scratched behind her ear, which I took as a tell.

"Let's assume you did," I said.

"What I will mention is that he's lawyered up way beyond his financial capability." That would be Badem, I thought, protecting his interests.

"He used the Taser on the woman before she jumped out of the car," I said.

She thought about that. "There's a witness presumably, someone who was in the car?"

"Yes, but they won't talk to the police, for good reason."

"They? I'm assuming it's Aurora de la Cruz, who I've just learnt has outstayed her welcome in the UK by several months."

It was my turn to try and remain inscrutable.

"You think she's believable, this woman, the one you've seen naked?"

I rolled my eyes and she raised her eyebrows at me. Her phone beeped. She retrieved it and squinted at the screen.

"We haven't finished but I've got to go back into the factory," she said, standing up. "I expect you to bring me something a bit more substantial by the end of the day."

"How about tomorrow morning?"

She stared at me while she buttoned her suit jacket. Her phone rang but she ignored it.

"End of day," she said.

42

STANDING AT THE OFFICE WINDOW SIPPING A COFFEE BOUGHT at Antonio's on the way back from Stubbing I thought about what she'd told me. I didn't know what Kristina and Badem had cooked up in his car yesterday, but either she'd known he had no intention of delivering Aurora to me (maybe she hadn't even asked him to) or he'd told her that he was going to do it and she believed him. But there was something about how she'd wagged her finger at him that made me think she was playing Badem. And now, knowing what Aurora had seen, things had a more sinister edge. I'd rung Rhianna and left a voicemail, so hopefully she'd get back to me soon.

Looking back outside, I saw Kristina's Range Rover pull onto the drive, parking where I could see that the scrape on top of her car was starting to rust. She got out, dressed in white, and disappeared from view before ringing through on the intercom.

"I'm on the top floor," I said. This would be interesting. I tidied up a bit but couldn't fix the worn carpet or the flaking paint. The *Argus* was face up on the desk, so I covered it with a sheet of paper – if she hadn't seen it, it was a card I could play to get a reaction.

She appeared upstairs dressed in an off-white linen trouser suit and black shirt with the buttons undone enough to allow for the long pendant at her neck to rest against the pale skin. She smiled, but it was the sort of smile you put on when you go in to see the dentist. We didn't shake hands. I waited for an ugly head to pop out of her large bag.

"No Misha?" I asked, just to have a crack at the ice.

"He's in the car."

"Didn't want to come up? I get the sense that he doesn't like me." Unable to raise a smile I tried a different tack. "You know you've lost the antenna from the top of your car?" I gestured to the window.

"Really?" We went to look. I pointed. "It would explain why the radio has stopped working," she said, her voice soft, like melting butter. She exuded a musky, jasmine smell that rendered me immobile. "I must have done it in the multi-storey car park," she added, as we stared down at the car. Was the Russian accent thicker again? I was aware of her pushing stray hair from her face.

"There are a couple of places where it's lower than the stated height," I said. My voice seemed to have dropped a register. She turned to face me and was too close but I couldn't bring myself to step back. Pull yourself together, George.

"I came into town to buy a new record player from that place round the corner on Trumpington," she said, "to replace the one I broke yesterday. Bill will be back from the States this afternoon."

"You don't want him to know."

"It might be difficult to explain how it happened."

"I can see that. You want to park on my drive?"

She grinned sheepishly, in the way attractive people do when trying to charm you into a favour. "Do you mind? It's double yellow lines on Trumpington."

"Of course not," I said. This wasn't why she was really here of course. I pulled myself out of my reverie by reminding myself of who I was dealing with and led her to the chair across the desk from mine.

"Is that today's newspaper?" She pulled it out from under the sheet I'd covered it with.

I could discern no reaction on her face, which meant she must have already seen it; no one was this good at playing it straight.

"Horrible business," she said, tapping Bogdana's photo. "Do you think the police know what happened?"

"If they do, they're not saying."

"I thought you might have contacts in the police?"

I shook my head. I couldn't have wished for a smoother segue into the topic of Bogdana being at her house. But I didn't – forewarning her about any police interest in her and her husband was out of the question.

"You know this reporter?" she asked, looking at me from under those long black eyelashes.

"No, why would I?" I asked, every ounce of my being on alert.

She shrugged and put the paper back on the desk, but with Bogdana face down so the bottom half with the picture of the makeshift shrine to the dead girl was visible.

"I'm surprised to see you here, I must say, Mrs Galbraith."

In the office of this seedy little Armenian.

"You mean after yesterday? You did what you had to do, I guess." A strained smile settled on her lips as she worried at the pendant.

"It didn't work though," I said, again studying her reaction. She didn't even pretend to be surprised.

"I'm sorry Badem didn't deliver on his promise," she said. "But I fulfilled my side of the bargain."

"You don't seem surprised. That he didn't deliver, I mean."

"I would have been more surprised if he had kept his promise, to be honest."

"What do you think he's done with her?" I asked.

"I've no idea," she said, shrugging – she obviously didn't give a shit. I could feel the impatience rising in me.

"Why are you here, Mrs Galbraith?"

She leant forward and whatever sparkly thing was on the end of the pendant swung free over the desk. "Why do you think I'm here?"

"You're wondering about the photos?"

"Yes, you know I am."

"Nothing will happen to them until Aurora is back with her dying daughter."

"Do you want me to speak to Badem?" she asked, her lips thin with anger.

"It didn't work the first time, why would it work again?" I asked.

She just stared at me and it took a few seconds for what she was saying to sink in.

"I see, you think he might have better luck getting the photos back from me. The photos are safe. I've deleted them all from my system and sent them to a lawyer. When Aurora is safe then the lawyer will be instructed to destroy them. If anything happens to her, or me, then the pictures will be released to the tabloid press. The lawyer doesn't know what's in the files I've sent, by the way." This was all off the cuff and I'd done none of it of course, but saying it out loud actually made it sound like something I should do.

She attempted a relaxed smile, but it barely suppressed the emotional agitation churning away. "That all seems a little over the top for some photos," she said.

"Everything about this case seems a little over the top."

When she left I tried to work out why she'd come – surely she had bigger concerns than having a lover on the side exposed, like the identification of Bogdana. Maybe she thought Aurora was safely out of the way and harmless, or maybe someone like her understood that exposing one secret often led to the exposure of others – that like a house of cards the carefully constructed lies would come tumbling down.

I went to the window to watch her leave. She had the car door open and was standing on the sill to examine the damaged roof, but she still wasn't high enough to get a proper view. She glanced up at the window, saw me and got down. Opening her cavernous bag she let Misha jump in, locked the car and walked down towards Trumpington Street, making a call as she went. I just hoped it wasn't to Badem.

I remained at the window, watching a man cycle onto the drive, presumably a client of one of the therapists. It reminded me of the dream last night, about cycling in a low tunnel. Something niggled, something brewing in my unconscious that had yet to be handed over to the part of my brain that could make sense of it. I went to the desk, saw the newspaper with the photo of the makeshift memorial at the car park barrier at Byron's Pool. The barrier was a height restriction barrier: 1.8 metres, it said on the middle of the bar. I took it back to the window and looked down at the car. I looked back at the photo. I shook my head. I told myself to get a grip.

43

I QUICKLY LOOKED UP KRISTINA'S MODEL OF RANGE ROVER AND checked the height: 1.835 metres. I took a small evidence bag from my desk drawer and ran downstairs; Kristina was unlikely to be that long at the hi-fi place. The Range Rover was a beast and the only way to get access to the roof was to stand on one of the large wheels. With the evidence bag in one hand I took the small tweezers from my Swiss army knife, then clambered onto the back wheel. I wanted to remove a flake of paint to check against the barrier at Byron's Pool car park, because it looked like a lot of it had been left behind. My thinking was that it might be enough to convince Stubbing to have a more forensic test done. Up high I could see the scrape was down a raised bit of the roof in the middle. I spotted a bit of paint I could peel off but it was just out of reach. I had to move onto my left foot and then on tiptoe in order to stretch. I got the tweezers underneath the flaking paint.

Because I'm an adult I don't wear trainers; I wear leather shoes with leather soles. They're designed for pavements, pubs and to go with adult trousers, but they don't really provide enough grip when clambering on cars. I slipped, and my foot got caught in the wheel arch as I went down, twisting me onto my back as I hit the tarmac. My lungs had the air forced out of them and I lay there, fighting for breath, unable to move, the tweezers and evidence bag still in my hands. I chuckled to myself, looking up at the sky: cloud cover with no chance of rain. I put the tweezers away in the penknife. I heard someone's feet approach the car on the other side. Turning my head left I could see, under the Range Rover, a woman's shoes and ankles: another client of one of the therapists. Something caught my eye underneath the Range Rover, near the passenger door – a small box with some gold markings on it partially obscured by mud. At first I thought someone had fixed a GPS tracking unit to the car but when I rubbed off the dirt the gold marking turned into a picture of a key. I slid the box open and a car key dropped out. I stood up and brushed myself off.

Thankfully Kristina had taken Misha with her so I pressed the key fob to unlock the car with a satisfyingly engineered thunk. I opened the door with my sleeve and took a moment to appreciate the luxurious interior before checking the door pockets. I found an open bag of dog treats (organic, no less) and an almost full bottle of sugar-free Coke. Some scrunched-up chewing-gum wrappers covering hard balls of discarded chewing gum littered one of the pockets, as well as some blackened cotton wipes, the type women use to remove makeup. I closed the door and went round to the passenger door. The glove compartment yielded a mess of receipts, old parking slips like the one in the window now, empty Weight Watchers snack bar wrappers and some leaflets advertising her salon. I took out the receipts and parking slips, spread them on the passenger seat and snapped them with my phone – she parked at the station a lot. I put them back and checked the door pockets but all I found was a compact umbrella and a small black plastic bag tied at the top. Curious, I lifted it up to examine it – one of Misha's turds, now gone hard. I replaced it and had a look in the back but it was pristine, like nobody's arse had ever made contact with the seat. Next I opened the tailgate, releasing the aroma of fabric cleaner. There was nothing in there but an open cardboard box, inside of which were the remains of the old turntable. Otherwise it was clean carpeting that looked brushed and unused. I started to pull down the tailgate and the interior of the glass bounced the sunlight inside and something at the back, where the floor carpet met the back seat, caught the reflected light. I lifted and lowered the tailgate until the light caught it again. I heard a cough behind me.

I turned to see Maggie standing next to her bicycle.

"New car?" she asked, raising her eyebrows. I pulled the tailgate down and closed it with my elbow.

"Not really my kind of thing," I said, locking the car.

"No, I wouldn't have thought so." We stood there for a second, me grinning stupidly. I hadn't spoken to her since the night I'd spent in her office with Aurora.

"I owe you a drink and an explanation, for the other night," I said.

She shrugged. "When you're ready," she said.

I waited for her to go in then got back onto the ground and put the car key back in its place. I was dusting myself off as Kristina approached followed by a young man carrying a large cardboard box. I got into my own car without acknowledging her and drove to Byron's Pool.

Parking on the road I walked up to the barrier at Byron's Pool and examined the faded flowers. The place was empty in contrast to the weekend, just one car in the car park. I studied the underside of the barrier and my idea of checking the paint sample from the Range Rover with the barrier immediately seemed stupid. There were scrapes of all colours from drivers either not reading the barrier limit or just willing their SUVs or four-by-fours to be lower than they actually were – the white paint of the steel barrier had been almost stripped bare so trying to match paint had apparently been a silly idea. I walked back to the road where I'd parked and saw an elderly man staring at me from the end of a track near the Grantchester Road. There was a small house camouflaged in ivy down the track which I hadn't noticed walking up to the barrier.

"You the police?" he asked. He was stooped but alert.

"No." I pointed at the house. "You live here?"

He nodded. He was unevenly shaved and wore his trousers high up his waist.

"You must be glad the crowds have gone," I said.

"Gawpers, the bloody lot of them. You a reporter?"

"No. Not very high, the barrier, is it?"

"Stops the wild campers," he said.

"Doesn't stop a lot of cars trying to get underneath," I said.

He pointed to a large dirty blue bucket on his drive. "I

pick up antennas that have been knocked off."

"Do you mind if I have a look?"

He spat into a bush. "Depends who you are."

"Insurance company. Investigating a claim of an antenna ripped from the top of a Range Rover. You seen one come down here?"

"I come out once a day to pick up the leavings, that's all," he said. I gestured to the bucket and he nodded. I went over to it and looked inside. It was half full with a collection of different types of car antennae.

"What's the last one you found?" I asked him.

"Whatever's on the top. I call the council when the barrel's full and they come and take them away for recycling." He spat into a different bush.

I picked up a black triangle-shaped antenna with a flat base from the bucket. It was dented at the sloping edge, where it had hit the barrier.

"Shark's fin," he said. "That could be from a Range Rover." It looked like something in the picture when I'd checked the height online.

"Do you mind if I take it?" I asked. He looked dubious and pulled up his trousers. "It would help with the claim," I said. "Once in a while we like to pay out."

"Help yourself," he said. As I walked off I heard him hawk and spit, presumably into another bush.

Back in the office I put the shark-fin antenna in an evidence bag on the desk and double-checked the phone to see if

Rhianna had called. She hadn't. Recalling Sandra's news about the Toyota lease car I decided to satisfy my curiosity by bringing up the Cambridgeshire Constabulary website. Since I assumed Kristina's lover to be someone senior I went through the site to see if I could spot him amongst the photographs of the good and the great. But he wasn't to be seen, and since I didn't know his name I couldn't search for him.

I transferred the snaps of Kristina's receipts from my phone to the computer and looked through them. On the night that Bogdana had been at the house she'd parked at the railway station at 11.25 p.m., which corresponded with what Aurora had said about her leaving to take a guest there. But why park if dropping someone off? Plus, looking at it more carefully, it was a twenty-four-hour ticket – why park for so long? I printed the picture of the ticket off and put it in a clear folder. I was about to check the antenna online when Rhianna rang.

44

"I'M HAVING LUNCH SO THERE WILL BE CHOMPING," RHIANNA told me in her deep, slightly hoarse voice, and I could picture her, bespectacled with cropped silver hair, probably dressed in something shapeless that did her short stature no favours. She'd once told me that she was shooed away from the entrance of a court because, with her plastic carrier full of case files, she was mistaken for a homeless bag lady. "I'm at the magistrates' court on St Andrew's Street all day and have twenty minutes."

I explained, as concisely as I could, Aurora's situation.

"Blimey, you've got your hands full. Well, let's see... She's under no obligation to make any statement but given your relationship with the local police I wonder if you going to them with what she's told you will be met with some scepticism, especially given we're talking about a figure in the public eye here."

"It is possible that I might not be taken seriously, yes."

"So what's your endgame?"

"Erm, I suppose it's to get Aurora out of the country and point the police in the right direction."

"Hmm." There was the sound of chewing, but out of necessity Rhianna had mastered the art of talking with her mouth full. "There's no reason that she has to go to the police to make a statement. I can take one from her; I do it all the time."

"OK."

"But, if it ever led to the situation that there was a case that the Crown Prosecution Service thought worthy of taking to court, and she was unable to attend a trial, any statement by her would be treated as hearsay and probably be deemed inadmissible by the judge. Having said that, if there's anything worth taking to court, it would have to be based on a lot more evidence than what you're telling me."

"Even regarding the woman killed on the A14?"

"Hmm. Again, if she's not around to testify then it's hearsay, her word against his. Besides, she's not saying he pushed the woman out, is she; the best you can do is use her statement to get the police to investigate, and maybe have a look at the house she was taken to. Look, I have to go to the loo before my next recidivist appears. When did you say she was due to leave?"

"Tomorrow morning."

"Can you bring her to my office at five this afternoon?"

I agreed to do so, thanked her and hung up.

Back at the computer I double-checked Kristina's model of Range Rover and revealed that it had the same shark-fin radio antenna on the roof that was now sitting on my desk. It wasn't proof exactly but I wondered whether it could be forensically matched to the car – it had a distinctive jagged pattern where it had been ripped from the roof. Otherwise it was just a coincidence.

Aurora's testimony about Bogdana being at the house, the scraped top of Kristina's car, the missing antenna found at Byron's Pool, the freshly cleaned luggage area in the Range Rover. It all added up to something, even though I wasn't sure what. And was that a pearl I'd glimpsed in the boot? Maybe, but more likely it was wishful thinking. After all, I was prone to wishful thinking.

I rang Sandra and asked if she could find someone to look after Ashley so she could bring Aurora over to the office by taxi for four-thirty. She agreed, and I was about to go and get something to eat when Jason appeared at the door in the outfit he wore to snare tourists for punting: red waistcoat over white shirt, and navy shorts. He was carrying a straw boater.

"Boss." He gestured towards the window as he sat at his mother's desk and switched on the computer. "I see you finally managed to get rid of the redundant technology. Told you one person could carry it down."

"You mean the fax machine? Yes, you were right, it was a doddle. How's the rip-off punting business?" I asked.

"The council want to crack down on touts. They claim it's getting out of hand and ruining the town for tourists."

"Never mind the locals," I said. I was fed up with being mistaken for a tourist and approached by a good-looking young person wanting me to go on a punting trip. I took some amusement in seeing how quickly they lost the charming smile when I told them to piss off. From the desk I retrieved the clinical audit report I'd brought from home and passed it to him.

"Can you scan that in for me?"

"Sure."

"And you know that stuff you cobbled together on the Galbraiths?" I asked him. "Have you emailed it to me?"

"No, I put it in the Galbraith folder on the shared drive, boss. Remember we talked about this – no more emailing documents around?"

I rolled my eyes unseen and pulled the keyboard to me. Determined to find the folder without his help I embarked on a game of digital hide and seek.

"How's things otherwise?" I asked, to distract from my file-finding struggles. He leant back in the chair and looked at the ceiling.

"I can't get a proper job and so I'm still living with my mother who takes calls from perverts to make ends meet. Other than that I'm fine."

"Excellent," I said, finally pulling up the document he'd created. I read through it, concentrating on the section concerning Kristina Galbraith. Her previous nail salon, the one which had been closed down, had people living above it. Had Bogdana worked for her? Had she been living over the new salon? I thought about going down there since Kristina was busy with the turntable but if I turned up and started asking questions she'd be alerted immediately. I looked at her husband's section. There were numerous online links. He had a Facebook page where people posted selfies with him and a Twitter account related to his TV show.

"Does Kristina not have any kind of online presence?" I asked Jason. "I mean for her salon or something?"

"If I found something it would be in the file. There's no Twitter account, or Facebook page, no Instagram, nothing. It's like she doesn't exist."

"Because you don't exist if you're not online."

"Exactly, I've been saying we should at least have a website."

"Sure, and people can leave star ratings," I said.

He laughed. "The only thing I found relating to her salon is the reviews submitted by customers, mostly on TripAdvisor. The link should be there."

"Found it," I said.

I read through some of the reviews relating to shellac pedicures and the wonders of the massage chair. All positive. I had my suspicions about the veracity of some of them, but that's just me sitting in cynics' corner. There were some small photos submitted by customers, mainly of people's brightly coloured nails, but there was one titled "friendly staff!!" and a selfie of some woman next to the receptionist, the one I'd met, although it was difficult to tell due to the size of the picture. She was wearing the same white coat and was blond.

"Jason, how do you make a photo bigger on here?"

He sighed and scooted over in his chair.

"Download the original file by right-clicking on it," he said, as he did it. The photo filled the screen in high definition. I recognised the reception desk. But that wasn't the young woman I'd spoken to when I was there, the one who Kristina said was new. I found the newspaper and held Bogdana's photo next to the screen to compare them.

"Same girl you think?" I asked Jason.

"Definitely, boss. She worked at Kristina Galbraith's salon?"

"Looks that way."

He scooted back to the other desk. "I've scanned that report and put it in the Galbraith folder, on, the, shared, drive," he said, with exaggerated slowness. He put his straw boater on and placed the physical report on my desk. I hadn't really thought about how I'd get it back into Galbraith's briefcase without him knowing it was missing. Since he was back today it was likely he would find out it was gone, ask Kristina about it and she'd realise it was me who'd taken it. Would she tell him? I decided I didn't really care; besides, I had more important things to think about, as would they. I printed off the picture and put it with the parking ticket from Kristina's car – it was amounting to a neat little package to give Stubbing along with Aurora's statement and the antenna from Byron's Pool. Not exactly evidence, any of it, apart from potentially the antenna, but it should be more than enough for Stubbing to start digging.

45

IT WAS NEARLY TWO WHEN I POPPED OUT TO GET A SANDWICH and spotted Maggie smoking by the bike shed.

"I hope that hasn't become a habit?" I asked.

She ground the unfinished cigarette out with the heel of her flat shoe. "So do I."

"To be honest with you it doesn't really suit."

"Does it suit anyone?" she asked.

"Smokers tend to have an air of desperation about them, like they're trying to recover something they've lost."

She laughed. "Well that sums me up at the moment, although I admit the smoking is an affectation."

I moved off then stopped. "I'm about to get some lunch…?"

Fifteen minutes later we were sitting on the warm steps of the Fitzwilliam Museum with sandwiches and cold cans of soft drink, watching groups of tourists stand and stare at the impressive facade.

"So," Maggie said, after we'd had a few bites. "What's your excuse for sleeping with that woman in my office?"

"That's one way of putting it."

"I'm pulling your leg. I saw your face that night, I know it wasn't that."

"It was a case I was working on. She was in trouble, had been through a lot and was exhausted. I'd seen you had a sofa in your office and I had a feeling you'd be understanding."

"Really? Because I'm a counsellor?"

"Because you're the only person in the building who gives me the time of day."

She affected to look bashful. "So what happened to her, the woman who slept on my sofa?"

"She's trying to get home to her daughter in the Philippines."

"And you're helping her?"

"I'm not doing a brilliant job."

"Is that what happened to your face?"

I felt my eye which I'd forgotten about. "I fell down the stairs," I said, which was sort of true.

She laughed. "You might as well say you walked into a door."

"Ah, you think I'm in an abusive relationship?"

She studied me. "No. I wouldn't have said so. Not that it doesn't happen to men, although it's mainly the other way round, at least when it comes to physical abuse."

"I read somewhere that what men most fear from women is being laughed at, while what women fear from men is being killed. Do you think that's true?" I asked.

"If memory serves, last year forty-seven per cent of murdered women were killed by a partner or ex-partner, whereas for men I think it's nearer five."

"Damning statistics," I said.

She tipped her head back and glugged her drink.

"Doesn't it make you despair, dealing with failed relationships day in day out?"

"No, not really. They're not failed, necessarily; in fact if they're seeking help then there's still hope. Don't you find the same?"

"I'm trying to get out of marital work; when people come to me about a partner it usually means things have gone over the edge. You develop a jaundiced view of things."

"You're cynical when it comes to people?"

"I find I question people's motives all the time, which I'm guessing isn't healthy."

"It's bloody exhausting at the very least. But you're right, it does become difficult to take some people at face value. Professional hazard, you might say."

We ate and drank.

"So why have you taken up this new hobby?" I asked.

"What do you mean?"

"The smoking."

She laughed. "It's a sort of displacement activity." She drained her can and crushed it. "I was shaken to learn that my own relationship isn't immune to the problems I see in others." This was said without rancour or edge, just matter-of-factly.

"Sorry, you don't have to talk about it. You hardly know me."

"You slept in my office, so I think we've broken the ice. And besides, it's often easier to talk about these things with a stranger. That's why I'm in business, after all."

I picked at my sandwich, glad to be in the moment and not trying to process all the stuff that I was supposed to be processing. She leant back on her elbows and lifted her face to the sun, closing her eyes for a few seconds.

"The problem is that he's a charmer," she said, sitting back up.

"Who are we talking about?"

"My partner. Correction, my ex-partner. I was thinking about this while in the middle of a session this morning, and I remembered that charmers are sociopaths, psychopaths even, given the right circumstances. I mean I knew this stuff of course, but knowing it doesn't make you immune. Charmers make you feel special, they have charisma, but it's always about persuading you to do something or buy something or believe in something."

"Like politicians, or TV celebrities?" I asked, thinking of Bill Galbraith.

"Exactly. They communicate well, even though when you think about what they've said afterwards you realise it lacks substance."

"But not all politicians or TV personalities are psychopaths, surely. Aren't psychopaths violent?"

"Yes, but psychopaths and sociopaths share common traits. They're conniving, manipulative and deceitful, remorseless, to name just a few. Think of all those well-known people now exposed as abusers of children and women. Psychopaths are simply sociopaths who are willing to cross the line." She picked up the plastic detritus from lunch and stuffed it into the small bag it had come in. "Sorry," she said.

"I'm just working through some stuff."

"Always happy to be that stranger," I said.

She smiled and punched me playfully on the arm.

As we walked back to the office I thought about what Maggie had said. She was obviously upset but there was something to it nevertheless. Had Bill Galbraith crossed that line with Bogdana, or perhaps it had been Kristina; as far as I was concerned she also fitted the criteria for sociopathy.

Anxious, I stood at the window, waiting for Sandra and Aurora to appear. Rhianna wouldn't hang around if we were late. The landline rang, I strode over and picked up.

"What the fuck do you think you're fucking playing at, Kocharyan?" I pulled the phone several inches from my ear but Bill's screeching voice was still perfectly clear. "You better bring that fucking report back as soon as possible. And I mean today, otherwise you're in deep fucking shit. That's a confidential draft that hasn't been signed off and if it gets in the wrong hands it can easily be misinterpreted. Do you fucking understand? Have you shown it to anyone? If anyone has seen it you're fucked. As soon I hang up I'm calling my lawyers and if I don't—"

I hung up, blowing out some air since I'd forgotten to exhale while listening to his tirade. I was pretty certain that when he caught his own breath he'd rethink calling any lawyers, especially when his wife showed him the front page of the *Argus*.

Sandra and Aurora came into the office. The landline rang again. I lifted the receiver an inch then put it down. In addition to the jeans and T-shirt Aurora now sported a baseball cap with "Just Do It" printed on it and sunglasses that covered most of her face.

"Here we are," Sandra said, smiling. "That's Aurora in case you didn't recognise her." She put the receipt from the taxi on her desk. The mobile rang. I checked the screen – my personal number, so thankfully not Bill trying to get through on the office mobile.

"Hello?"

"Mr Kockaryman?" A young man's voice.

"Kocharyan, yes."

"We have your father's ashes ready for collection."

"OK," I said, hanging up before he could deliver some well-meaning but platitudinous compassion. Suddenly exhausted, I felt a sudden need to sit down. Sandra and Aurora looked at me expectantly. For the life of me I couldn't remember why they were here. I needed to lie down, preferably in a cave.

"How about a cup of tea?" Sandra asked, frowning at me. "Before we go round to Rhianna's?" I stared at her, remembering what was going on. "Aurora, why don't we go and make some tea," she said, making eyes at me.

"Mr George OK?" Aurora asked as they walked out.

"Mr George just needs a minute."

They disappeared and the mobile buzzed with a text.

found the key! got wine and something to bung in the oven. Lxx

How was London? I replied.

: (

Oh dear. Should be home in a couple of hours and you can tell me all about it. Gxx

It felt comforting to know Linda was waiting for me at home, I—

"What's up, Kocky?" Jesus. I looked up to see Stubbing leaning against the open doorway, arms folded. "It's end of day, matey. Whatchya got for me?"

46

SHE CAME INTO THE ROOM AND IDLY PICKED UP THE ANTENNA in its sealed bag from the desk.

"Where do you get these bags?"

"You can buy them online."

"Makes you feel like real police, I suppose?"

I said nothing – the best option when she's like this.

"What is it?" she asked, sitting down and holding the bag up, letting it swing a little.

"Why are you here?" I asked. Behind her Sandra stopped at the door. She muttered to someone out of view in the hall, presumably Aurora. Stubbing followed my gaze and Sandra came in alone, carrying two cups of tea. She put one on my desk and went to hers.

"Give us a minute, love," Stubbing said to her. Sandra, to her credit – it must have taken an awful lot of willpower – ignored her and turned to me.

"What shall we do about your five o'clock?" she asked, gesturing to the clock on the wall. It was a five-minute walk round to Rhianna's and there were fifteen to spare.

"How long will this take?" I asked Stubbing.

"How long is a piece of string?" she asked, examining the antenna through the plastic.

"If I'm not done in five can you go ahead?" I asked Sandra. "You know what's involved and we can't afford to miss it."

"Of course," she said. She took her untouched cup of tea and put it in front of Stubbing, smiling sweetly. "Don't burn your mouth. It's hot."

"Where'd you find her?" Stubbing asked when Sandra had gone.

"Shall we do this?"

"You said you'd have something for me by end of day."

"Actually I said tomorrow morning. You said end of day."

"So here I am."

"Give me a couple of hours."

"I've got boxercise in an hour," she said, deadpan.

"Really?"

"We can sit here until I have to go to it if you like."

"OK then. Aurora de la Cruz is having her statement taken by a solicitor as we speak."

"Saying what?"

"I told you this morning. About what happened in the car. And some other stuff."

"What other stuff?"

My plan, when I'd spoken to Stubbing this morning, was to tell her about what Aurora had said last night and to give her the statement that Rhianna would hopefully very soon be recording, ideally after Aurora's departure was an irreversible act. But now that I had a little more to add to it, like the antenna, the photo of Bogdana at Kristina's salon and the parking ticket confirming Aurora's story, things hinged less on her testimony.

So I told Stubbing everything that Aurora had revealed last night and this morning with just enough context for it to make sense but without complicating matters by mentioning Badem or the audit report – I was still worried about Badem's threat against Linda. When I finished she sat back, not looking terribly excited.

"Let me get this straight. This domestic, who worked at Bill Galbraith's… and, just to be clear, this is the life-saving surgeon and TV celebrity Bill Galbraith we're talking about… this domestic ran away, stealing his briefcase, and told you that she'd seen Bogdana alive at his house on the Tuesday night."

"Correct."

"And where is Aurora de la Cruz now?"

"I told you, recording her statement," I said.

"You're not hiding her in your bedroom, are you? A little live-in Filipino maid. That would be considered harbouring an illegal immigrant."

"The Galbraiths had her passport, so she didn't know the visa had expired."

"So basically I'm unable to speak to her to verify this wild tale?"

"She's going back to Manila to see—"

"Please stop," she said, face-palming me. We sat there for a few silent seconds while she studied the cracked ceiling. She looked at me sideways.

"Given that she'd run away from her employers," she said in a knowing voice, "it would make more sense if Bill Galbraith was your client and you were asked to look for her, or this briefcase that she stole. Am I right?"

"Does it matter?"

"You never know if something matters until it does," she said, which sounded annoyingly like something I would say. "The facts matter," she continued. "Besides, since when can a domestic afford to hire a private eye? Was she paying in kind? Is that how you saw her naked?"

I rolled my eyes.

"She has no reason to lie about what she saw," I said.

"Uhm, I beg to differ. Sounds like she had every reason. Disgruntled employee who runs away, wants to dump her employer in the shit with the police as she leaves the country, but won't talk to us? Give me a break. Did you fall for her or something?"

I had to support the weight of my head with my hands, something I was prone to do when being with Stubbing for any length of time.

"Look," I said. "Galbraith was very keen to find her and for her to leave the country. He made up some bullshit about having an affair and not wanting her to go to the tabloids with it but it's nonsense; he moves the goalposts every time I talk to him. Think about it, why didn't he report the theft to the police?"

"I understand where you're coming from. He's a successful professional, good-looking, is on TV, probably even has a trophy wife. You subconsciously compare yourself to him and come up short, and are unable to attain the same heights so you want to destroy him instead. You've got nothing except a case of penis envy."

"For god's sake, Stubbing, spare me the pop psychology."

"I don't think I've heard the whole story, and what I have heard is certainly not enough for me to go knocking on the door of someone in the public eye. Even if I did, what do you think will happen if I ask him about it?"

"He'll deny it. His word against hers, and his word is gospel," I said, feeling deflated.

"Exactly, and that's even if I interview Aurora myself, which I need to do if you want me to take this seriously."

It was time to play my other cards.

"That antenna in the bag?" I said, nodding at it.

She picked it up again.

"I believe it comes from Bill Galbraith's wife's Range Rover." I turned over the newspaper and jabbed at the picture of the barrier at Byron's Pool. "The height barrier is just that bit lower than her model of Range Rover which has a lovely scrape along the top."

"Where did you get this?"

"From Byron's Pool. There's an old guy living near the entrance who collects the antennas knocked off cars. The point is you could match it to her Range Rover."

"First you point the finger at him, now it's his wife?"

"I'm just giving you facts – they matter, right?" She opened her mouth to speak but I pushed on. "Here's another fact: Bogdana worked at Kristina Galbraith's salon on Green Street." I handed her the photo I'd printed off from

TripAdvisor and flipped over the newspaper so she could see Bogdana's photo. Gratifyingly, she was genuinely surprised. I told her where I'd got it. She pulled a face.

"It sort of looks like her but it's not exactly evidence; neither is this antenna, which you could have picked up anywhere. Let me explain something," she said, her voice rising a register. "Unlike you I have to actually build an evidence-based case that I can present to the Crown Prosecution Service who will then tell me whether I have enough for them to take it to court with any chance of prosecuting successfully. Do you understand?"

"I know how the bloody system works," I said, my own voice now raised. "I wasn't suggesting this was evidence of anything. It's a lead. Isn't your job to turn leads into evidence?"

She looked at me with murder in her eyes. I braced myself, but she started to breathe and studied the photo.

"I'd like to speak to Aurora myself; a solicitor isn't going to ask the right questions," she said.

"She was locked in her room, so all she can do is establish that Bogdana was there that night, as well as what happened to her in the car on the A14."

"That's another thing I'd like to talk to her about. I'd love to know where Leonard Diski was taking them when the woman jumped from the car?"

"What does he say?" I asked.

"Nothing. I had to release him on bail not thirty minutes ago. He had a decent solicitor and no priors. What does Aurora say?"

That wasn't good news about Leonard being released.

"Well, what does she say?" she asked.

"He took her to a house in the Fens. It'll be in her statement," I said.

"How soon can I get this magical statement, and don't say tomorrow."

"Fine, tonight if you like. After your boxercise class?" I asked, unable to resist a smirk.

Ignoring me she took a biro from her jacket and wrote down a mobile number on the newspaper. "Call me when you have it," she said, picking up the antenna and the clear folder with the photos in it. She stood up and rolled her shoulders. "Do me a favour. Don't mention any of this to Linda – I don't want her running around investigating Galbraith, or worse, publishing something."

"You didn't have to say that," I said.

She moved to the door.

"Just out of curiosity," she said, "what was in the briefcase that everyone was so keen to get their hands on?"

I saw no reason why she shouldn't know. "Just a clinical audit report and a broken necklace belonging to his wife."

Stubbing froze, drilling her pale eyes into mine. It was disconcerting, even at a distance. Her voice came from somewhere deep in her chest.

"What sort of necklace, George?"

"Pearls," I said. "Why?"

47

STUBBING STOOD AT THE DOOR, LEAVING MY QUESTION unanswered.

"What's the significance of the pearls?" I asked her. She removed whatever tied her hair back, which I've never seen her do, then pulled the hair really tight with both hands and reapplied it. It all took less than thirty seconds but she seemed transformed by it, recovering her impenetrable professional face.

"Did you say the necklace was broken?" she asked, her voice neutral.

"Yes. The pearls were unstrung, in an envelope. Kristina thought Aurora had stolen them but she didn't know they were in the briefcase. It was locked."

"You saw them yourself? This isn't something Aurora's told you?"

"Yes, Galbraith showed them to me when I gave him the briefcase. Although Aurora did tell me she found a single pearl in Galbraith's study when she was cleaning it."

"Please let me speak to her, George," she said, almost pleading. "It doesn't have to be at the station, could be here or wherever she feels comfortable."

"Are the pearls important?"

"I won't know that unless I speak to her."

"She's leaving for Manila in the morning," I said.

"Then tonight."

"She's quite fragile. Her daughter is dying of cancer and she's been through a lot."

"What are you trying to say?"

"That she needs handling with some sensitivity."

"And I can come across as insensitive?" she said.

"Occasionally," I said. Something flickered in her face and I wondered if I'd hit a nerve.

"That's only when I'm dealing with arseholes and the criminal underclass," she said. Touché. "I've had training, I know when to dial it down. What's-her-name can be there if you want," she said, gesturing at Sandra's desk.

"I'll talk to Aurora, see what she says, but she'll have been through the mill already with the solicitor. I'll call you as planned when I have the statement; you'll want to read that anyway before you talk to her. If she agrees."

Stubbing nodded and disappeared. I checked my phone: it was gone five-thirty and I'd missed a call from Linda. There was a text.

wheres the stash? nothing in the tin in hall.

I rang her.

"What's that thing in the hall drawer, Georgie? Looks like a stun gun."

"Ah yes, forgotten about that. It's a Taser, I wouldn't fiddle with it."

"You planning some kinkiness?"

"Not with that. It's more Guantanamo Bay than *Fifty Shades of Grey*. Anyway, I rang to say I haven't got any stash; you took it home 'cause I couldn't handle it. Was today that bad?"

"It was embarrassing. It was obvious that they were seeing me out of courtesy, because I knew someone at the paper. When I went through my pieces they felt cringeworthy really. I need a meaty story. Something with legs."

"The Bogdana story might be that."

"I'm just regurgitating what the police are telling me. I need a scoop, something that will trigger an investigation or something, not just reporting one that's already happening," she said, the words coming fast. She really wanted out of Cambridge, I realised, wanted to be in London. If only she knew what I knew. Of course I would never tell her anything that would jeopardise an investigation and was genuinely affronted that Stubbing felt it necessary to—

"When are you coming home?" Linda was asking.

"Not sure. A couple of hours maybe. Will you be OK?"

"Of course, I've got a bottle of wine to keep me company."

"Oh dear, we are feeling sorry for ourselves."

She laughed, a little too loud, and I suspected she'd already found company with the wine. "Just get your arse back here as soon as poss," she said.

I spent almost five minutes keying Stubbing's number into my phone then looked at the clinical audit report on my desk which Galbraith desperately wanted back. He seemed more exercised about it than the pearls, which, judging by Stubbing's reaction, had more significance than I'd realised, but then he had the pearls in his possession and was unaware that the police knew about them. Had they found a pearl on or near Bogdana's body and kept quiet about it? They sometimes keep certain things out of the public domain as a way of keeping one step ahead of a murderer but also to eliminate the people who feel compelled to confess to a crime they didn't commit.

I put the report in an envelope and sealed it with brown tape, then wrote his name and hospital address on the front and stamped it "Private & Confidential" – I would drop it off at the hospital tomorrow. I had no desire to leave it in the office overnight, scanned or not scanned.

But as I locked up to go to Rhianna's an idea started to percolate, something that would help Linda. The timing was critical though, as I needed to neutralise Badem. I rang Sandra as I walked up Lensfield Road.

"How's it going?" I asked.

"Fine. We're just having a break. Are you coming?"

"I just need to make a quick stop."

Standing in Kamal's kitchenette I watched Chris put a ready meal in the microwave and set the timer. It was an unpleasant reminder of my own efforts when I was alone for any period. Kamal was on an evening shift so we had the place to ourselves.

"I'm sorry about my tantrum last time," he said. "I've been under a lot of stress. Kamal explained that you weren't working for Galbraith in that way."

"No worries. Any developments at work?"

"Not really. I mean, they returned our computers. But all

342

the work the director had commissioned to get the medical notes transcribed has gone. Nobody will be doing that again – the time and cost make it prohibitive. So the report might as well no longer exist."

"I've been thinking about what you said and making things right," I said. "It's a matter of how it's done, though."

"What are you proposing?" he asked.

"Well, I need to work out some of the details and timing but one of the things needed will be having someone who can explain the report when asked to. Like you did with me. You wouldn't have to give your name or—"

"I'll happily give my name."

"Well, it's your decision. You might want to think about how it will affect your career."

"I don't want a career if it means biting your tongue because you don't want to upset the status quo. Does success have to come at the price of integrity?"

I smiled, loving his youthful idealism. Where did it go?

"OK, give me a personal email address and number." As he wrote them down, I said, "I have another favour to ask which will enable all this."

"Name it."

"It's not very ethical."

He snorted and looked at me expectantly.

"I need you to check your operating theatre system to see who carried out an operation on someone. Not the named consultant, who is Galbraith, but the actual surgeon. And I'll need proof in the form of a photo or screenshot or something."

"That's easy enough."

"The thing is, I need it tonight."

"No problem, I'll pop back into work. Just give me a name, man."

I took out my notebook, ripped out a sheet and wrote down Iskender Badem's name as well as my email address and mobile number.

"If you're going to the hospital can you take this and leave it at Reception?" He clocked the name on the front and frowned.

"You're giving it back?"

"Don't worry, it'll give him a false sense of security before the shit hits the fan."

He smiled as the microwave pinged.

From Kamal's I walked back down Mill Road towards Parker's Piece, intending to cross it to get to Rhianna's office. I was about to cross Mortimer Road that led down to the university cricket grounds and glanced over my shoulder without breaking stride to check nobody was turning onto the road when a white transit van did just that, at speed. I glimpsed Derin was at the wheel. Stepping back onto the pavement as it came to a stop in front of me, the side-loading door slid open. I felt a hard shove at my back and stumbled forward as hands reached out from the dark interior of the van. I was pulled inside and someone pushed in behind me. The door slid closed as the van moved off. It smelled of stale sweat.

"What the fuck?" was the first and only thing I managed to say.

The answer was a punch to the side of the head that lit up the darkness briefly, but then my brain went dark.

48

COLD WATER SPLASHED MY FACE AND I WAS PANICKED INTO taking in gasps of air. Someone laughed behind me. The back of my scalp stung. I opened my eyes to see Badem sunk into my sofa like before except this time he was engrossed in his Sudoku. Somebody was holding my head up by my hair, which explained the pain. I tried to move but was tied to a kitchen chair with cargo straps, like before. My left temple throbbed where I'd been punched in the van. The hand released my hair and I looked round to see Derin. He showed me his bad teeth. He was in a red weightlifter's tank-top with "No Pain, No Gain" on the front. I felt woozy and couldn't remember coming into the house. Why had I been out so long? Not from just a punch, surely?

"There you are," Badem said, putting down his magazine and pen. He rested his hands on his stomach, fingers drumming. Unlike last time the curtains were closed and the overhead light on. Half a bottle of wine and an empty glass with the pink imprint of Linda's lips on the rim sat on the coffee table. Was she still here? I silently prayed that she'd got bored and gone home before they'd arrived.

"She's in the kitchen," Badem said, smiling. "With Leonard."

With superhuman effort fuelled by adrenalin and rage I managed to get to my feet, chair and all, before being yanked back down by Derin, who pressed his hands down on my shoulders. I felt dizzy.

"Don't worry, Mr Kocharyan," Badem said. "We just need her for insurance. We'll have a little chat first. You tell me what's what and she won't be harmed unless absolutely necessary. If and when that happens she'll be brought in so you can watch." He squirmed into the sofa. "It was rather fortuitous that she was here, really. An added bonus if you will."

"What do you want?" I asked, trying to keep my tone civil; my ear still remembered Derin's previous clouts. My arms were pressed against my sides but my hands could grasp the seat of the chair. My attempt to get up did at least give me hope that movement might be possible if unchecked. What I could usefully do once on my feet and hunched over with a chair strapped to me was another matter, but a straw is a boat to a drowning man. As Linda had reminded me, the Taser was in a drawer in the hall, but might as well have been at the bottom of the Bosphorus. I tried to focus on Badem, but my vision was off.

"What do you want?" I repeated.

"You know what I want," he said. Before he could expand Leonard came into the room, sleeves rolled up, carrying Linda's large smartphone, which he put next to mine on the table.

"She's a handful but not going anywhere," Leonard said as he sat in an armchair. I noticed a fresh scratch next to his left eye. A scratch Linda had the nails for. In a film my character would yell some clichéd macho bullshit about how I'd kill Leonard if I discovered that he'd laid a finger on her, then get slapped around for my trouble. I needed to use my words carefully; they were all I had right now.

"This is kidnapping, at the very least," I said to Badem. "Not something the police take lightly, especially since your boy here is out on bail."

"They don't take blackmail lightly, either," he said.

I said nothing and he smiled.

"Yes, I know about that. Incidentally, was that your doing, Leonard's arrest?" Badem asked. "Didn't I warn you to keep away from the police?"

"I had nothing to do with it."

"To be fair," Leonard said, touching his scratch, "from what the cops said it was Derin's fault, driving over the railway crossing when the lights were flashing. We were caught on CCTV." He made a face at Derin, who snorted and removed his hands from my shoulders.

"You told me to hurry," he said, like a reprimanded twelve-year-old.

Badem raised a hand in warning then looked at me.

"So, what have you done with Aurora?"

"What do you mean?"

A big mistake. I was never sure whether it was better to try and relax into a blow or not, but if you know it's coming you instinctively tense, and if you're sucker-punched it always seems worse. But this time Derin, rather than clout me, caught hold of my sideburns and was attempting to lift me and the chair up by them. This is a lot more painful than I'd imagined and my whole body tensed in an effort to rise up and relieve the pressure and to avoid giving Derin the satisfaction of crying out. Just as I thought the hair would be ripped from my face he let go. I grunted in relief, my eyes watering.

"Leonard found a message from the family you stole her from when he was released tonight. They want a refund, believe it or not."

"She's in police custody," I said.

He smiled. "Really?"

"She's in the country illegally," I said.

"And you just handed her over," he said, demonstrating with his hands.

I didn't have an answer to that.

"She's not with the police," he said. He nodded to Derin who gave me the sideburn treatment. This time I couldn't help but cry out. Tears were running down my face. I took in deep breaths.

"Why do you want her so badly, this maid?" he asked.

"Her daughter is sick, dying, and she wants to go home to see her."

"Ah, so you're a humanitarian as well as a blackmailer? You didn't want to use Aurora against Bill, threaten to go to the tabloids and expose his affair. Earn yourself a little tax-free cash?"

"I don't know what Kristina or Bill have told you but they both lie." It was the wrong thing to say as I was rewarded with a cuff round the head, but it was actually preferable to the hair pulling.

"What do you mean they lie?" he asked. How much to tell him? He probably supplied Bogdana to Kristina, but did he know she'd been at the house? Was this all about protecting himself from his association with the Galbraiths?

My phone rang and Leonard picked it up.

"Someone called Sandra," he said to Badem. It stopped ringing.

"Does Linda know about this Sandra?" Badem asked me with a little smile. The three of them had a chuckle but it was reassuring to learn that they didn't know who Sandra was. He tapped Leonard's knee. "Why don't you bring her in and we'll find out," he said. "I haven't got all evening to spend on this nonsense." Leonard grinned and winked at me and disappeared. My heart sank.

"Look, she doesn't know anything," I said.

"It doesn't matter," Badem said. "You know where Aurora is so we'll find out which of them you're more loyal to."

"I thought you were more cultured than this."

"Culture doesn't work with you people. Aha, here she is."

Linda staggered in, staring at Badem and Derin but seeming unable to acknowledge me. She was in my bathrobe. Her mouth was gagged and her hands tied behind her. Her pallid face looked momentarily relieved when she did see me but then clocked the cargo straps round my middle. Leonard gave her a push into the room and followed, dragging another kitchen chair.

My phone rang.

"It's that woman again," Badem said, looking down at it. Leonard placed the chair at right angles to mine and pushed

Linda onto it. She looked at me, a question in her eyes. I tried to look reassuring – difficult under the circumstances. The bathrobe had fallen open to expose her thighs. We were both sweating.

"Remove that thing from her mouth," Badem ordered. Leonard obeyed, also pulling a balled sock from her mouth. She worked her dry lips.

"Water," she said.

"Here," Derin said, throwing some water in her face. He laughed.

"Pig," she shouted. Derin stepped over and slapped her hard. She came off the chair and Leonard had to pick her up and sit her back down. Badem said something curt to Derin in Turkish but he was in a world of his own, looking bright-eyed and dangerous, like he was excited to be hurting Linda. He stood close behind her, pushing the bathrobe aside to rest his hands on her bare shoulders. I gritted my teeth.

"I thought you were better than this," I said to Badem.

My phone buzzed with a text.

Leonard picked it up and read, "Where the hell are you? We're tired of waiting." I prayed that Sandra didn't mention Aurora. "We're tired of waiting?" he repeated. "Do you think she has the maid with her?"

"Maybe. Ask her," Badem said, looking at me. "Wait, don't ask her, he would already know that, it'll make her suspicious. Tell her to bring the maid here." Leonard tapped away on the phone.

"Now then, dear lady reporter," Badem said. "Tell me how close you are to Kevork here?" Linda, her left cheek crimson, just looked blankly at him as Derin stroked her hair.

"Kevork?" she asked. Leonard's text whooshed off. Linda tried to shake Derin's hands off.

"Kevork is Armenian for George," Badem said. "Is he fond of you?"

"What a stupid question," she said, with bravado. Derin reached into a pocket and pulled out a flick knife. Luckily Linda couldn't see it but things were going bad quickly. My phone received another text.

"Mr Badem," Leonard said. "You should see this." He was holding my phone as he stepped over to the sofa. Shit, maybe Sandra had replied to say they were coming. Badem peered at the small screen and frowned.

"This isn't from Sandra," he said. He looked up at me. "What's the meaning of this?" he asked, looking more bewildered than angry.

"What is it?" I asked, my mouth dry.

"It's from someone called Chris. It says your hunch about Badem op was on the money."

The landline in the hall started ringing.

49

"THAT'LL BE SANDRA," I SAID, AS THE LANDLINE RANG. "AND if I don't answer it she'll get worried. I was supposed to meet her earlier."

"She's probably on her way with Aurora," Leonard said.

"Did she reply to your text? What did you say, exactly?"

Impatiently he read it out. "'I'm at home, bring the maid here.'"

"Then she's definitely not coming. I would never call Aurora 'the maid'. Most likely she'll call the police if I don't answer the phone."

Leonard looked at Badem, who glanced at him.

"Idiot," he muttered.

"Let me speak to her," I said, "then I'll explain about your operation. Bill's been lying to you." The landline stopped ringing but the mobile started to ring in Badem's hand. Startled, he looked at it.

"Let me speak to her," I repeated.

"Shut up," Badem said, thinking. The phone went silent. "Let her do it," he said, nodding at Linda. "I don't trust what you might say to her."

"It'll look odd if she rings from his mobile," Leonard said.

"She can use her phone, or better still, ring from the landline, that way this Sandra will see it's his number," Badem said. This could be a chance. I knew that Linda had self-defence training after her stalking experience but using it under pressure was another matter. But if she was going to the telephone table in the hall...

"What should she say? Why would she ring her?" Leonard asked Badem.

"Must I think of everything... Let's see. George is in the bath and she's seen that Sandra's been calling. Oh, and she sent the text from his phone on his instruction – it might explain using the word 'maid'. If this Sandra's worried she probably works for George. Do you know this Sandra?" he asked Linda.

"I've never met her but she knows who I am," Linda said, sounding confident. Was she thinking what I was thinking?

"Don't tell him anything," I said.

Derin grinned at me over her head. "It would be better if I did it," I said to Badem.

"I don't think so," he replied. Sometimes reverse psychology worked.

"Will the phone reach in here?" Leonard asked.

"No, not in here," Badem said. "George might decide to partake in the conversation."

"How can we trust her not to say something, to warn her?"

"Because if she puts a word wrong George here will get

hurt. It'll be a test of her dedication."

Derin clapped his hands.

"I'll do it," Linda said, "but not tied up like this."

"Watch it, she's vicious," Leonard said, touching his scratch.

Derin laughed. "I can handle her." Badem wrote down Sandra's mobile number from my phone onto a page in his Sudoku book and ripped it out.

"Untie her," Badem said, giving the sheet to Leonard. "You should go with Derin," he said.

"I can handle her, Uncle, I don't need him," Derin said, annoyed. He opened his knife and cut through the duct tape around Linda's wrists, then flicked the knife closed. With two of them she had no chance, even if she remembered the Taser in the drawer of the telephone table. She pulled the robe closed and rubbed her wrists.

"Linda," I said, waiting for her to look at me. "We'll be released from this little Guantanamo Bay soon." Our eyes met and I saw a flash of understanding.

"I know, it'll be stunning," she said – she'd remembered our telephone call. She stood up with Derin clasping her elbow.

"Go with him," Badem said, tapping Leonard's knee. "I need to speak to George alone about this text from whoever Chris is."

Derin, fury burning his face, let go of Linda and stepped forward, slightly in front of me to my right. He was shouting at his uncle and Leonard was watching him, smiling.

It was now or never – both of them accompanying Linda would make going for the Taser impossible. I grabbed the seat of the chair with my hands and got to my feet. Hunched double by the chair, I kept going. In my peripheral vision I glimpsed Linda making for the door as I crashed into Derin's hip with my right shoulder. Derin, who'd been working on his upper body strength and neglecting his legs, went down onto the coffee table. Leonard spotted Linda exiting the room and jumped to his feet, trying to step over Derin who was flailing for his knife which he'd thankfully lost. I tried to get up but had ended up on my side. Leonard disappeared from view but I heard the familiar buzzing and a guttural grunt. I heard him go to ground. Derin, knife retrieved, came for me on hands and knees, blind to Linda who appeared behind him. She stood, legs astride his, mouth set in grim determination. Badem – who had somehow extradited himself from the sofa – shouted a warning, but it was too late as Linda bent over and applied the Taser to the back of his sweaty shaved head. She kept it pressed there until I had to yell at her to stop.

Badem must have moved fairly quickly because I only realised he was gone by the sound of the front door closing. Released by Linda from the chair, I recovered Derin's knife and with Linda wielding the Taser I got Derin and Leonard back to back on the floor and tied the cargo strap too tight around both of them. Linda handed me the Taser. She looked pale.

"You OK?" I asked.

"I'm getting dressed," she said, avoiding my eyes. Derin started swearing so I retrieved the duct tape in the kitchen that Leonard had used on Linda's wrists and used it over both their mouths.

I closed the door on them and called Sandra from the landline.

"Where the hell have you been?" she shouted. "What the hell was that text you sent?"

"I'll explain later. Stubbing wants to talk to Aurora, do you think she'd be up to it?"

"If Stubbing can pretend to be human."

"Can you wait at the office?"

"We're already here. Came here when you didn't turn up. What happened?"

"Later. Listen, any chance you can find out where Iskender Badem lives?"

"Sure. I'll text you the info."

Next I rang Stubbing and told her to come to the house.

"You got that statement for me?"

"I've got more than that, I've got the recently released Lenny and his friend trussed up in my living room. They were both carrying weapons." The Taser was Leonard's, after all, even if he hadn't brought it with him. I hung up before she asked questions. Linda, dressed, holding her overnight bag, was waiting for me to come off the phone.

"You're leaving?" I asked.

She nodded. She was trembling.

"Linda, I'm sorry this happened." I reached for her but she moved away to the door.

"Are you OK?" I asked.

"Any chance you can keep me out of this… mess?"

"I'll try my best."

She opened the door and stepped out, taking a deep

breath. She pulled the door closed behind her without looking at me and I was left with the hollow feeling it was the last time she would come to the house.

I gently rubbed my sore sideburns as I sat with Stubbing at my dining-room table. Derin and Leonard had been handcuffed and removed by uniformed officers, much to the excitement of the neighbours. There was no car or van outside so I assumed they must have been dropped off with me and Badem had arrived separately. Stubbing wrote down my version of events. Basically I told her that they'd come to the house looking for Aurora. I didn't mention Badem because I had unfinished business with him, and I didn't mention Linda because she didn't want me to. My story contained holes large enough to drive a tank through, the least of which was how I'd overpowered two armed men on my own. But the odd thing was that Stubbing didn't seem to care, or was distracted. She just nodded and wrote it all down.

"Aurora might be willing to talk to you about Bogdana," I said, when finished. "She's waiting at my office."

"Bogdana's not my case any more," she said, shrugging.

"Why? What's going on?"

"I met with my DCI and went through the reasons why I should talk to Kristina Galbraith. He decided that, given who she's married to, he should do it, because I'm obviously not to be trusted to handle it sensitively."

"He said that?"

"Not exactly, but what other reason could there be? You

said the same yourself." I preferred any Stubbing to a self-pitying one but let it ride.

"And?"

"I've been told to abandon any line of enquiry regarding the Galbraiths. Seems they're untouchable. For the moment, anyway."

"But the pearls, the antenna, the picture of Bogdana at the salon?" She picked up the king from the chessboard. I made a mental note of its position.

"The DCI had a chat with Mrs Galbraith. I wasn't present. She told him she scraped her car at the multi-storey in town trying to park in one of the low spots."

"And what about the antenna?"

"It doesn't matter, George. She's got an alibi for the night in question."

"What alibi?"

"She was with someone apparently. It's sensitive, so I assume she's having an affair."

A horrible thought had struck me. "Who was she with?" I asked, moving round to the computer.

"I don't know, but my boss says he personally checked the alibi and it seems kosher. She left after dinner on the night and didn't get back for hours. The parking ticket just confirms it."

"This is all coming from your DCI, is it?" I asked, printing off the sheet I'd used to blackmail Kristina with.

"What is that? Is there something else you haven't told me?"

"He's not Asian, is he, your boss?"

"No, what you on about?"

"I happen to know that Mrs Galbraith is seeing someone who works at the station. I saw him this morning in fact when I was waiting for you."

Stubbing's jaw actually dropped.

50

STUBBING PUT THE CHESS PIECE DOWN NEXT TO THE BOARD.
I gave her the printout showing Kristina and her lover
getting intimate.

"Those were taken at the Galbraith house," I said.

"I'm not even going to ask why you have these," she said,
studying the pictures. "He's not police."

"Management?"

"No. He's not based at the factory but visits regularly."

"Who is he?"

She stared at the photos and shook her head as if I hadn't
spoken. "This explains a lot. My boss would have spoken to
him after she'd told him who she'd been with."

"Are you going to tell me what you're on about?"

She looked up at me. "You have to keep this to yourself,
George."

"Come on, Vicky, you can't doubt my discretion."

"He's a senior lawyer in the Cambridgeshire Crown
Prosecution Service."

I stood up. She, however, seemed to have slumped into
the seat.

"This was in her house?" she asked, waving the sheet.

"Yep, just last week. His DNA will be everywhere."

"Jesus. This is the lawyer who'd decide whether any case against the Galbraiths is worth prosecuting or not."

"You think he's the alibi?"

"He must be."

She bent over and spoke to the floor. "I mean I can see why my boss wants me to back away from this. The embarrassment factor alone would make him cautious. She's married to a high-profile guy – the tabloids would have a field day. But I can't see him inventing alibis, or just taking this guy's word for it. That's a step too far and career suicide. It would explain what he said about needing more time or having something more tangible. He has to refer this upwards, to see how they would handle the fallout. They'd probably need to sort things out in the CPS before the shit hit the fan, get this guy recused or whatever they call it."

"The parking ticket proves that she parked at the station," I said.

She clicked her fingers. "I remember speaking to this guy while we were parking our bikes up outside the factory. He told me he lived near the railway station, in one of those new flats springing up everywhere. And the ticket doesn't prove she stayed there all that time, only that she parked there."

"You're right, there's no barrier to record comings and goings, it's a pay-and-display car park," I said.

"It's back to Kristina and her lover's word against Aurora's. Guess who'll win that face-off?"

"OK. Assuming the alibi is legit the focus should be on

Bill, right? Something happened to Bogdana in that house involving the pearl necklace." I studied her for a reaction. "Did you find a pearl in her clothing or not?"

She nodded imperceptibly, still focussed on the floor.

"How did she die exactly?" I asked, thinking he might have strangled her with them.

She looked up at me, deciding what to tell me. "Blow to the head." She touched her left temple.

"Was she raped?"

She shook her head.

"So what now? You can't just leave it like this. You and I both know he is likely Bogdana's killer."

"Likely isn't going to cut it. The CPS are going to apply the full evidence test to this one, and they're going to want to see the evidence, not just take what the police tell them at face value, which is what usually happens."

"So what are you going to do?"

"What I'm told, of course, what else? Short of Galbraith confessing or a real witness coming forward I'm going to focus on the woman who jumped into the path of an eighteen-wheeler and get to the bottom of why this low-life Leonard was driving Filipino women around. I'm working on the theory, and I'm hoping Aurora's statement will bear this out, that there's some sort of trafficking going on."

I remembered the house in the Fens. The police needed to get to it before Badem moved the women. "He was delivering them to a house out in the Fens. Let me get you the address. There might be other women there."

"For fuck's sake, George."

I found my notebook in my jacket and she rang the Fenland cops. I took the opportunity to put the king back on his correct square.

"Anything else you haven't told me?" she asked, when she'd finished.

"This is all in Aurora's statement and like I said, she's in my office waiting to speak to you. But Bogdana is connected to this somehow, since it looks like she was lured to work here. If that is Bogdana in the photo at Kristina's salon, then there's a good chance the rest of the women working there are also working illegally. Mrs Galbraith has form in that regard, it's in the public record." Of course I knew they were illegal from what Badem had said, not to mention Kristina herself.

She nodded wearily. "I'll go and read Aurora's statement and speak to her." She waved the sheet. "Can I keep this? It might come in useful."

"Don't see why not, although it didn't come from me." She folded it, stood up and put it in her jacket.

"As for what happened here…" She shook her head.

With Stubbing gone I stared at the chess problem without seeing it. I was working under the assumption that something had happened to Bogdana at the Galbraiths' house and Bill had decided to get rid of her body using his wife's car, or even perhaps with her help. The Porsche didn't have much of a boot so it would make sense. Plus it was far too conspicuous, whereas Range Rovers in Cambridge are two a penny. How to prove it happened though? I was too tired to get any further; too much had happened too quickly. The pain in my shoulder, which had been gradually subsiding after the injury sustained in the pub car park when first meeting Leonard and Derin, had now returned after colliding with Derin. Something was bothering me on my neck, like an insect bite. I went to the mirror and took stock. A new contusion on the side of my head where I'd been punched, and a red mark the size of a five-pence piece on my neck, with a puncture wound in the middle, just like an insect bite. Had the bastards injected me with something? It would explain being out for so long and the dreamlike nature of what had happened when I woke up, events I still couldn't quite believe. Linda had been amazing, and probably saved me from being knifed. I hadn't even thanked her. When she'd left she'd looked in shock. But it was Chris's text that had saved us both. I found the phone and scrolled up to the message – *Your hunch about Badem op was on the money. Have emailed theatre records.* At the computer, I found it and printed it off. Bill Galbraith had not been in the operating room.

I grabbed a beer from the fridge. I was starving, but all I could find was a chunk of dry cracked cheddar which I nibbled at. The mobile phone, which was charging in the hall, beeped. A message from Sandra.

cant call cause stubbing here but badem called me!!?? He must have kept the sheet of paper he wrote Sandra's number on. *wants to meet you asap.* She'd provided a Cambridge number. I rang it.

"Efes, can I help you?" an English female voice said. Efes was a Turkish restaurant on King Street. The real deal, not one of these all-encompassing "Mediterranean" places.

"Erm, can I speak to Iskender Badem, please?"

"Just one moment," she said, seemingly unfazed by my request. The place didn't sound busy but it was Monday night. There was a delay as either Badem made his way to the phone or the phone was taken to him.

"Mr Kocharyan." Badem sounded confident, even chipper.

"Mr Badem. Can we meet?"

"Have you eaten?"

"I'm not hungry." No spoon was long enough to sup with Badem.

"Leonard and Derin are in custody?"

"Yes."

"But interestingly, I'm not."

"We have unfinished business," I said.

"Yes, that we do."

"You've been misled," I said.

"You said something about Bill lying to me?"

"In fact they've both been lying to you."

"You can prove it?" he asked.

"Yes, but I think we should give them a chance to explain themselves. Shall we go and see them?"

51

I'D AGREED TO MEET BADEM AT THE GALBRAITHS' HOUSE (he'd ring them to say he was going over) but arrived early, standing in the Weasel and Stoat pub garden in Fulbourn where I could see the gate to The Willows, trying to calm my nerves at what was to come and resisting the temptation for Dutch courage. I held a large folder to my chest. Inside was a copy of Kristina and her lover's photos, a printout of the operation sheet from the theatre system Chris had emailed and some printouts from the *Argus* website, since I'd left my copy at the office, along with my car. I was early because I assumed Badem must have other Leonards and Derins he could call on – at least three people got me into the back of that van. But he turned up solo, in a taxi. Not wanting to give him too much time with the Galbraiths I walked quickly up to the house, slipping through the already closing gate and catching up with him as he lumbered up the drive. An open bottle of spirits was clutched in his right hand.

"We might need it," he said, breathing charcoaled lamb into my face.

Kristina was waiting at the open front door in a zippered

jumpsuit and headband, like she'd stepped out of an eighties pop video. She looked puzzled when she caught sight of me but didn't say anything. She glanced at the folder in my hand.

"He's been drinking," she said as we entered the white hall. We followed her up the stairs, me behind Badem who was wheezing with the effort. I took the opportunity to take out my fully charged phone, which I'd set to silent, and dial Stubbing's number. As agreed she didn't speak, and I put the phone back into my jacket pocket, microphone facing out.

Misha, oddly subdued, waited at the top of the stairs. He padded to the sofa in front of Kristina. Bill leant in the doorway to his study, an iced amber drink in hand. Unshaven, red-eyed, in a torso-hugging T-shirt that showed off his flat stomach, he stood barefoot in carefully ripped jeans. His grin was loose, his eyes shiny.

"Ah, good," he said. "Someone to drink with." He didn't slur, just spoke louder.

He gestured expansively to the armchairs. I sat opposite Kristina on the backless leather cube while Badem opted for something more comfortable at right angles to me.

"I brought raki," Badem said, putting the bottle down. "The good stuff, the Altınbaş." Bill went to a cabinet and came back towards the sofa quite deliberately, the way drunk people do, like they're walking on a narrow ledge. He had four fingers stuck in four glasses and a bottled water, chilled. Kristina flinched as he banged them on the table and sat down too quickly beside her, Misha darting out of his way onto her lap. He poured raki and splashed water into the glasses, turning the contents milky. He handed me a glass, then Badem, then offered one to Kristina, who declined. He shrugged and raised it, held it there until Badem and I raised ours. We drank – rather Badem and Bill drank; I took a sip and put it down. A sip was enough to burn my empty stomach.

Kristina sat upright, poised, turned slightly towards her husband. He took her hand. They seemed to want to project a united front, despite whatever was coming. I was almost looking forward to it.

"Is that the report you stole from my case?" he asked, nodding at the folder I'd placed next to my drink. He looked at me, waiting.

"No, that was delivered to you at the hospital earlier. I didn't really understand it, I just wanted to confirm it wasn't Mr Badem's medical records." From the folder I pulled out the theatre system printout that Chris had emailed me. His expression didn't change as he glanced at the sheet in my hand.

"Mr Badem's medical notes were never in the briefcase," I said to him. "You lied to him so he would find her and the briefcase when I wouldn't hand her over." I turned to Badem. "I checked at the hospital: your notes have been in the medical records library since your operation."

He looked at Bill. "In clinic you sat there and told me they were missing, that she'd taken them," he said. Bill grinned boyishly and half-shrugged as if it would be enough to get rid of the accusation. Badem stared at him but Bill was looking at me, as was Kristina, who was kneading Misha with one hand and her husband's hand with the other.

I passed the operation sheet to Badem as I addressed Bill. "And why did you tell Mr Badem that you carried out his

369

operation?" I said. Badem read the sheet as Bill pulled his hand from Kristina's clasp.

"Because I did," he said, his voice flat.

"No, you didn't," Badem said, softly. He handed Bill the operation sheet but he refused to take it.

"Those things aren't accurate," he said. Kristina reached over for it but Bill ripped it from Badem's hand and threw it to the floor.

"You wanted to create a bond," I said to him. "Because you wanted Mr Badem to feel beholden to you."

"But why?" Badem asked him. "Because you wanted Aurora back? Because she'd seen you having an affair with a colleague?" Bill refused to meet Badem's eyes.

"No, there was no affair with a colleague," I said.

Badem frowned, his bushy eyebrows almost covering his eyes, then turned to Kristina as he hoicked his thumb at me. "You told me yesterday that this guy was blackmailing Bill, threatening to go public with his affair, which is why you needed Aurora gone." She was frozen, unable to speak.

"What?" I said, understanding what she'd done. "No, I was blackmailing Kristina, not Bill." I took out the sheet of photos showing Kristina in flagrante with the crime prosecution lawyer and put them on the table. Both Badem and Bill leant forward. Kristina went pale, staring at me like it could kill me. Bill looked away and picked up the other glass of raki.

"So the maid knew about this?" Badem asked, tapping the photos. "That's why Kristina wanted her gone?" he said, but there was a change in his voice, like things were slotting into place.

"No, maybe that's what you thought when Kristina lied to you yesterday, but I think you had a suspicion today why she desperately wanted Aurora gone, right? You didn't kidnap me, torture me and terrorise an innocent woman because of an affair the person you thought was your surgeon was supposedly having. That's over the top, even for you." I pulled the printouts from the *Argus* website from the folder and laid them out, Bogdana's smiling face on top. "I'm guessing you saw the newspaper today, started to worry, and felt exposed, especially when you learnt from Leonard that I had Aurora." They were all staring at Bogdana's picture.

"I tried to call her today to ask about it," Badem said, as if she wasn't here.

"I'm guessing you sourced Bogdana for Kristina's salon, which is why you were worried."

He and Kristina exchanged a look. If I wasn't careful they were going to close ranks.

"Aurora saw Bogdana here at the house the night before she was found dead," I said. That got his attention. "That's why they wanted her gone. The irony is that Aurora didn't realise the significance of what she'd seen until she saw the newspaper this morning."

"Rubbish – she was never here," Kristina said.

"Really? That's the best you can come up with? You had people here for dinner, you think nobody saw her?" I asked.

"You've told the police all this?" Badem asked me.

I nodded. "As has Aurora – she's with them now, so it's no longer containable."

Badem nodded. Bill looked like he was about to vomit.

"Was that Bogdana's real function?" I asked Badem. "To provide sex to people like Bill?"

"No!" he shouted, slapping his hand on the table. "I do not provide that sort of service."

I was going to make a jibe about nominating him for most principled people-trafficker of the year award, but my better judgement prevailed.

"There's something else," I said. "A pearl was found on the dead girl, in her clothing I imagine. There are some pearls in the briefcase Galbraith wanted to recover."

"I don't understand," Badem said.

"Aurora found one in his study, but I don't know how the other ended up on the body. All I know is that Bill had something to do with it."

Badem stood up with surprising agility and looked down at Bill. "Why do English men in positions of authority prefer young girls?"

"It wasn't like that," Bill said, sounding like he was in a stupor.

"Be quiet, Bill," Kristina said, her voice shrill.

"I didn't touch her," Bill shouted. "Not like that. I just wanted to… to see what Mother's pearls looked like on her since you wouldn't wear them."

Kristina spat something in Russian. "Really? You're blaming me?" she asked, incredulous.

"But Bogdana also refused to wear them, didn't she?" I said, pressing him. "Didn't she?" I urged Bill. "She wouldn't wear them for you and that made you angry."

Bill shook his head. "You're wrong. She did. I thought

she'd look nice in them. She was so perfectly innocent. I didn't want to hurt her. I just wanted her to look nice for me. To see them on her bare neck and shoulders. That's how they look their best, on a bare torso."

Badem slapped Bill hard across the face. His drink went flying, as did Misha, who darted to the stairs.

"You pervert; she was a child!" Badem screamed. I stood up.

"Did you kill her?" I shouted. Kristina put her hands to her husband's mouth. Badem slapped them away. Bill was blubbing, snot bubbling at his nose.

"It was an accident…"

Kristina looked at me, her hands clenched. "What do you want from us? Money?" I saw a glimmer of hope in Bill's teary eyes, and even Badem studied me with interest.

It was him I addressed. "Remember what you told me when we first met, sitting in your car?"

He shook his head.

"You wittered on about honour and how there should be consequences to actions. Remember that? Or did that only apply to the Auroras and Bogdanas of this world?"

I took out the mobile phone, relieved to see that it was still on a call.

"Did you get all that?" I asked Stubbing.

For a heart-stopping few seconds there was silence at the other end.

"Yes, we're at the gate."

52

AURORA DISAPPEARED INTO SANDRA'S EMBRACE OUTSIDE HER
house. I took her small case to the car.

"Passport?" I asked a teary Aurora. She showed it to me.

"Ticket?" She patted her breast pocket.

"Money?" She patted the front pocket of her trousers.
We got in the car.

"Call me when she's through passport control," Sandra
said. She waved us off.

The drive to the airport was mostly in silence. I was
exhausted, not having slept, but I wasn't going to delegate
this job to anyone else.

"How long since you've seen your family?" I managed to
ask.

"Three years," she said, then silence.

We reached the airport car park with plenty of time to
spare. I wheeled her case into the terminal and we checked in.
On a whim we popped into a mobile phone shop and I bought a
pre-charged phone. I got the shop to put in a prepaid SIM card
then I rang my number with it so it was in the phone. I gave
it to Aurora, saying, "Call me when you are through passport

control." She seemed to perk up at this idea. I walked her to the departures barrier, beyond which only travellers can go.

We stood there for a minute grinning stupidly at each other until I decided enough was enough.

"You better go, Aurora."

She quickly put her arms round me, pinning my arms to my torso, her head resting on my chest.

"Thank you, George," she said. "I call you soon."

I watched her disappear behind the barrier. I checked my phone was on and wandered round, devoured a burger, then, having had enough of the holidaying hordes, made my way to the car park thinking that I might as well wait in the car.

My phone rang as I was checking the integrity of my home-made duct-tape-and-plastic hatchback cover. I got inside the car.

"Aurora?"

"No problem from passport control. I am on the plane," she said.

I could feel the tension rush from my shoulders, like releasing the top on a bottle of fizzy water. I started to laugh, and then I was bloody crying.

"You OK, Mr George?" She was still there.

"I'm OK. No, I'm happy."

With no way for me to check that the plane had actually taken off I headed back to Cambridge where I sent (with Jason's help) an anonymous email to Linda, complete with the scanned copy of the audit report and Chris's contact details. Then I went home and soaked my shoulder in the bath, then lay on the bed, looking up at the cracked bedroom ceiling trying to get some sleep but my shoulder was too painful, even with painkillers. Then Linda rang. I took her call on the bed.

"Did you send me that report?" she asked.

"What report?"

"I thought it might be you. This Chris guy seems to know you."

"Don't know what you're talking about, but I hope it's useful, whatever it is."

"You'll see, probably the day after tomorrow."

"In the *Argus*?"

"No, think bigger. Think sleazy national." She couldn't hide the excitement in her voice.

"How are you doing?" I asked. "After yesterday."

"I'm OK; I'm in London to do the story. I'll probably stay on here. I think I need to be alone for a while."

"Gone off men?"

"You could say that."

"Can't think why."

She laughed, and it was good to hear.

"I had a good time," I told her. "Up until yesterday that is. But you did good; you probably saved me from being horribly disfigured."

"Well there's that. Will you be OK, Georgie?"

"I'll be fine."

The next day in the office I received an email from an unidentified email address. The subject was "from Aurora".

There was no text in the body of the email, just an attached photo – a selfie showing Aurora cheek to cheek with a jaundiced-looking bandana-wearing girl in a hospital bed. From the identical smiles I deduced the girl was Aurora's daughter. Aurora's smile, her whole face, was relaxed and unselfconscious, like I'd never seen it before.

Stubbing came to the office around midday. She came in without knocking and sat opposite. I took my feet off the desk.

"What's with the sling?" she asked.

"Have a seat," I said, but she ignored my tone. "Occupational hazard." I'd spent the morning waiting to have it x-rayed and bandaged up.

"Thought you might like some closure," she said.

"It's all I'm ever looking for." She pulled a face.

"Bill Galbraith's been charged with manslaughter," she said.

"Not homicide?"

She shook her head. "Not enough evidence for that."

"Did he tell you what happened to Bogdana?"

"Well, his version of it. She came into his study after the dinner party and saw the pearls which happened to be on the desk."

"So far so dodgy," I said.

"It gets worse. Aurora had gone to her room—"

"He locked her in."

"That's what she says, yes, he says not. Anyway, according to him Bogdana asked if she could try them on. He said yes then asked if she'd take her shirt off so he could see what they looked like against her skin."

"He actually told you this?" I asked, astonished.

"Privileged men like him truly believe that they are entitled to whatever they want. He thought it was a reasonable request. Still does, which is why he's happy to admit it."

She told me how he'd said Bogdana was reluctant and that he'd jokingly insisted, trying to undo her shirt. She panicked and tried to remove the pearls while he tried to calm her down and undo them at the hasp – there was a struggle and they broke in the process. She slipped and hit her head on the corner of the glass desk.

"Her head wound is consistent with the corner of that desk," Stubbing said. "Forensics found minute traces of blood on it which will probably turn out to be hers."

"You'd think he'd have cleaned up properly. He's a surgeon after all."

"Even intelligent people screw up under stress."

"So, basically he's claiming it was an accident."

"Yep. Bogdana wasn't sexually assaulted. Her shirt was pulled open but defence will argue that it happened during their struggle for the pearls."

"But he tried to dispose of the body."

"Yes, there is that. He says he panicked, thinking he'd never get a fair trial because of the media interest."

"He used her car?"

"We did find a button from Bogdana's shirt in the back of the Range Rover," she said.

"A button, not a pearl," I said, more to myself.

"Excuse me?"

"Nothing."

"You'll be pleased to know the antenna might prove useful after all," she said.

"You think he moved her on his own? Did she help him?"

"She says not, he says not, her alibi says she was at his flat all night, so…"

"CCTV at the station?"

"Disabled, what with all the renovation going on there, but my suspicion is that she did help. I don't think he would have faced it on his own."

I agreed with her. His story was that once he'd realised Bogdana was dead he drove to the station in the Porsche, borrowed his wife's car while she was visiting her lover, then took Bogdana's body to Byron's Pool. He then returned it to the train station and drove home.

"It doesn't marry with what Aurora says she heard. She'd have heard the Porsche leave. Besides, he'd have to have known she'd be parked there all night."

"He says he thought she was in London; she does park there a lot and that was her story."

"I dunno, I mean—" She put her hand up.

"If I could stop you there, George. I think you can let it go now. I'm all over it."

I laughed. "Sorry."

She sighed and looked over my shoulder.

"What is it?" I asked.

"He's managed to get bail, despite the manslaughter charge."

"What the fuck?"

"He has patients booked in for surgery – comes under

exceptional circumstances, so he'll be out pending a psychiatric report to make sure he's not suicidal. He was interviewed by a doc at lunchtime so I'm sure he'll be released by the end of the day."

"I'm hoping those exceptional circumstances will be voided very soon."

"What do you mean?"

"You'll have to read about it tomorrow like everyone else."

"I guess that explains why Linda's gone AWOL." She stood up and I walked her to the door.

"What about Badem?" I asked.

"Ah, yes. Fenland police tell me they found seven women at that farm. We found their passports at Badem's house. I've put Immigration onto the beauty parlour – it's not really my jurisdiction."

"Please tell me Bill and Ben are indisposed."

She snorted. "No worries there, they'll be caught up in the system for a while."

As will those poor women, I thought, as I closed the door behind Stubbing. I wondered whether we'd done them any favours? All I knew for certain was that we'd probably cut their families off from much-needed income. Aurora herself would be back in the Gulf or wherever as soon as her daughter had passed – as she'd said, she had no other choice.

Later that same evening, over drinks at the pub near the office, Maggie told me that her partner had decided to go and make house with someone twenty years younger.

"How boringly predictable," I said. "How long were you together?"

"Long enough that it hurts." We sipped our drinks.

"Sounds like an arsehole," I said.

She smiled. "I was thinking that myself."

We drained our glasses and I picked them up with one hand.

"One more?" She thought about it, then nodded.

"Can you manage?" I nodded and went to the bar. I didn't really want to be striking something up with Maggie while she was in this state. And it wasn't exactly as if I was ready myself. I took the drinks back to the table. She was going through her diary as I sat down. The painkillers I'd been given were prescription only and I probably shouldn't have been taking them with booze.

"Sorry, just checking the rest of the week's sessions," she said.

"Are you free for a couple of hours this week, during the day?"

She looked down at her diary. "Tomorrow afternoon, actually. Why?"

"How do you feel about a trip to a crematorium?"

She pulled a face and laughed, unable to tell if I was pulling her leg.

"I have to pick up my father's ashes," I said, patting my sling. "And I can't drive."

"Can't drive, George?" she asked, with a knowing, appealing smile.

"You're right. I don't want to go on my own."

ABOUT THE AUTHOR

E.G. RODFORD IS THE CRIME-WRITING PSEUDONYM OF AN award-winning author living in Cambridge, England. Rodford writes about the seedier side of the city where PI George Kocharyan is usually to be found.

Twitter: @eg_rodford

THE BURSAR'S WIFE

A GEORGE KOCHARYAN MYSTERY
E.G. RODFORD

Meet George Kocharyan, Cambridge Confidential Services'
one and only private investigator. Amidst the usual jobs
following unfaithful spouses, he is approached by the glamorous
Sylvia Booker, who fears that her daughter Lucy has fallen
in with the wrong crowd.

Aided by his assistant Sandra and her teenage son, George soon
discovers that Sylvia has good reason to be concerned. Then
an unfaithful wife he had been following is found dead. As his
investigation continues—enlivened by a mild stabbing and the
unwanted attention of Detective Inspector Vicky Stubbing—
George begins to wonder if all the threads are connected…

"A quirky and persuasive new entry in the ranks of crime
fiction" BARRY FORSHAW, *Crime Time*

"A worthy addition to the private eye genre" *Crime Review*

"An absolute delight" STEVEN DUNNE,
author of A Killing Moon

TITANBOOKS.COM